A LOVE LIKE Pumpkin Spice

HAILEY FROST

Content Warning

A Love Like Pumpkin Spice *is intended for adult readers. It contains mature themes and sexually explicit content and is not intended for readers younger than 18 years.*

Welcome to Wayward Hollow - Where strangers become family and love finds a way.

After catching my fiancé tangled up with my sister (yes, my sister), and being told by my parents I was "overreacting," I packed my best friend and what was left of my dignity to flee to Wayward Hollow - a picturesque little town that looks like it was plucked straight out of a Hallmark movie.

I try to put myself back together. People-pleasing? Officially retired. Love? Off the table.

At least that was the plan.

But Chaos unfolds when my attempt to save a stray cat leads me to Henry. The town's beloved veterinarian is gentle, ridiculously attractive, and seems to have a sixth sense for broken things...including me.

Just when I start to believe in new beginnings, the past comes knocking—loud, uninvited, and far from finished.

Published by: Hailey Frost, c/o Block Services, Stuttgarter Str. 106, 70736 Fellbach.

Cover Illustration by @melxartz

Editing by EJL Editing

Contents

Author Notes

Dear Reader,

thank you so much for picking up "A Love Like Pumpkin Spice." While it's a cozy read, it comes with some warnings, namely:

- Emotional abuse and manipulation (by a former romantic partner and family members)
- Cutting ties with family
- Toxic family members
- Cheating ex
- Animal death
- And, to no ones surprise: Cursing and On-page sex

It is recommended for a mature audience. Reader discretion is advised. Please feel free to check my website for additional information on the animal death part (though it might contain minor spoilers).

However, this book also comes with a FMC with a very shiny spine and spice. There will be a happy end and the whole storyline will be resolved, though all characters may appear in future books.

I'm so excited for you to read it and I wish you all the cozy vibes as you dive into Nic's and Henry's story!

xoxo,

Hailey

Playlist

Carole King - Where You Lead
Taylor Swift - Fearless
HUNTR/X - Takedown
Bring Me The Horizon - Throne
Sabrina Carpenter - Manchild
Taylor Swift - thanK you aIMee
Set It Off - Wolf in Sheep's Clothing
Dove Cameron - Too Much
Sabrina Carpenter - Lie To Girls
Taylor Swift - Bejeweled
Ilene Woods, Mike Douglas - So this is Love
Shinedown - Enemies

To the black sheep, the misfits, the ones who always felt like they didn't quite belong.
It was never you, just people not realizing your worth.
This one's for you. Welcome to Wayward Hollow, I hope it feels like home!

And to you know who you are:
Turns out, spite ***does*** *make a wonderful motivator.*

Prologue

Nic

"Oh my God, you're a fiancée!"

With a giant smile on her face that I'm all too happy to return, Lauren pulls me into a tight embrace. "Nic! It's been too long."

"It has been." I release my best friend from the bone-crushing hug. She steps back, keeping her hands on my upper arms, and beams at me, cheeks red with excitement. "What am I even supposed to congratulate you on first? Retiring from acting, that pretty ring on your finger, or your birthday?"

"My birthday isn't until tomorrow, so one of the other two," I tell her with a giggle and grab her hand to pull her inside the house.

Retiring.

The word still sounds weird to me. I'd rather describe it as refocusing, living life in the shadows of fame instead of the spotlight. After fifteen years of acting, I need a break, some time to focus on my private life, and to start the family I always wanted to have.

But hey, whatever the media wants to call it.

"There are... a lot of people," Lauren points out with a sigh and shifts her weight. She brushes a strand of her ash-blond hair behind her ear, while the fingers of her other hand nervously play with the fabric of her pink summer dress. I shoot her an apologetic smile and give her shoulder a reassuring squeeze.

“I’m sorry. Since Jay’s family is hosting, they insisted on inviting a bunch of people I’ve never even met. Trust me, I’m as thrilled as you.” She tenses under my fingers, and I gently turn her to me. Her eyes dart around the room, and I quickly reach for her hand. “Will you be all right? It’s not too late to run. No hard feelings.”

I know she doesn't do well with large groups of people in small spaces, but bless her heart, she nods slightly, takes a deep breath, and straightens her shoulders.

“I’ll be okay,” she assures me with a small smile. “But speaking of Jay, where’s your fiancé? Arguably, he deserved the congrats even more now that he gets to spend the rest of his life with you.” Her face softens as she stretches her neck to peek into the adjoining living room. Most of our families are gathered there, happily chatting and sipping on the overpriced champagne we splurged on for the occasion.

“I could swear he was with them a moment ago.” I tilt my head and scrunch my eyebrows. Where could he have wandered off to? “Maybe he’s upstairs. Let’s go find him.”

I pull her with me, taking her mind off the loud chatter coming from the living room.

“By the way, how come I haven’t seen any new movie announcements from you?” I ask her as we climb the stairs, trying to distract her. “I heard you were in talks for some amazing roles.”

She twirls a strand of hair around her finger and looks at me sheepishly. “I’m taking a page out of your book and having a break. I have no idea what I’ll do with myself but damn”—a deep sigh falls from her lips—“I’m exhausted, Nic.”

“I get it,” I say with a soft nod and stop when we reach the top of the stairs. The light in Jay’s childhood room is on, and I nod toward it. “There he is.”

We walk down the dark hallway, our footsteps muffled by the soft carpet. I am about to reach for the door handle to open it, but the sound of two voices talking makes me freeze, my hand hanging in the air as if stopped by an invisible wall.

"You know it's not for long, babe."

Babe.

His nickname, for me, which normally wraps around my heart like a warm, comforting blanket, but now?

Now it makes my skin tingle as if spiders are crawling up my spine. My stomach churns and nausea creeps up my throat.

Lauren steps closer. Her eyes flicker towards me, wide with shock. I press a finger to my lips. Pain tightens my lungs, but I have to keep listening. She nods immediately, and I feel her tension ease. Her fingernails dig into my forearm.

We remain motionless, and I strain to hear better. The blood rushes in my ears louder than a waterfall, trying to drown out the meaning of the words. Maybe it wasn't his voice after all?

"Am I supposed to stand by helplessly while you marry that bitch?"

My lungs forget how to work, and my knees buckle when I recognize the high-pitched voice. Only my back leaning against the wall stops me from collapsing. I hoped maybe the TV was running, or he was listening to one of his weird podcasts.

But the fact that he's talking to Marissa?

My own damn sister?

That is much worse. And here I thought she peaked when she told my third-grade class during recess that I pee my pants at night. Guess she was only warming up to making my life miserable.

At first, my brain refuses to process it. I mean, maybe I'm having a stroke, maybe I'm imagining things. It just … doesn't make sense. I've been thrown into some cruel parallel universe where up is down. Where monsters wear my sister's face, and I'm falling, like Alice, down the rabbit hole.

From the corner of my eye, I see Lauren rustling in her bag, and she takes out her phone. I shoot her a glare. What is she going to do, livestream my engagement going up in flames?

This time, it's her turn to motion for me to shush as she pulls up her camera.

"You know I have to do this." The lights dim briefly as Jay walks past the door and my heart races, the fear of getting caught twisting my stomach.

Hold on—why the hell would I feel bad about getting caught?

"Once the papers are signed and the period for an annulment is over, I'll divorce her, take half of her money, and we can be together. We talked about this, baby. I'm doing this for us."

Every single word stabs at my heart like a knife, like I'm the final girl who didn't run fast enough from the killer.

Of all the things … it's about money? A cold wave washes over me, and I cover my mouth with my hand as tears form in my eyes.

"I hate having that skank between us." I hear the sound of lips smacking against each other, and bile rises in my throat. Hell, the thought of having kissed the same man as my sister drains all the blood from my face; makes my hands tremble with a mix of disgust and the urge to break her nose.

"Me too, babe. But I'll make sure she sets us up for life. We're going to take all the vacations we talked about—on her dime. Just imagine, the two of us on a beach in Hawaii, cocktail in hand, laughing at her miserable life." Lauren reaches for my hand and gives me a reassuring squeeze, watching me from the corner of her eye, probably afraid I'm about to have a panic attack right here. It wouldn't be an unfounded worry.

"You better. I need to cut that shrew out." My sister takes a deep breath. "For twenty-eight years, I've been dreaming of the day she'd disappear. I can't believe it's almost here." They giggle. I force myself to take calm breaths. "All thanks to you.

It's laughable how you have her wrapped around your little finger."

"Right?" His chuckle makes the hair on my neck stand up. "It was almost too easy to convince her to skip the prenup."

"She's not the brightest tool in the shed. It's embarrassing to be related to her, honestly. Give her a crumb of attention, and that's all it takes to have her trotting after you like a lost puppy, minus the charm."

I inhale sharply. She's not entirely wrong.

She always outshone me. My childhood was the Marissa Show, and I was the underpaid, emotionally neglected production assistant that was supposed to be happy about being allowed to be there at all. Even on my birthdays, she managed to walk away with more presents than I did.

"It wouldn't be fair otherwise," my mom used to say. You know, because celebrating my birth was apparently a scandal itself already.

For the longest time, I hoped I was adopted. Hell, I'd have been fine with being an affair baby. At least that meant there was a reason for them to hate me.

But nope. No hidden letters, no torrid backstory. Just pure, uncut resentment. Turns out, they just hate me for the crime of existing.

Marissa was the wanted child, while they acted as if I decided to show up out of nowhere without any input from them. If she got a D, it was the teacher's fault. If I got a B, I lost Wi-Fi privileges for a week and had to "reevaluate my priorities."

The older and more independent I got, the worse they became. I started acting at thirteen so I could get out; going from school straight to auditions, only involving my parents when I needed their signature once I got a job. They managed to make even that seem as though I'd asked them for a pony. Yet they were happy to take any money I made until I was finally old enough to open my own bank account and forge their signatures well enough.

"You should be thankful for having a roof over your head. Contributing is the least you could do." They used to say whenever I complained, while Marissa spent the day lounging in front of the TV instead of going to her university classes or finding a job.

All I wanted was to move out. I dreamed of it for years, how I'd live my best life, all on my own. But there was always some reason to not do it. Birthdays, Christmas, Thanksgiving.

Like a complete idiot, I still wanted their love. Still bent myself into a thousand emotional origami shapes, hoping they'd notice me.

Now look where that got me.

"It's pathetic." Jay's cruel chuckle pulls me back to my nightmare of a reality. "She's super dumb. She believes every word I say."

How fucking dare he?

I want to storm in, give him a piece of my mind, slap the smug smile off his face. But Lauren tightens her grip on my arm and turns me to face her.

"No," she whispers harshly, and with that little word, I deflate like a balloon, slowly crumpling into myself.

"People like her are meant to be used. She's always been a joke. Way too emotional and way too stingy with her money." Marissa lets out a deep sigh. "Fucking annoying that she had her breakthrough when she was of age. My parents and I could have used that money a lot better than her."

"Just be glad she didn't spend it. Think of all the millions she's saved up, for us," Jay says, still laughing. "And I can't wait to spoil you with it, baby."

I glance at Lauren. She sees the meltdown loading behind my eyes. I've heard enough.

My eyes are stinging with tears, and my hands are shaking with anger. How could I have been this damned blind?

The sound of clothes rustling from the other side of the door almost makes me vomit. It doesn't take a lot of brain cells to know what they're doing.

Fucking in Jay's old room during our engagement party.

I knew Marissa hated me. Hated that, all of a sudden, she wasn't an only child anymore. But even for her, this is a new low. My bar for her was in hell, and holy shit if she didn't fucking limbo under it.

"Let's go," Lauren whispers, pulling me away from the door as if it's the edge of a cliff.

I follow her, but my world is packed in cotton. The walls are closing in on me, every laugh from downstairs hitting me like a slap to the face. The pictures hung on Jay's parents' walls mock me with every step down their stairs. Us at the beach. Jay's birthday. His proposal. We reach the bottom of the stairs, and Jay's mom suddenly appears before me.

"There you two are!" she says brightly, holding a plate. "Come have some cake, honey. Jay was asking for you"—she looks around, confused—"a while ago. No idea where he wandered off to now, though."

My mouth opens, but no sounds come out. I'm not sure if it's bile or a scream I'm holding back.

I gulp and force myself to focus. I need to get out of here. I don't know where, but I can't stay here, in the house where my fiancé is currently fucking my sister.

"I …" I stammer and shoot Lauren a helpless glance. She squeezes my arm and answers for me.

"She realized she forgot something at home," she jumps in with the kind of parent-charming smile I've only ever seen her do successfully. "A surprise for Jay. We're going to get it, and we'll be back in a flash."

“Of course,” Nora says and shows me a warm smile. “That is so sweet! I can’t wait to see it. I’m sure he’ll love it.”

“Oh, he’ll be ecstatic,” I force myself to reply, not quite able to swallow the bitterness in my voice and try to return her smile. Lauren pulls me outside, then pushes me into her car’s passenger seat.

“Fuck.” I completely deflate as soon as Lauren shuts the door behind her as she climbs into the driver’s seat. Reality crashes over me with the force of an avalanche. “Fuck, fuck!”

“I can’t believe them,” Lauren adds, cursing them out under her breath. I bury my face in my hands and force myself to take a deep breath in a feeble attempt to gather my thoughts.

It was all a lie? Every single second?

How could he?

And how did I not see it?

Lauren’s hand lands on my shoulder and draws reassuring circles over my back as I fight back my tears. And after a few more deep breaths, I lower my hands and turn to her, the ice in my veins replaced by burning hot anger.

“Lauren, I need your help,” I admit with a sharp inhale. “Help me deal with this smartly. I can’t think straight.”

“Are we going the calm route or escalating?” When I glance at her, I notice a mischievous sparkle in her eyes. I'm so glad she's here.

“Calmly but nuclear.” I pinch the bridge of my nose. “I want it to hurt. Want them to hurt. But I don’t want either of us to go to jail.”

“Got it.” She nods and pulls something out of her pocket. “Remind me, did you and Jay live together yet?”

“Not officially,” I say and lean my head against the backrest. Right. She was never his biggest fan and at some point, I stopped bringing him up during our calls. “We were planning on it, being engaged and all that. He has a bunch of stuff at my place, though.”

No wonder he hesitated about finding a place together. I still don't get it. How could I not see it?

"Good. That's good," Lauren says with a solemn nod and hands me her phone. "Call Gus from my contacts, please."

"Huh?"

"We're having your locks changed."

Barely an hour later, we're on our way back, all of Jay's stuff thrown into trash bags and piled into Lauren's backseat.

I would have been fine with ghosting him, shutting him out without wasting another word on that turd on two legs. However, Lauren rightfully pointed out that he'd want his stuff back and knows where I live. Ergo, back to his parents' house we go.

"I don't think I can do this without puking," I mumble when their driveway comes into sight. My heart beats into my throat as I fist my clammy hands in the hem of my shirt.

"Even better, in my opinion. Throw up on his shoes." Her jaw ticks as she puts the car in park. "He'd deserve it."

"His parents don't, though," I point out and she sighs. "They've always been lovely to me." Gulping, I try to swallow the emotions threatening to surface.

Jay's parents showed me what it could be like to have parents who love you. His mom jokingly called me "the daughter she never got to have" and cooked my favorite meals when she invited us for dinner. I could barely mention finding new snacks I enjoyed without his dad having boxes of it ready for me on our next visit, his face lighting up as he showed me.

"I hate it when you're right," Lauren grumbles, then points to the back. "Then open one of the trash bags. Throw up on his things."

"Great idea."

We wrestle all the trash bags out of her car, mostly filled with his clothes and random stuff he left around my house, such as his chargers or Tupperware. Though I couldn't help myself and dumped a pack of glitter into one of the trash bags. Whoops, didn't know that was hidden between his clothes and all that.

Among the two of us, we manage to carry the seven bags to the front door in one trip before ringing the doorbell.

Nora opens the front door, her eyes widening in surprise, then eyebrows creasing in confusion when she sees everything we've brought.

"Nora, I'm sorry in advance," I whisper to her, and she tilts her head in response, utterly confused, as we carry the trash bags inside.

"There you are, baby!" Jay pops his head around the corner, and I fight against the invisible force that wants me to freeze in my spot and cry while hitting his chest and dramatically sobbing, "How dare you?" Taking a deep breath, I try to brace myself. I have to do this.

Slowly, I glance up at him, putting all the hate that's searing through my veins right into my eyes.

Suddenly, I notice every single detail. His brown hair is more ruffled than this morning. His lips are red from kissing. There's lipstick on his cheek, almost hidden by his stubble. His usually perfectly ironed designer shirt is crumpled. There's even a hint of a goddamn hickey on his neck and it's not even subtle. Either I've been literally blinded by love, or they think they're winning already and have become careless.

Whichever it is, soon it's not going to be my problem anymore.

"Here I am." I want to scream, but I can't bring my voice above a whisper. I force a smile on my lips as I walk into the living room, throwing the trash bags into a corner. The clutter makes all heads in the room turn to me. My parents, his uncles, cousins, and so many people I've never even met before, all of them stare at me as if I just grew a second head. The room is suddenly so silent I could hear a pin drop.

"What's going on?" Jay asks cautiously and steps closer, reaching out to grab my arm, but I quickly take a step back. The smile on his face tenses as he speaks through gritted teeth. "You're acting strangely."

"You know," I raise my voice, making sure everyone in the room hears me. It might only be less than thirty people, but I might as well be in the spotlight in front of a sold-out arena.

It doesn't matter. Nothing matters.

"It's funny you should say that." I cross my arms in front of my chest. "I mean, considering I learned you've been fucking my sister less than an hour ago, I think I'm pretty calm."

A sharp gasp from my left leaves me feeling strangely vindicated.

"I don't know what you're talking abo—"

"Save it, Jay," I interrupt him and roll my eyes. Oh, the anger is back, baby. "At least have the balls to admit it. I heard you. Well, I left once you undressed each other." Color drains from his face, and he opens and closes his mouth in a pretty accurate fish-imitation. "And at home, I found the deleted messages on your tablet." I step closer to him and add in a whisper, "All of them. And I have a backup of every. Single. One. So, I suggest we do this amicably. I might not be the brightest, but trust me, I'm not as dumb as you might think."

Jay gulps, a muscle in his jaw twitching, anger burning in his eyes. He doesn't appreciate being backed into a corner, and that's exactly what I'm doing. Because I'm now well aware that if I wasn't doing this publicly, he'd probably find a way to gaslight me into thinking I imagined everything.

"Anyway," I add loudly. "Here's your stuff. Don't bother trying to come back to my place—your key won't work anymore. For the record: It's over." Then I turn around to the side of the room where my so-called family is standing, leveling Marissa with a cold stare.

She stands straight as an arrow, her blonde hair combed back strictly, her makeup flawless, as if she had dressed up for a glamour photo shoot rather than a family gathering. No smile. No emotion. Just slightly smudged lipstick and the same dismissive, slightly pitying look she always gives me.

"You're dead to me."

"Pfft," she laughs and looks around the room. "Cute how little Nic is trying to stand up for herself."

I eye her up and down. What a miserable witch. She thinks because she is beautiful and has perfected her fake laugh, the world is lying at her feet, just like our parents. It's laughable to think that I ever wanted to be friends with her.

Now I know better. Suddenly, it's easy to ignore her jab and turn my gaze to my parents instead. "You seem awfully unsurprised." I cross my arms in front of my chest, a wave of disappointment washing over me. "You knew?"

When all they do is shoot each other an annoyed glance, I can't help it—I break into a hysterical giggle. Anger bubbles in my throat, and suddenly, I can't find it in me to keep it inside.

"Of course you knew. God, this is next-level betrayal. Shakespearean. No, worse—reality TV level. Even the producers of the worst soap operas I've acted in would be like, 'Hey, that's a little much.' Let me get this straight. You"—I point at my parents angrily—"knew that my fiancé, the man who got down on one knee and promised me forever, was sleeping with her." I point at my sister, who rolls her eyes as if to say that all of this is just a big inconvenience to her. "The family's sweet little princess, the sun that the rest of us are supposed to orbit around like obedient little planets. And you just… what? Crossed your fingers and hoped I'd be dumb enough to go through with the wedding so all of you could get your part of my hard-earned money?" You can hear my heart cracking, but I'm far from done, years of frustration and desperation wanting to break free.

"I can't believe it. You even congratulated me. God, I can't believe you'd stoop that low. Most families emotionally manipulate their daughters into bad marriages for, I don't know, social status or a nice country club membership, but all of you went full-on con artists." I shake my head, pinching the bridge of my nose.

"Now, for the record, don't think you're getting a penny from me. Not a dime. No more shopping sprees, no more vacations, not even a fucking quarter for parking. Which won't be hard because I don't intend to see any of you again after today. You want money? Go ask your precious daughter or future son-in-law. Oh, wait—they don't have any! That's the only reason you still tolerated me, right?"

I can't be hurt anymore. As soon as I truly realized the extent of Marissa's betrayal, I knew they couldn't have been clueless. After all these years, I shouldn't be surprised anymore.

I'm just done. So. Fucking. Done.

"Oh, please." My mother rolls her eyes, her perfectly shaped eyebrows creasing, and meticulously lined lips thinning. "We knew you'd overreact and be dramatic. We didn't want to deal with that. Now look at you, proving us right." She waves her hand at the trash bags in a corner.

I take a deep breath, the words hurting more than I anticipated. "How could you? I know she's your golden child—"

"Ah, there it is. Always playing the victim." My father interrupts me.

"Surprise, in this case, I quite literally am," I say coldly, shaking my head. "And you know what? I'm done. And when you're old and Marissa puts you in the cheapest care facility available, leaving you to rot without necessities and die alone while she spends your money, I hope you remember this evening and how you screwed me over. Maybe someday you'll realize that you've lost the one daughter that actually gave a fuck about you. Because I assure you, the moment you are of no use to her anymore, she will cast you aside."

"How dare you—"

"That's enough," Nora interrupts and steps between my parents and me. God bless her. Then she turns to her son, hands trembling and eyes shining with disappointment. "Is she right? Did you do that?"

Instead of an answer, he stares at the ground to hide his face, turning red with shame.

Her eyes land on me, and the sadness on her face almost makes me tear up, despite the anger still raging through my veins hotter than a wildfire.

"I'm so sorry, hun. We had no idea," Nora rushes to assure me and funnily enough, she's the only person in this room, along with Lauren, who I'm inclined to believe.

"Thank you for everything, Nora," I tell her with a sad smile, the fight leaving me as I let her take my hand in hers. "I'm sorry it had to end this way, but please know that I am incredibly thankful for the way you accepted me into your family. I'll miss you."

She squeezes my hand, tears shimmering in her eyes. I bite the inside of my cheek, fighting to keep my own tears at bay.

"Don't be a stranger," she whispers, and that gets the first genuine smile out of me since I stumbled over Jay and Marissa.

"Thank you," I assure her just as softly. Then I pull my hand out of her grasp and let Lauren link her arm with mine as she guides me out of the house.

"You did great," she whispers and squeezes my upper arm. And as soon as the front door shuts behind us, I silently let the tears I held back fall.

This day was supposed to be one of the happiest of my life.

Instead, it became the day I lost everyone.

Okay, almost everyone.

Lauren maneuvers me into her passenger seat and drives off, and I can't shake the feeling that I'm reaching the end of a chapter.

Let's hope it opens the door for a new, better one.

Chapter 1

Nic

"It's going to be a fun new beginning,"

At least that's what I've been telling myself since I started the engine a few hours ago. I drum my fingers on the steering wheel, let out a deep sigh, and relax my shoulders. The last freeway exit is finally in sight.

"So. Much. Fun," I reiterate through clenched teeth, the kind of smiley-grimace you force your face into when someone says "Everything happens for a reason" while your life is on fire. If I repeat it often enough, maybe it'll start to feel real. Maybe I can gaslight myself into optimism. Either way, it's cheaper than therapy.

It's been rough. After leaving Jay's parents' house on that evening, three months ago, I couldn't bear returning to my own. The house where memories waited in every corner, sending flashbacks of catching him with Marissa piercing through my heart with a dull force equivalent to a barely sharpened pencil. A dull kind of pain that hits with force, fighting to pierce the skin and making it all the more painful.

Lauren took me in. Like a stray puppy abandoned in the streets after the new owners decided the Christmas present was too much effort. She drove me home, tucked me tightly into a blanket, fed me pizza and kept my glass full with vodka-mixers throughout the evening.

And then the next day, she picked me up like the big sister I'd always wished for and didn't let me continue the pity party any longer.

"You know what? Maybe we both need to get out of here," she said, spoon halfway to her mouth, piled with what was definitely our third tub of ice cream and absolutely no longer dinner adjacent.

"That sounds wonderful," I'd replied through a tight throat and burning eyes, still swollen from all my crying the night before. "I could really use a new start." Preferably somewhere far away from the celebrity hustle and bustle of Los Angeles.

Because there is no way I can go back to acting. I retired because I was ready for a new chapter, to enjoy the results of my hard work and plan my wedding or spend time with my family.

Well, that fell through.

But it doesn't change the fact that I'm done with that chapter of my life. Maybe for good. Maybe in five or ten years I might revisit it, but right now, I need something new. Something that helps me find out who I am, aside from Nicola Duncan, world-famous actress.

"As do I." When I lifted my gaze up to her, it was to find her with a faraway expression on her face. A different kind of pain reflected in the tightness of her eyebrows.

"Hey, I'm sorry for this mess. Fuck, I'm a bad friend. Is everything okay?"

"You're not a bad friend. And it will be." She turned to me with a sad smile. "Let's do it. Let's disappear. Or at least, dramatically relocate."

We clinked our glasses together as if we were sealing a pact with cocktail-based magic.

And damn it if I didn't fall in love at first sight with the lake house she showed me. It has a cute wraparound porch and the most stunning view of a lake with mountains in the distance.

Next thing I knew, although in reality it took a few weeks, it was a done deal, and we owned two houses in a small town that is home to a bookstore, a café, a flower shop, and an antique shop that might or might not have a ghost problem.

"I could see myself having extremely meaningful morning coffees out here," I said, squinting at the porch like it had just whispered life advice to me. "And you know what, maybe I need more early morning romance. Let's romanticize the fuck out of life," I'd said solemnly, and we clinked glasses one more time. Only that time felt more charged with determination.

Next stop: spontaneous life decisions disguised as self-care. A.k.a. the hair salon.

She'd been joking about a breakup haircut and honestly? I was three seconds from cutting my own hair with nail scissors anyway, so this felt safer.

I was more than ready for a change. I've been dying my hair darker for work—my manager insisted my natural blonde would only get me "dumb blonde" or sex bomb roles—but I've had enough of it.

I told the stylist to take out the extensions, bleach out the dye, and bam - now I'm back to blonde. Golden blonde. The real me kind. Now it brushes just past my shoulders, my natural waves breaking free, like it knows things are changing.

And weirdly? There's a weight off my lungs. I can finally breathe again.

Oh, how much lighter life can become when you're not surrounded by people trying to tear you down. As torn down as I was right after my breakup, now that I've blocked my family and Jay, I feel so … light.

No more scrutiny over what I decide to spend my money on. No more snide comments over my purchases or how much I'm spending on a hairdresser.

Turns out, when you take the emotional vampires off your invite list, life gets a whole lot shinier.

And quieter.

And *mine*.

And I intend to do exactly as I said: Romanticize the fuck out of it. And reclaim it. I'm not sure how yet, but I'm excited to find out.

Now here I am, driving down a winding road lined with trees that hide the sky, toward my new home, my new life. And, hopefully, my freshly assembled furniture. If I get there and it's not built the way I'd asked and paid handsomely for, only a mountain of IKEA packages mocking me, I might just burst into tears.

There was no way I was bringing *that* bed with me. The one my ex probably fucked my sister in. No fucking way. It's cursed, and it filled me with way too much satisfaction to watch it fall down the landfill.

I hide a yawn behind my hand, glancing at my GPS.

Less than thirty minutes to go. God, I can't wait to flop on my new mattress and have a nap that would make sleeping beauty jealous. Hours of driving are more taxing than I remembered—one of the few advantages of having a job that requires regular travel and a schedule so tight that you can only manage it with private jets.

I'm humming along to a Taylor Swift heartbreak song—because apparently that's who I am now—when suddenly something catches my eye. Right in the middle of the road.

A bag?

No. Oh no.

It's a lump.

A furry lump.

Holy shit, that's a cat. And it's not moving.

I slam on my brakes, tires screeching the way I do when watching a horror movie and come to an abrupt halt. Thank God this is Bumfuck, Nowhere, and the only other souls around are probably cows and the occasional deer. No danger of someone rear-ending me.

I throw the car into park and launch myself out like a woman in a made-for-TV movie. My brain's already spiraling.

What if it's dead?

Wait—lone woman being stopped in the middle of nowhere ... isn't this how horror movies start? I check the bushes at the side of the road as if the branches will spell out "Danger hiding here" with some cute little arrows pointing to the masked killer.

Then again, I've survived a cheating fiancé, toxic relatives, and a dramatic hair transformation. If I get taken out by a fake cat trap on a rural road, at least my funeral portrait will look amazing.

"Hey, sweetie," I coo in a high-pitched voice that I hope signals that I come in peace and cautiously move closer to the black-furred animal.

What if it's not a cat, after all?

What if it has rabies?

The closer I get, the more my heart races until I hear a soft, miserable *meow*.

I gasp, my pulse racing; first, because I'm relieved it's actually a cat and not a small bear with its mother waiting nearby. Being mauled to death right now would put a serious damper on my romanticizing life plans. Second, because there's blood everywhere and soft, agonized breaths make adrenaline kick in, and I spur into action.

"Oh no, sweetie." I immediately take off my jacket and put it over the cat, grimacing when it makes a pained sound. "I'm sorry, cutie pie, but I have to move you." My eyes scan the area for more cats, but it seems this little animal was all alone.

I bite my lip to refrain from crying as I pick it up to agonizing meows, carrying it to my passenger cradled to me as I would hold a baby, softly talking to it and stroking its head.

My heart beats in my chest like it's about to chisel a hole into my ribcage as I search for the closest vet office on my phone. Then I set the GPS to lead me there on the quickest route.

"You'll be all right," I continue cooing at the cat softly, reaching over to gently stroke its head as I turn the key in the ignition. "Stay with me. We're going to find someone who can help you."

Tears spring into my eyes as the little creature, despite being weak with pain and shaking in agony, purrs under my fingertips.

"I'm going to save you," I promise her and clear my throat, clogged by emotion. "Don't even think about dying on me, sweetie."

I repeat it. Like a mantra. Though its breaths turn weaker and weaker, and the purring stops as she mobilizes her strength to survive.

Trees and fields fly past me as I follow my navigations directions to the closest veterinarian.

When I glance over, I catch it staring at me with wide yellow eyes as if saying, "It's okay. Thank you for trying."

Fuck no. She can't die on me. Ten more minutes to the vet—I decide to make it in five. A life's at stake, and if ambulances cannot give a shit about speed limits, I shouldn't either.

"Fuck, you've got to make it, sweetie pie." Another weak meow, and I notice her moving under my hand.

I can't check on it, though, because I am breaking every speed limit on these empty streets as I attempt to save the cat's life and try to keep mine. Suddenly, it tries to climb into my lap. And it takes every ounce of strength to not fucking lose it and break down while speeding down these curvy roads.

"No, no, sweetie," I glance down but let's be real, there's no way I'm going to stop it. The small creature clumsily makes her way over the center console and climbs into my lap, curling her tiny body into itself until she all but disappears in my shirt. She's covering my favorite pants in blood, but I don't care about that right now.

"Don't cry, Nic," I mutter to myself and softly stroke the cat's soft head. It's the only thing I could see that wasn't covered in blood.

"Turn left in one mile, then you will reach your destination in 100 feet."

"We're almost there, sweetie," I whisper, glancing down at the cat. Its eyes are closed, and it's shaking in my lap. "Oh, shit."

A flash of red and blue lights suddenly floods my rearview mirror, and my stomach drops to my knees. "Oh, great," I mutter, eyes flicking between the cop car behind me and my phone's GPS. "Of *course* this would happen. Heroically saving a cat, only to get arrested. Very on brand."

I glance down at the lump of fur on my lap. "If I get a ticket, you better make it, whiskers."

Brakes screeching, I come to a halt in front of the vet clinic, a protesting meow coming from my lap as I unbuckle and turn in my seat to jump out.

"Ma'am—"

"All's in here!" I shout at the cop without even looking, flinging my wallet onto the roof of my car. "License, registration, my entire life savings. Take your pick—but let me save the cat!"

And without waiting for a reaction, I run into the vet's office, only glancing over my shoulder once to make sure I'm not getting Tasered. Thank God, the front door is open.

"I need help!" I storm inside frantically, and scan it, but there's no one here. "Hello? Fucking help!"

"Whoa, hey, calm dow—" My head whips around as a man rounds the corner to what I assume are the treatment rooms. "Oh."

"Don't 'oh,'" I snap and run over to him. "Are you the vet?" He nods slowly, clearly confused, and I all but thrust the cat into his arms. "Good. Fantastic. Then *save this cat*. Please."

Without a word, he takes the cat out of my arms, confused frown turning into pure focus right before he turns around and walks away with quick steps.

And I stay where I am, frozen to the spot, watching him disappear into one of the rooms.

It's only now that everything hits me. I lean my back against the reception desk, crossing my arms in front of my chest, trembling fingers digging into the fabric of my shirt as I try to calm my breaths.

God damn it. My life is giving me fucking whiplash.

"Miss, here's your wallet."

I bite the inside of my cheeks. Hell, I completely forgot about the cop already. Taking a deep breath, I straighten my back and turn to him.

"Thank you." I can't quite force a smile on my face as I accept him handing me my wallet. But his eyes widen ever so slightly, and with a deep sigh, I slowly run my hand over my face. Right.

"Huh. I was wondering if your ID was fake, but you're—"

"Yes," I interrupt him, gaining me a small, unimpressed eyebrow raise. "Sorry. I would prefer we keep that quiet." I force one of the corners of my mouth upward. "And I'm sorry for speeding; I had to get that little guy here as soon as possible."

"All right." He takes a deep breath, and now it's his turn to cross his muscular arms in front of his chest. Wait, his muscular what?

It's only now that I take a better look at him. He's young. Early thirties, I'd estimate, built like a mountain of a man. Seriously, that uniform fits him tighter than a glove. One flex and the seam on his arms might rip and reveal more of his tattoos that I can only catch small glimpses of.

And he's tall. When my eyes wander up to his face, I notice his knife-sharp jawline hidden by the most subtle scruff. His hair is short but tousled, thick and sandy brown, as if he ran a hand through it and left it that way on purpose. Finally, I meet his green eyes.

"You're good. Nothing happened, and that's a valid reason. Just don't do it again."

"Thank you, officer—"

"It's Erik. Everyone here calls me that."

"Okay then, thank you, Erik." My smile is turning more genuine as the stress of the past hour slowly rolls off me. "I appreciate it. And so does the cat, although it can't quite voice it."

"Are you one of the lake mansion buyers?" He lifts his eyebrow at me curiously while mine scrunch together in confusion. In all the chaos, I hadn't even realized—

"Wait. Is this Wayward Hollow?" I point at the ground.

"The one and only."

My shoulders sag in relief. No matter what happens, at least I'm almost at my new home.

"Good. That's good. Then yes. I think I'm one of the lake mansion buyers."

He nods, then extends his hand.

"Then let's do this the proper way. I'm Erik Madden, the Sheriff of Wayward Hollow. If you have any issues, please don't hesitate to reach out. Happy to help."

"Nicola Duncan," I say nervously, shaking his hand. "Which, uh, you know already, and I'm happy to be here." He's got a nice grip. I can't say how icky I find weak handshakes—I've encountered more than my fair share in show business. Mostly from egotistical men who sneered down their noses at you yet had the grip of a dead fish.

Erik's eyes trail behind me and widen ever so slightly. I let go of his hand and whirl around to find the vet emerging from the hallway. My heart beats in my throat, and when he lifts his gaze, his expression makes my heart sink.

"I'm so sorry," he speaks softly and subtly shakes his head. "There's nothing I can do for her. From her injuries I'd say a car hit her at full speed. She's bleeding internally, and I can barely find a bone that isn't broken."

"No." The word comes out in a broken whisper. "Listen, I don't care about the costs. I—"

"I'm sorry," he interrupts softly but firmly at the same time. "The kind thing here is to let her go. Even if by some miracle she survived, it would be a life full of pain."

"Fuck," I whisper, letting my head fall back, desperate to hold it together.

It's not working, though.

"Will you stay with her? I'm sure she'd appreciate you being with her as she … goes," he asks, and I nod before I even fully register his question.

"Of course." I angrily wipe away the tears streaming down my face. I already imagined out life together, cozy and cuddly evenings in front of the tv with the first friend I made in my new life. Just why? Fuck, I feel so helpless.

He leads me to one of his exam rooms where the cat is lying on a stainless steel table, ears perking up the tiniest bit when I enter.

"Did she have a microchip?"

"No," he says softly and motions for me to walk closer. "And she's extremely thin. I'm pretty sure she's a stray."

"She?" I step closer, fighting with more tears as I lean over her. "Does that mean you don't have a name, sweetie?" She immediately nudges her head against my palm, her whole body trembling in pain. I force a smile on my face as I try to keep myself together. The thought of her dying without even a name tears my heart apart piece by piece.

"We can't have that," I say softly, taking a moment to think. "I think you're Chaos, little lady," I whisper, then nod to myself. "Yes. I like it. Chaos."

As if she understands, she closes her eyes, her tongue darting out to lick my palm. And the tears I've been trying incredibly hard to keep in check overflow again.

"Are you ready?" The vet asks, and I nod silently. As much as I want her to live, as much as I need some fucking positivity in my life, she's suffering. She doesn't deserve that.

I can't watch the vet give her the injection. All I can focus on are her ragged breaths and the way her whole body suddenly relaxes at once.

Then there's silence. Deafening silence.

Her breathing stops and her head becomes a heavy weight on my hand, and I can't help the sob escaping me.

She's gone. And now I'm all alone again. Any hope I had in a positive outcome has shattered, like the universe embodied a cat and swiped a glass off its kitchen island.

"Hey, are you okay?"

Chapter 2

Nic

I lift my head slowly until I meet the vet's gaze.

Okay? Am I *okay*?

I can't help it. Before I even realize what's happening, I'm laughing hysterically.

"Am I okay?" I repeat through tears and take a step back, gingerly setting down Chaos's lifeless head on the sterile steel table. For one last time, I run my fingers over her tiny, soft forehead. "What a great question, Mr. Vet." I don't know what to do with my hands, until finally, I clutch the hem of my shirt.

"No. No, I'm not okay. My whole life is going to shit and this little creature dying just became the tip of the shitshow fate is throwing my way." I start pacing the cramped little room, everything breaking out of me.

"You know, one second, I had a good life. Then I caught my fiancé cheating with my sister, and now I get to pick up the pieces. And I thought she was it." I point at the lifeless Chaos on the table, more tears falling from my eyes. "She was well on her way to becoming my living, breathing omen that everything would be all right. I believed so strongly in her recovery, I already imagined how we would navigate this new life together. Hoped some cosmic, I don't know, entity sent her specifically for me, a sign that there was hope. The universe saying, 'Welcome, weary traveler. You've made it to Wayward Hollow, and life here will be good.' She was going to be the first new friend I made here—the adorable sidekick to this new life."

I wipe tears off my cheeks while the rant continues to bubble out of me.

"And now she's dead. Actually dead. I haven't even seen my new house yet, not unpacked a single box, and my sign from the universe is just … gone. This tiny glimmer of hope, yanked away like 'Whoops, sorry, never meant to get your hopes up!' And if my hypothetical good omen is now lying dead on this table"—I take a deep breath and turn to face him, all the fight and hope I had, falling from me as my voice breaks—"what does that mean for me?

"Everything is a mess, and I can't think of anything to make it worse—I know saying that out loud is daring the universe to one-up itself, but I don't get it. Was she a sign that things would get better or that I still have a way to go to rock bottom?"

I stop, breathing heavily, my eyes burning with even more unshed tears.

"Fuck. I'm sorry, I don't know what I'm saying!" I sob, and my eyes jump to little Chaos on the table once more. "Ignore me. Please, for the love of God, pretend you didn't hear that." I take another deep breath and square my shoulders, wiping my face before facing him. "So, what now?"

"Eh …" I finally truly look at the man, and it takes everything in me to contain a gasp.

Why is every man in this town so goddamn attractive? First the Sheriff and now the vet?

Obviously, I noticed that he was roughly my age. But in my panic, I never realized he appeared to be fresh out of a fashion magazine. His dark green shirt stretches slightly over his muscular shoulders, the sleeves rolled up to just below his elbows. He's got a jaw that looks sharper than the scalpels I can see in the corner of the exam room. But what makes my cheeks turn red are his eyes.

Beautiful blue eyes that radiate kindness and calm, even though the rest of his face is marked by worry.

His tousled dark blond hair seems intentionally imperfect, every strand laid down with the right precision to make it appear effortless, like he ran his fingers through his hair.

And here I am, probably with mascara running down my face and definitely wearing clothes covered in Chaos's blood. Because that's just me and the perfect first impression I intended to make on my future neighbors. All part of my plan. Obviously.

"Would you like to … bury her?" he asks, and my eyes dart back to the table, more tears gathering in my eyes. God, I can't take my eyes off her. Poor little Chaos.

"You know what?" I clear my throat and blink a few times before I continue. "I think I would like that." Then I sigh and deflate. "But I wouldn't even know where, I haven't even—"

"Been to your house, I know." My eyes jump back to him, and I open my mouth to apologize again for my earlier rant when his warm hand on my shoulder makes me shut up.

"Don't worry about it. You had a rough day. Get to your new place and have a warm cocoa." He tilts his head, then softly shakes it, giving my shoulder a soft, reassuring squeeze. "Maybe a spiked one. I can keep her until tomorrow if you'd rather come to collect her then?"

"That—" I pause as my emotions well up again. "I—"

"You're welcome. Now, I have to fill out some paperwork. Why don't you stay with her a bit longer? I have one of the best cuddlers to keep you company."

"And then he brought me to the waiting room and told me to stay put for a minute, promising he had something to make my day better. And, *yes*, I know how that sounds, Lauren, but he did not whip his dick out. Nope, he sent in his dog, an adorable husky with the most striking blue eyes," I tell Lauren, words tumbling over each other.

I'm not doing great by any means. But I can at least pretend to myself that I have a grip on my emotions again.

She appeared at my place only minutes after I pulled into the driveway, quicker than a raccoon sensing an unattended snack. And now, she's helping me carry the rest of my boxes into my new home.

They hold the kind of mementos I wouldn't dare trust a moving company with. My electronics, my movie collection, and some photo albums from my childhood I couldn't bring myself to sort through and burn yet.

"And he didn't lie. That dog provided peak emotional support. Soft fur, face-licking, the whole nine yards. Definitely made me feel better. I should have asked for its name," I continue as we walk outside to grab the rest.

"Better consolation than any man could offer," Lauren says approvingly and snickers. "I'm glad you're better now. That sounds like a rollercoaster of a day." She opens the trunk to take another box. "I never knew you had such a big heart for animals, though." She steps aside so I can grab the last one. "And you already met the town's hotties."

"If I had a free hand, I'd fan myself," I admit sheepishly, my cheeks burning. "You should have seen them. With the current quota, this little town must be full of hot guys. It's two for two. How did you find this town again? A magazine pointing out a single's dream destination?"

"Swear to God, I was only checking out for cute houses far away from big cities, and the lake was a bonus. Now stop acting as if meeting hot guys is some kind of punishment."

A deep sigh falls from my lips as I kick the front door to my new home open. "It's not. And, I mean, they're nice too. I can't imagine dating so soon again after …"

"Those who shall not be named?" Lauren sets down her box in the living room, then shoots me a scrutinizing stare. "I get it. For now. Let's revisit this conversation in a few months."

"My answer will be the same," I tell her with an eye roll and lock the car behind us. "Anyway, what are you complaining about? More hotties for you."

"Yeah, sure," she scoffs, but thankfully drops it.

"Thank you for helping me, Lauren."

"Of course." She makes her way through the labyrinth of boxes and assembled furniture to give me a tight hug. "We made it," she mumbles right next to my ear, and I release a deep breath as I throw my arms around her.

"Yeah. We sure did."

She releases her tight hold on me and takes a step back, a small happy smile playing on her lips.

"It will be great." I lift my eyebrow, but she puts her hands on my shoulders and gives them a reassuring squeeze. "It will. Just look." She pushes my shoulders until I turn around. "This house is even more gorgeous than in the photos!"

"Maybe because I've paid a good penny to have it renovated and furnished," I quip, but a spark of optimism is slowly igniting inside me. "Do you want a tour?"

"Obviously." She rolls her eyes and follows me back to the hallway leading to the front door.

We walk through the ground level, and I make a mental to-do list that I will forget by the time we're through. Page one: unpacking my movie collection and books and printing some pictures for all the frames I bought for the living room and hallway.

It's the perfect mix of modern and whimsical. My furniture is made of thick, sturdy wood, created to last forever, the walls adorned with subtle floral wallpapers.

"It's giving modern fairy," Lauren whispers at one point, and it makes my lips stretch into a grin. "Or flower witch. The cutesy kind that raises plants and brews love potions instead of casting curses."

"That's exactly what I was going for." I pull her to the kitchen, and the sight takes both of our breaths away.

"Who was your interior designer again?" she asks, voice low in awe. Huge arched windows provide a perfect view of the lake, only a few trees between my house and the water. It's a clear day, allowing us to see all the way to the other side of the lake, where forests turn into mountains, snowy tops shimmering in the evening sun.

"Me. I came up with all this." I wave my hand around vaguely. "It took forever to find just the right furniture and wallpapers."

The kitchen is illuminated by the orange evening light, turning the white cupboards and shelves a beautiful peach color.

"Are those … decorative plaster?" Lauren lays back her head and stares at my ceiling. "Nic, this is *fancy*, fancy."

"I figured if this becomes my forever home, I should go all out from the beginning," I whisper with a shrug. "How is your house doing?"

"I'm committed to DIY," Lauren says with a happy giggle that makes me smile right along with her. "Don't laugh! But maybe keep your interior designer skills close—and your guest room, well, guest ready."

"Will do. Just let me know at what point you need a key." I laugh and slowly walk through the kitchen, drinking in every detail. They even put away all the new cutlery and dishes I bought.

Suddenly, I hear something shuffling somewhere in the house.

“Oh my God, what was that?” I freeze, my gaze jumping around the room in panic.

“What?”

“I heard a sound … a shuffling?” I say and tilt my head, straining my ears and flinching as if I was a balloon dog at a porcupine convention. “There! Did you hear that?” My panicked eyes meet Lauren’s wide ones as she slowly nods.

“I think it’s coming from your front door.” Lauren takes my hand, and as quietly as possible, we creep back through the kitchen, trying not to make a sound. "Is this how we die? An ax murderer on our very first day here?"

"We're not going to get killed by an ax murderer," I whisper back. 'Hopefully' I add, only in my mind.

“There it is again,” Lauren whispers once we reach the front door, and we stare at each other with fear-ridden eyes. Slowly, I peek through the peephole, but I can’t see anyone on the other side of the door.

“Do you actually think an axe murderer would stay in sight?” Lauren hisses, and I shoot her a glare, placing my finger in front of my lips to shut her up.

“A salesman would,” I whisper softly and grab an empty vase, weighing it in my hand. Yes, this can do some damage.

“Good thinking,” she answers equally softly and grabs an umbrella that’s leaning against the wall next to her to use as a weapon.

Lauren and I exchange a glance, and I lift a hand to slowly count down from three with my fingers.

God, this feels like we’re in the middle of a horror movie.

I tear the door open, shouting“Haaaaah!” to surprise the perpetrator, only to reveal … “Nothing?”

"What?" Lauren pulls the door open wider, also stunned when there's nothing on the other side. "I heard it crystal clear. What the hell?"

"Oh my God, please don't tell me I bought myself a haunted house." I close the door and stride over to the kitchen, pinching the bridge of my nose. Nope, I will pretend the last five minutes never happened. "Did they—ah. Thank God. They also brought my groceries." I find a bottle of wine in my fridge, and after opening five drawers, a corkscrew as well. "God, I need a drink."

"And I'm right there with you." Lauren nods and opens the cupboards to find wine glasses. Then she grows impatient and grabs the first thing she finds, which are mugs with little cartoon crocodiles on them. "It's a small housewarming party."

"Nobody I'd rather have it with." I fill them up, then I clink my mug against hers and take a sip, grimacing when it hits my tongue. "God, that is awful."

"Still not a wine girlie?"

"Apparently not." I take another sip, much to Lauren's amusement when my face stretches into a grimace yet again. "Nope."

"You have lemonade in your fridge. Just mix it." She takes a sip of her glass, humming happily when she tastes it.

"Good idea." I jump off the bar stool at my kitchen island and open my way too big fridge. If doomsday ever comes—as long as I have power—this baby will feed me for months once filled. Holy hell. "Don't tell anyone from France, though. They'll have my head."

"Nah, I think they banned guillotines a while back."

I giggle as I grab the lemonade from the fridge door.

"Also, the wine is from Italy. You're good."

"Thank God," I chuckle and fill up my mug to the brim, then take a sip. "Yeah, that's better."

"Well, here's to a new start, pretty men, and a peaceful life." She lifts her cup again.

"Yeah. To that." The two cups make a deep sound as they clink against each other. The two of us keep sipping while enjoying the silence, looking outside where the sun disappears behind the mountain tops on the other side of the lake. Gentle waves flicker in the orange sunlight and trees sway in the soft wind.

"Where did summer go?" Lauren asks suddenly and sets hers down.

"Fitting though, isn't it? New season, a new beginning …"

"Right."

We shoot each other smiles, then startle again when we hear a scratching at the door.

"Nic, I hate to say it, but you might—"

"Yup. Guess I've got a haunted house."

"So cool. I'm sleeping over." She reaches for the wine and pours herself some more. "If you don't mind."

"You are always welcome to my haunted guestroom."

"Speaking of ghosts. We should find a spot for your little, short-lived friend while there's still light."

"I guess we should." My eyes dart over the grass reaching from my home down to the lake. "Let's go."

Chapter 3

Henry

The bell above the entrance door to Caleb's Café rings and his eyes dart to me as soon as I enter.

"So you met the new guys?" Caleb asks me gruffly, a coffee machine behind him announcing a finished espresso.

"Damn." I chuckle and walk right past him. "Word travels fast. Can't a guy sit down for his after-work coffee first?" I ask over my shoulder as I slide into my usual booth, beckoning my dog along. "Come on, Jensen Ackles."

"I still can't believe your dog is named after an actor."

"Look at him. The resemblance is uncanny." Caleb rolls his eyes at me, but I shrug it off.

I first saw a video of him online a few months ago, so thin he could barely stand up and fur riddled with ticks. One whimper and I knew instantly that brown husky with the sad eyes was my soul dog. When I finally got to meet him, it was love at first sight. He already had this name then, thanks to his foster mom being a huge fan of the actor.

I tried to get him to respond to Loki, but he wouldn't have it, and there were far more pressing matters, such as getting him to a proper weight. So, Jensen Ackles it is, and now he might be the most spoiled dog in the county.

I truly think adopting him was my destiny. From being raised by parents who were famous for taking in strays, saving even the most hopeless cases, to becoming a vet and carrying on their legacy by saving animals like Jensen. Those who have been discarded, left to die by the people who were supposed to love and care for them. Those who experience the kind of cruelty only humans can show.

They say dogs resemble their owners, and I can't deny that with Jensen. But Caleb? If he were a dog, he'd be a German shepherd. He always sports a grim expression, and he is constantly alert and in tune with all his senses. If something is off, he'll know it before anyone else and be ready to step in.

Yet, I'm sure that somewhere behind those sharp cheekbones and lady-killer scruff, there's a giant golden retriever hidden in him.

"Better than naming him after me," I retort, shooting him a pointed glare, considering I'm sitting in a café called Caleb's. "Henry Mason the Second doesn't quite have the same ring to it, does it?"

"Touché." He sits down with a sigh, crossing his arms in front of his chest, and watches me with that unnerving, emotionless stare of his.

"So?"

I bite the inside of my cheek to keep from smiling. I can't believe he's nosy. Mr. *I don't give a fuck about gossip* is curious about the town's newbies.

"She's pretty," I mumble, averting my gaze as heat crawls into my cheeks.

"Pretty" is almost understated—she was fucking stunning. Even with mascara smudged on her cheeks, messy hair, and her nervous ranting. "I'm sure you'll see her around soon."

"That's all you've got?" he asks, lifting his eyebrow slightly, and I shake my head.

"Really? You're prying for information without even giving me coffee first? What lousy service in this establishment."

"You know I'm closed already." He shoots me a glare that comes from the depths of his soul.

"Don't try to kill me with a look. Jensen Ackles will avenge me."

"Nope, Jensen loves me." Caleb leans down, adjusting his cap to keep it from falling off. And, of course, my dog immediately perks up when Caleb begins to pet him and licks his hand. "Who's a good boy?"

"Traitor," I whisper, making Caleb's eyes soften. "Don't get cocky. Jensen loves everyone. Now, get your hands off my dog and get me a coffee." He shoots me another sharp glare until I add, "Please."

Only minutes later, he's back with my signature cappuccino decorated with a white middle finger on the foam and a biscuit on the side.

"Thank you," I say pointedly, and pop the biscuit into my mouth.

"So?" He lifts his eyebrow expectantly, and I sigh, motioning for him to sit down again.

"Okay. But you need to keep this on the down low." He lifts his eyebrow, unimpressed. Caleb is not one to gossip. He's not even one to listen to gossip, even though he's right at the center of it. Whatever happens in Wayward Hollow, it *will* be talked about right here, within these four exposed brick walls.

Like when the first person moved into the lakeside mansions. Kieran. All tattoos and the dark, brooding type, but only on the outside from what I've heard. I haven't met him beyond a quick introduction a few weeks ago.

Nobody knows where he came from or what exactly he does, but, boy, there sure is a lot of speculation. I remember precisely how Courtney, the owner of the flower shop two houses down, sat right by the window and all but shouted her theory into her phone as she told her sister. She lives overseas and judging by how loudly Courtney likes to talk during their calls, I think she's trying to eliminate her phone as the conversation-middleman.

She thinks Kieran is a mobster hiding from law enforcement. Since he is tall, muscular, has dark hair, tattoos, and is giving a bad boy vibe, that was her best guess.

God, I love this small town and its nosy people.

"She rushed into the clinic earlier," I tell Caleb, after scanning the room to ensure we're alone. I enjoy our town gossip as much as the next person, but losing a pet is not something that should make the rounds. "Had a cat with her, which, sadly, was a hopeless case. The poor thing got hit by a car—" I take a sharp breath and gulp, wrapping my tense fingers around my mug. It never gets easier to lose an animal. "There was nothing I could do but end the pain for her."

"I'm sorry, man." The slightest hint of worry washes over his face, and I quickly shake my head.

"It was the kind thing to do." I clear my throat. "Anyway, that's the extent of our meeting. "But if you're curious, she's coming to the clinic tomorrow. You can catch a glimpse then."

He tilts his head, eyeing me like I'm crazy. Then suddenly, his expression softens.

"Maybe I will."

"Did I miss the notice for a town meeting?" Kieran suddenly appears beside us, startling me when he suddenly speaks. Even Caleb, the unmovable giant of Wayward Hollow, flinches.

I'm waiting for Wayward Hollow's newest addition to collect her furry friend. But Jensen kept whining at the door to be let out, so I decided to enjoy the sun for a while in front of my clinic. Caleb joined us quickly once he saw me sitting outside. I can't believe even the town's anti-gossiper is curious about our new town members, even if he's hiding it behind a nonchalant expression.

"Holy shit, newbie, you scared the shit out of me." I clutch my chest and shake my head at Kieran.

"Sorry, didn't mean to. What are you two doing out here?"

Before we can answer, Jensen Ackles weighs in with a high-pitched *awoo-woo*, making Kieran smile.

"Oh, hi there, sweetie. Can I pet him?"

"Sure. Kieran, this is Jensen Ackles. Jensen, this is Kieran." I chuckle as I introduce them while Kieran kneels on the ground, and my dog loses no time making a new friend.

"I shall call you Squirrel," he whispers as Jensen licks his face.

"Here she comes," I whisper to Caleb and nod toward our left where the same black car with tinted windows she arrived in yesterday pulls up.

Today was a slow day. I only had an appointment in the morning. My cousin Ethan lives two towns over and asked me to come over to check on one of his cows who was behaving strangely.

It's incredibly rare to have someone bring in their pet without having chatted with me first, and this town doesn't exactly brim with emergencies. Yet, you better bet when they do, shit's going down.

Just like yesterday.

I shoot the box with the cat's body a wistful glance where it resides on my reception desk inside. Young cats are tough, and this cat couldn't have been older than two years.

No matter how often and to which animal it happens, their deaths always hit hard.

Kieran's low whistle pulls me right back to reality. "Now I see why you're waiting out here. They're gorgeous!"

"They?" I turn my head right as the driver and passenger doors of her car open. Her blonde, wavy hair pops up from the driver's side, and another, slightly shorter woman with lighter and longer blonde hair climbs out from the passenger side.

They're chatting happily, and a part of me is relieved that the beautiful stranger seems to be in a way better place than yesterday.

She was so shaken up. I got worried about whether she made it home okay.

"Hi there," she says when she stops next to our little group, sounding nervous. "I need to apologize again for yesterday. I'm sorry. Let's try this again. I'm Nicola, but please call me Nic."

Baffled, I take a deep breath. She's even prettier than I remember. Today, her sharp blue eyes aren't smudged with makeup or red-rimmed. She's wearing subtle makeup, the kind that makes her seem to glows from within. She has a faint blush on her high cheekbones and a shimmer along her narrow nose, making her look as if the sun shines on her, even indoors. Her lips have the slightest tint, as though she's been biting them—and I can't take my eyes off them.

From the corner of my eye, I see a grin tug at Kieran's lips and quickly refocus.

"A pleasure to meet you, Nic. I'm Henry." I smile and nod toward the others. "And that's Caleb. To nobody's surprise, the owner of Caleb's, the café two doors down."

"That makes sense," Nic says with a chuckle. "Good to meet the person who will feed my caffeine addiction."

"And that's Kieran." I nod toward the third guy in the group. He plasters a smooth smile on his face before he gets up, my dog jumping up his side to get more attention.

"And this is Lauren, my best friend."

"Nice to meet you all," her friend adds. She's also gorgeous, with a wide grin on her heart-shaped face, soft bangs down to right above her eyes. She seems vaguely familiar—but I can't put my finger on it. Maybe she was in town before to scout the lakeside mansions? I feel like I've seen her before.

They didn't resemble each other much apart from their hair color, but their mannerisms are so similar that I would have pegged them as sisters. The same dimple appears in their cheeks when they grin and both their eyes keep darting to my dog.

"And who is this wonderful creature?" Lauren leans down and holds out her hand for Jensen. "Hello, you handsome boy. I heard a lot of good things about you."

"That is Jensen Ackles," I say, unable to help my chuckle when my dog whines for more attention.

"No way." Nic and Lauren burst into laughter. "I didn't even realize you named your dog after an actor!"

"To be fair, he already had the name when I adopted him, and he's incredibly stubborn. Even if I'd wanted to, I wouldn't have been able to rename him."

"Okay then, Jensen Ackles." Lauren kneels to play with him while I walk inside and retrieve the box the two of them are here for.

"Here," I say and hand Nic a palm-sized card. "Again, I'm sorry. If there had been any way to save her, I would have."

"Thank you." Her lips tug into a smile that doesn't reach her eyes. "I'm sure you would have." She peeks at the card and turns it in her hands, her eyebrows furrowing in confusion. "What is this?"

"I do a final nose and paw print for all of my patients," I explain and watch her open the card, her eyes widening when she sees the small prints. "It's something for owners to remember their pets by. You might have just found her, but she obviously meant a lot to you."

"Yeah," Nic whispers with glossy eyes, staring at the card. "She did. Thank you, Henry."

I inhale sharply. I adore the way my name sounds from her lips. Sweet and melodic, like wind chimes on a quiet, sunny morning.

Lauren takes the box from Nic's hands and smiles mischievously at me, Caleb, and Kieran. "You know what? You should join us for her funeral."

"I don't—" Caleb starts, shaking his head.

"Absolutely," Kieran interrupts him quickly. He tries his best to appear solemn, but I can see the corners of his mouth twitch with amusement. "We would love to pay our respects to …" He motions at the box.

"Chaos," Nic completes his sentence. "You don't have to, though. It's—"

"Oh, we'd love to," Kieran assures her, and even Jensen Ackles whines his approval, nudging his head against her leg.

"Great! Then that's settled." Nic giggles and absentmindedly scratches my dog's head. "Follow us, gentlemen."

"Why did you do that?" I hiss at Kieran the second the two girls are out of earshot. We walk over to my car, since I've installed safety features in it to make sure my dog's protected if we get into an accident. Not that many happen in Wayward Hollow, but you never know. There's enough dumb or borderline suicidal wildlife around that likes to pop up in front of fast-driving cars.

"One, because they're pretty." I roll my eyes when he wiggles his eyebrows, and Caleb pinches the bridge of his nose. "And two, because they are new here, and as a newbie myself"—he gives us a pointed look—"I know life is more fun here if you make friends."

"We got plenty of friends," Caleb mumbles, making Kieran break into barking laughter.

"Sure, coffee boy. But can you ever have enough friends?" He leans closer to me. "Also, I saw how you stared at the taller one. Go shoot your shot." A knowing grin is on his lips as he takes a step back. "Friend."

I keep my eye on him as he climbs into my backseat, while I open the trunk for Jensen Ackles. This might be the first time I've exchanged more than a greeting with him. That must have been the stereotypical small-towner in me who meets new people with a healthy amount of skepticism. Turns out Kieran might just be an all right guy.

One that might be way too observant for my taste.

"You only asked us over to get us to shovel the grave, didn't you?" Kieran asks Lauren as he heaves another heap of dirt out of the hole, and I can't help but chuckle. Nic has the other shovel in her hand, and we are digging a grave for the little creature.

Well, Nic and Kieran are.

I'm standing to the side and shoveling the dirt into a neat pile to prevent it from messing up Nic's whole garden, while Caleb is keeping Jensen Ackles in check. He'd be all too happy to help with the digging. However, I don't want him to make a habit of it at and turn my garden into an excavation site as a result.

"I'd help you, but I need to hold on to this." Lauren lifts the little box with a grin and shrug. "She'll be in the cold, dirty ground soon enough, so I think it's fair to hold her in my warm arms until then."

"This should be deep enough," I interrupt their banter and assess at the hole they've dug. "Three to four feet is the rule of thumb and slightly deeper than half of you"—I nod at Kieran—"seems about right."

Nic struggles to find footing to climb out of the hole and grimaces, eyes jumping from the muddy ground to her hands and light beige coat.

"Here, I'll help you," I say, stabbing my shovel into the dirt and bending down to her.

She tilts her head, puzzled, but quickly catches on, looping her arms around my neck. I slide my arms around her waist, plant my feet, and push upward.

She lets out a tiny squeak as her feet lift off the ground, clinging tighter. With a low chuckle, I shift her weight easily, and in one fluid motion, we're standing. Her body presses against mine, not an inch of space between us.

For a second, neither of us moves. Fuck, she's beautiful. Her eyelashes flutter nervously, her breath feathering over my throat, and …

"Now me!" Kieran shouts, ruining the moment, and extends his arms, lifting his face to the sky, presumably waiting for me to lift him out too. Reluctantly, I let go of Nic and take a step back from her.

"You get a hand." I shake my head at him when he purses his lips in a pout. At first, he tries to pull me down there with him, but I fully expected that and counter it. After a short scuffle, he gets out of there almost by himself.

"You picked a great spot, though," he says to Nic as he pats dirt off his jacket. His face contorts into a grimace once he realizes the mud is clinging to him and soaking through the fabric of his jeans. "It's a beautiful view from here."

And he's right.

Everyone in town knows that the lake is the most beautiful spot around. It's where we used to go with our dates if we needed some uninterrupted time away from curious eyes in our teens.

The spot Nic picked for the cat is perfect. It's slightly elevated and not far from the lakeshore. From here, you can see the water, the mountains, and the forest on the opposite side of the lake.

"I'm sure she would have loved it," Lauren adds solemnly.

Nic nods and takes a shaky breath. "I bet she would have. But we'll never know."

We gather around the freshly dug hole. Caleb takes the box out of Lauren's hands and, together with Kieran, gently lowers it inside it. Jensen whines and attempts to throw himself into the mud, but I grab him by the collar and gently scold him to stay.

"Goodbye, Chaos," Nic mumbles and crosses her arms in front of her chest once the box is settled. Lauren steps closer to link her arm with Nic's and gives it a reassuring squeeze. "You're gone too soon, but I hope you're having the best time in cat heaven."

"May you be surrounded by tuna and treats." Lauren nods.

"See you in the next life."

Chapter 4
Henry

"On a scale of one to ten, how fun was your trip to Jacob's yesterday?"

"However 'fun' you'd scale shoving your whole arm into a cow's behind," I tell Caleb. I take a hearty sip of my coffee he set on the counter. Meanwhile Kieran, who's in the seat next to me, grimaces and proceeds to make retching sounds. "Very mature."

He turns to me with an apologetic grin. "Sorry, had that picture pop up in my head, and it straight-up stimulated my gag reflex."

I subtly lean my chin onto my hand and raise my middle finger at him.

"Don't be crass," he scolds me, and I shake my head at him.

Grabbing my coffee and the sandwich that Caleb slides over the counter to me, I carry them to my usual table. Jensen Ackles follows me diligently, with his eyes firmly on my food.

No matter how crowded Caleb's café gets, nobody ever sits here for some reason. Maybe this table has a haunted vibe that I'm oblivious to. But it's the perfect table. It has a clear view of the town center through the big front window. From here, I can see the whole café, with its brick walls, black metal accents, warm wood, and moody lighting, which definitely fits Caleb's equally moody demeanor. I can also stay mostly hidden behind a giant plant with leaves big enough to double as umbrellas. I can pop in headphones and be left alone or eavesdrop.

Anything going on in this city? There's no hiding it from this table.

Caleb might have unofficially called this one the "stalker table" for exactly this reason, but it actually became my usual table because it's always empty. At least, that's what I'm telling myself.

"Dang, it's full here." I hear a familiar light and melodic voice from the entrance, and I can't help myself. I stretch my neck to peek past the plant and catch a glimpse of Nic, watching her without being noticed. Her wavy blonde hair is loosely swept up into a claw clip, with soft strands spilling out in effortless waves. They surround her face like the prettiest golden frame of a picture I can't take my eyes off.

Caleb shoots me a look that says *get a grip*, and I shrug with a sheepish grin.

There's something about her that has me in a chokehold.

She came into my practice with a fire, every pore of her ready to fight to keep that cat alive. Ever since she shoved that little cat into my arms and pleaded with me to save her, she's been on my mind.

That tinge of sadness in her eyes that appears to be a permanent resident, the way she absentmindedly curls a strand of her hair around her finger when she's thinking.

She's a mystery I want to solve. I want to know how to make that sadness in her eyes disappear. What her soft hair feels like when I run my fingers through it, how her lips would fit against mine, and …

"Earth to Henry?" Caleb suddenly asks next to me, and I glance up at him. Even Jensen gives me a confused look.

"What?"

"Would you mind sharing your table?" He nods to Nic and Lauren, who glance around the café cluelessly, trying to gauge who might get up soon and free up their table.

The bad news is nobody will. It's the middle of the daily afternoon rush, which means everyone and their mother and grandma are in here, checking the special afternoon snack of the day. Today, it's cinnamon rolls with walnut pieces—since I'm Caleb's taste tester for pastries, I already know they're divine. I also know that one of them is reserved for me, waiting somewhere behind that counter.

"Yeah, of course," I say, trying to sound nonchalant, but judging by the amused look he shoots me, I'm failing spectacularly.

"Great. Then you're getting company. Over here!" He waves the two of them over, and before I know it, they scoot into the seats opposite me.

"Anyway, it wasn't a one-off. I'm about 92 percent sure my house is haunted," Nic continues their conversation as she scoots into the booth. "Hi, Henry. It's good to see you."

"Hi, Nic. Lauren," I greet the two of them with a polite smile. "Just an FYI, Jensen Ackles is under this table, and he *will* beg for food."

"You know, I will never get tired of that name," Lauren says with a giggle, then leans down to peek under the table. "Such a handsome boy!"

Jensen gets up from between my feet and trots over to her for some well-deserved pets. Meanwhile, I turn to Nic, only now realizing what she just told her friend.

"Wait. Your house is what now?" I ask before taking a sip of my cappuccino.

"Haunted," she declares with a sigh and a convinced nod. "And I'm pretty sure it's by the ghost of a maybe disgruntled, maybe attention-seeking cat."

I almost spit out my coffee, though I'm not sure if it's out of surprise or amusement.

"Wasn't it newly built? How can there be a ghost?"

"That's what makes it even worse," she groans and hides her face in her hands. "I mean, a two-hundred-year-old haunted Victorian mansion with cobwebs and creaking floor—sure, I'd expect that. I'd probably buy a velvet robe, get myself a fancy candle holder, and embrace the gothic lifestyle." She gets a faraway look in her eyes. "I'd spend my evenings reciting Edgar Allan Poe in the hallways and ask a skull whether to be or not to be. But the paint is barely dry on this house, and here I am, dealing with a ghost cat scratching my doors and pushing glasses off my kitchen counter."

"So, ghost kitty is, like, the official paranormal diagnosis?" Lauren asks with a chuckle, then nods at my dog. "We should call the Winchester brothers."

"I bet it's Chaos," Nic says with a deep sigh as she contemplatively gazes out of the window. "Come to think of it"—she turns to me and narrows her eyes—"shouldn't she technically be your ghost then, too?"

"Hate to disappoint you, but the only scary sounds in my home are this one's farts," I say with a chuckle and point to where I assume my dog is under the table. As if he understood me, he suddenly appears by my leg and pulls a face that resembles a smile.

"Yes, you are," I coo, brushing my hand over his head. "Such a scary creature."

"Please," Caleb scoffs, appearing at the table out of nowhere. "I've seen bread that was scarier than your dog. How are you two doing? Are you settling in okay?"

"*You* are scarier than my dog," I scoff back and grin at Jensen, who agrees with a soft whine. From the corner of my eye, I see Nic rummaging in her bag, then pulling out her phone.

She glances at it for a moment before swiping and making it disappear in her bag again.

"Henry and Nic are ghost parents. That's how we're doing." Lauren snickers and looks up at Caleb. "Can I get a pumpkin spice latte, please?"

"None of that sugar shit here. I have coffee and milk, and I can get you any combination of those."

"Then a regular latte macchiato, please," Lauren says, her lips pursed into a pout. Nic quickly adds, "Make it two, please."

"Coming right up—wait, what? Ghost parents?"

"That took a while," I tease him and duck when he lowers his notepad, without a doubt to slap it against the back of my head. What can I say? Gentle head slaps are a sign of love in this café.

"Nic thinks her house is haunted."

"I not only 'think', I *know*." She crosses her arms in front of her chest and glares at Lauren. "There are no cracks in my doors, and there is no way any wind is getting into my house. Yet I keep hearing those scratching noises. Lauren was there; she heard it too!"

When I glance at Lauren, I'm surprised to see her nod.

"At first, I thought it was probably a mouse. Or any other tiny, normal, non-paranormal creature. But then I realized no normal mouse would follow me from *room to room*. Every room I go into, *scratch, scratch, scratch*—she's there. It's like she's stalking me! Or judging me? I don't know. The scratching surely sounds judgmental."

"You've got issues," Lauren says lovingly, fighting a grin. "No cat would judge you, and ghosts don't exist."

"Oh, really?" She turns in her seat and shoots Lauren a glare. "Then how do you explain this? Every time I try to hang something up, I swear a chill runs down my spine. Like, she disapproves of my decor choices. Last night, I put up a perfectly normal picture from some premi"—she stops herself and clears her throat, giving Lauren a meaningful look—"some *event*. Honest to God, nothing offensive to the feline spirit realm—and I kid you not, the whole thing slid right off the wall. No nails loose, no breeze, only straight-up cat disapproval."

"Maybe you didn't put it up properly?" Kieran asks from his space at the counter before he gets up and motions for me to scoot over. "Make some space. This is better than any gossip about myself I could hear from over there."

"Oh, hi, Kieran," Lauren and Nic say in unison. Even Caleb is curious, crossing his arms in front of his chest, his notepad with our orders still in his hand.

"I'm ... oddly invested now."

"You should be invested in our coffees," Lauren teases him. "I wasn't kidding about my caffeine addiction."

"Shawna's got it." He looks over his shoulder at the woman who has been helping him work through the noon-rushes for years now, before leaving early in the afternoon to spend time with her grandchildren.

Her copper hair, streaked with occasional gray strands, is tied back loosely, yet it holds up surprisingly well—even though she moves between the counter and tables with the energy of a whirlwind. She's the kind of woman who can take six orders at once, clean the counter, and make you laugh—all in the blink of an eye.

Once he catches her eye, he moves his hand to signal their order to her, in what appears to be their own secret sign language. She pulls out a pencil tucked behind her ear and quickly writes down his order.

"Okay, good." Lauren nods happily, her fingers nervously tapping the table.

I pay the banter of Caleb and Lauren no mind, but I catch the corners of Nic's mouth twitch as she listens in.

"I definitely put it up properly, Mr. Science over here," Nic finally continues. "And try to explain the clear and loud meowing right next to my ear at three o'clock in the morning. Or the way something left an indentation in the blanket and kept my feet warm right after. Both scared the hell out of me."

"Maybe you dreamed it?" Caleb scratches his scruff, and I tilt my head. "Sleep paralysis?"

"That would be a cute sleep paralysis demon, though." Lauren giggles.

"Are you sure it's not creaky house sounds and guilt about Chaos's passing?" I wonder and sip my coffee, noting the way they wistfully stare at my mug.

"No, the place is sturdy. No creaks, no whistling. It's sturdier than my emotional state." She freezes for a moment, then shakes her head. "Which isn't saying too much, now that I think about it." She takes a deep breath, and then, finally, Shawna appears with their drinks, receiving grateful smiles from the two of them. Lauren's eyes light up as though she may just have found her new favorite person. Funny, Jensen does the same when I open a bag of treats. She wasn't kidding about her love for coffee.

"If it's a ghost, what's your plan?" Lauren asks, taking a sip of her coffee and releasing a deep, happy sigh. "Oh, this is good."

"Thank you," Caleb says gruffly, but from the corner of my eye, I can see the corner of his mouth twitch.

"Are you going to call a pastor for an exorcism? Ignore it? Draw salt circles around your house? Find a pet psychic that will show her the light?"

"I was thinking more along the lines of bribery. I ordered a bunch of treats and left some out in a little dish, you know, as a peace offering. But when I woke up, the dish was mysteriously tipped over, and the treats were all over the floor, but there were less than before. So now I'm paranoid that I've *encouraged* the ghost cat. Maybe I've accidentally opened some portal to the cat afterlife, and now I'm obligated to feed her every night."

"You realize you're talking about feeding an invisible, likely non-existent cat spirit?" I raise my eyebrow at her amusedly. She takes the little biscuit off the saucer and throws it my way. It bounces off my sweater, falling to the ground.

There's no use trying to retrieve it. Jensen barely lets it land before he devours it. Thank God the biscuits Caleb uses here are, well, not exactly dog-friendly, but not poisonous.

"Oh, I realize it, all right. But you don't get to judge my supernatural pet-care routine. Not until you have your own cat ghost that knocks over picture frames and gives you the heebie-jeebies in the middle of the night. Maybe she'll be at your place tonight, Daddy." I grimace at that last word, making the whole table laugh.

"God, I can't believe I've been here for only a few days, and this town is already making me a crazy cat lady."

"Welcome to Wayward Hollow, I guess," Caleb says dryly, and Kieran hides his wheezing laughter behind his hands.

Nic glances at Lauren and exhales a deep sigh. "Just what have we gotten ourselves into here?"

"Don't worry, you get used to it," Kieran says, chuckling at their skeptical expressions.

Chapter 5

Nic

"You think I'm crazy," I accuse Lauren as we walk along the lake, letting the cool autumn breeze play with our hair. "Hell, *I* think I'm crazy."

"I need context, babes. Did the ghost strike again?"

"All the damn time." I sigh and kick a pile of leaves, making them flutter through the air. The trees are turning a beautiful shade of orange, and it's finally the kind of weather to wear a cozy sweatshirt—a stark difference from the California sun all year round. And I have to admit, I'm finding this much better.

An hour ago, Lauren knocked and all but pulled me out the door for a nice autumn walk. She's holding a pile of leaves in her hand, the ones she deemed prettiest and intends to dry for a scrapbook – one of the new hobbies she decided to try out. I wonder if it'll stick.

"Yesterday, I sat on my couch, as one does, trying to read a book and not doom scroll on my phone, but I swear to you, an invisible cat jumped onto my lap." Lauren gives me a skeptical look, and I halt. "I swear to fucking God. She nudged her head against me, and I even felt it vibrating with a purr when I asked if she was Chaos. Don't look at me like I'm insane—you heard the scratching, too!"

"I did," she says calmly and stops walking too. "But it could have been, I don't know, a squirrel on your roof. Have you checked your carbon monoxide levels?"

"A squirrel on my roof when the scratching clearly came from my front door?" I ask her with a lifted eyebrow. "And yes. The fire detectors in my house also read carbon monoxide levels. If that were the issue, you'd probably hear the incessant beeping from your own living room." I roll my eyes. Why does nobody believe me?

"Hey, it sounds more plausible than 'A ghost cat haunts me.'" She exhales a deep sigh, then reaches for my hands. "I'm sorry, Nic. I know how sad you are about that cat and how much you wish she were haunting you. But ghosts don't exist."

"Logically, I know you're right," I say grimly and pull my hands from her grasp, slowly continuing to walk. "But I choose to believe I have a ghost pet now. At least it distracts me from my fresh heartbreak."

"Better, don't talk about it too loudly, or they'll Maurice your ass and put you in a padded cell." Lauren quickly catches up and links her arm with mine. "I bet they have one of those here. The town is way too idyllic so far; there must be a catch."

"Maybe the catch is ghosts," I point out with a giggle, making her groan and pinch the bridge of her nose. "And I hate to say it, but in this particular case, the available Jensen Ackles is not fit to exorcise demons."

"Then let's hope their dark town secret is some kind of swinger club," Lauren snickers, and I roll my eyes.

"Let's hope not. I mean, Henry, Kieran, and Caleb I could see myself fantasizing about, but the rest of the town?" I shake my head. "No, thank you. I do not need to be mentally undressing the guy we saw at Caleb's who still wears socks with sandals." I shudder. "Some things can't be unseen."

"Aw, come on," Lauren says teasingly, nudging me with her elbow. "You said the sheriff was eye candy, and I saw at least one more hottie at Caleb's."

"When?" My eyes grow wide. "Because when we were there, the average age of the other customers was probably eighty or above. Not that an eighty-year-old can't be attractive, but since when are you into men your grandpa's age?"

"I might have gone back to the café another time," she admits sheepishly, and I stop in my tracks, looking at her with betrayal in my eyes and mouth agape. "Or three."

"And you didn't tell me?" I ask loudly and clutch my shirt dramatically. "I can't believe it. You got coffee without me. The betrayal." I put the back of my hand to my forehead and sway, pretending to faint.

"Cut it out, you drama queen." Lauren laughs and gives me a gentle shove. "Hope acting is not your job or anything."

"Yeah, luckily not," I agree with a giggle that abruptly dies when my phone buzzes in my pocket. God, do they never give up?

With a heavy sigh, I study the cloudy sky for a moment, then pull out my phone, only to decline the call when I don't recognize the caller ID. Maybe I should change my number after all.

"What's that about?" Lauren asks and points at the phone in my hand. "Your whole demeanor shifted from happy-go-lucky Pooh to Eeyore, just like that." She snaps her fingers while I put my phone away.

"I've been getting all these calls," I finally tell her. "I'm not sure if it's Jay or any of my genetics-sharers, or someone from the industry. I haven't been answering them." I take a deep breath. "Someone apparently tattled about Jay and me breaking up, though. It could be many people."

"Oh, fuck," Lauren curses with wide eyes and kicks a stone into the lake. "Have you …?"

"Googled myself? Of course, I have." I sigh and blow a strand of my hair away from my face. "The internet is full of speculation. Will I make a comeback now that my retirement plans have changed? Where am I? Is the reason we broke up because I had an affair? Apparently, Massimo and I appeared awfully close on set."

"God, if they only knew you are pretty much the opposite of his type," Lauren quips with a giggle.

"I'm not planning on outing him, so let's keep them guessing." I shake my head at her when she continues to giggle. "Maybe it's time for a new number anyway—a clean cut from my old life."

"Oh, that's very final, though. What if you want to go back?"

"If the industry wants me to, they can deal with a new phone number." I roll my eyes and continue walking. We're almost at my place now, and it's getting chilly. "It's a decision for another day. Are you coming in for a hot chocolate or coffee?"

"Oh, absolutely. I hope your ghost cat won't scare me away." I stick my tongue out at her and climb the stairs to my porch.

Why do I hope that little Chaos will do exactly that?

"You have *such* a nice view from here," Lauren mutters, walking up to my ceiling-high windows facing the lake.

"Don't you almost have the same one?" I ask her, handing her a steaming mug of hot chocolate spiked with Bailey's.

"I mean, you have my house in view," she says with a giggle and immediately takes a sip.

"How is that going, by the way?" I walk over to my couch facing the windows and sit down, careful not to spill my drink. "Do you already regret DYI-ing it?"

"Oh, it's still fun," she says with a grin. "Don't get me wrong, I spend more time researching, watching tutorials, or browsing for materials, but I'm not tired of that yet. I'm calling that a win."

"Wait, you're doing everything from scratch?" I blink at her, surprised.

"I mean, it's only cosmetic. It's a new house, after all." She giggles, and the alcohol is tinting her cheeks pink. "No wiring or plumbing, but those bookshelves are driving me crazy. You assemble one and think you've got the hang of it, but then you completely mess up the next one and the first breaks down the second you try to put your books in it."

"I'd probably break my thumb with the hammer. Or get a bunch of splinters," I mutter and put my mug on the coffee table to pull my legs onto the couch.

"Hey, what are these?" She suddenly holds up one of the catalogs I had sent here, then starts flipping through the pages. "Interior design?"

"Yeah," I say, reaching for a pillow. "I had a lot of fun putting everything together, and I have a lot of free time. Maybe college is in my future after all." I shrug and take a deep breath. "I mean, I need *something* to do or work toward. You've got your house to keep you busy, but I have"—I wave my hand around vaguely—"nothing."

"There's nothing wrong with focusing on yourself first." She shrugs. "Take that break you've been talking about. Rediscover who you are outside of your family and a relationship. Find a new hobby. I just bought myself a pottery set. I mean who knows, maybe there's a clay master hidden inside of me."

"I know there's nothing wrong with that." I hug the pillow tighter to my chest. "I wouldn't even know where to start, though."

"What about 'romanticizing life?'" she asks with a raised eyebrow, and I softly shake my head.

"I can only romanticize so much on my own. And it's not exactly giving me *purpose*," I try to explain, when suddenly I notice a dip on the cushion right next to my legs.

"I knew it!" I say triumphantly, flashing a grin at Lauren, who blinks at me, confusion written all over her face.

"What's going on?"

"Come on, sit down," I say with the sweetest smile, patting the couch right next to me.

"Okay?" It sounds like a question, but Lauren sets down her mug, too, and sits. She gives me a suspicious glare while I keep the most pleasant smile on my face.

She calls me crazy for thinking a cat is haunting this house? Now is the time to prove her wrong.

Please, Chaos, don't disappoint me.

"What the—?" Lauren tenses visibly, and her head whirls to me as she stares at me with wide eyes and mouth agape. "Are you fucking kidding me?"

"I'm not doing anything," I point out, lifting my hands in the air to prove it.

"Did something climb into my lap? Why can't I see anything? What?"

"Told you." I shrug.

"I can't believe it," she mutters, shaking her head. "It's actually a ghost kitty." Then she shoots me a mischievous smile. "Do you think we could see her if we blow some flour over her?"

"I think the only thing that would do is make a mess."

"What else do you have your fancy robot vacuum for?"

But before I can answer, I sense a tap on my calf. The cushions dip as though she jumped off, and only a second later, we both hear a scratching on the door.

"I'm getting a mad sense of déjà vu," Lauren whispers, her eyes darting between me and the front door. "You better get that."

"I can't believe it. I'm taking orders from a ghost cat," I whisper and shake my head at myself, but get up to take check anyways. "The universe won't even let me be a crazy cat lady, I swear to—" I pull the door open, only to see … nothing.

"Hello?" I ask loudly and scan the area. All I see, though, are bushes, trees, and grass I should probably mow sometime.

Way to go, Nic. Maybe this one wasn't a ghost kitty scratch after all, but, I don't know, crispy leaves being blown against my front door.

"Hello?" I shout again and step out onto my porch. If it were my little paranormal friend, there must have been a reason she wanted me to go outside. "Why—" and then I suddenly hear it. A soft *meow* from under my porch.

Without hesitation, I hurry down the steps. "Come on," I plead. "Meow again." A beat later, I hear it—a tiny sound coming from right beneath the porch steps.

"Is everything okay?" I hear Lauren's footsteps approaching. She leans over the railing and gives me a quizzical look. Meanwhile, I lower myself to my knees and search the area under the stairs. "Here, take my phone flashlight."

"Thanks," I tell her, realizing I left mine inside. Fuck, it's dirty under here. There are leaves and some beer cans that the construction workers must have left, and …

"Oh no," I whisper and narrow my eyes when I see movement not too far under the stairs.

"What is it?"

"It's a cat," I whisper, and stretch my arm to reach the pile of leaves that just moved. "Only a little more …" Finally, I feel something non-leafy under my fingers. Soft. Warm. Gently, I grab the cat and retract my arm.

"She's tiny," I coo as I pull her close to me while I get up. My heart melts now that I see her. She must be super young. She's so small and has the most adorable orange stripes, covered in what I hope is mud and not blood.

"What's going on here?" Lauren asks amusedly. "Are you becoming a cat whisperer?"

"Seems like it." She's small. Looks like I need to make another emergency trip to Henry. My cheeks flush with heat at the thought.

I might have lost most trust in men. But hell if Henry's gentle demeanor and kind smile make me wish I hadn't.

"Oh my God." Lauren bursts into laughter, and I glance up at her. "You're a cat lady now."

Chapter 6

Nic

"Please be there," I whisper under my breath as I drive to town, under the scrutinizing eyes of the orange kitten.

Lauren and I found a shoebox and got her situated in there with a towel and a small pillow. The whole time, I was just praying for the kitty to be okay. I think she might be? And by that, I mean I see no blood, and it has all its limbs. That's about as much as I can judge.

However, she keeps *screaming*. Not cute, little meows or whiny complaints. No, she's full-on screaming, and I don't know why. She sounds miserable, and all the worst-case scenarios keep flashing through my mind. What if she's bleeding internally? Or has a painful tumor?

My heart is racing, my hands clammy as they white-knuckle the steering wheel, memories of little Chaos and her miserable whines flashing through my mind.

I can't go through that again. This little one has to be okay.

What if she doesn't make it? And what if she does? What do kittens even eat?

I may have a full fridge, but what if I accidentally give it something toxic?

I run through a million questions, each making me panic more. Finally, I reach the town center and throw my car into park in front of Henry's vet office, glancing at the windows and …

Oh no.

There's no light on. Fuck. Of course there isn't. It's after seven in the evening. Of course he's not working anymore.

"No, no, no," I mutter under my breath as I jump out of my car.

Having a good work-life balance is important and all that, but I really need him and his brain right now. I hurry to the entrance, pressing my face against the glass, but it doesn't make him magically appear, which is disappointing.

My eyes dart between my car and the dark window, anxiety making my stomach drop as I hear her even through the closed car door. What if the next vet is a three-hour drive away? What if the kitty won't make it that long?

Just as I'm about to bolt to my car and floor it to the nearest emergency vet, I see a little piece of paper stuck to the door.

Out of office. In emergencies, call my cell phone.

Before I even realize it, I have dialed the number and am pressing the phone to my cheek. I pace the sidewalk anxiously, biting my lip, and send a prayer to the universe with each unanswered ring.

Come on, Henry. Answer it.

"Hello."

God, I could cry when I hear his voice, relief making a weight fall off my shoulders.

"Henry, I need you."

"Huh?" I hear some rustling, as if he's getting up from a couch or something, and the soft whines of Jensen Ackles in the background. "Nic?"

"Okay, wait. Not like that! Not in the 'cue the romantic music and slow-motion run' way. More in the 'this is an emergency, and you're my only hope' way." I force myself to take a deep breath before I pass out by talking more than my breath allows. "Would you believe me if I told you the ghost cat brought me a kitten?"

"A kitten?"

"Yeah. Sorry, I should have led with that. I need your help, please." I stop and close my eyes for a moment, sorting my thoughts. "Let me start from the beginning: I found a kitten under my porch, and I can't tell if it's all right because it keeps screaming. And one ghost cat is already more than I can deal with. If you could take a look at it so I don't have another cat on my conscience, that would be fantastic."

"Where are you now?"

"Right in front of your clinic." I resume pacing up and down his storefront. "And let me tell you, it's eerily silent here in the evening. Does everyone in Wayward Hollow disappear at seven p.m. on the dot? I might as well be in a graveyard." I glance around the town square and the dark storefronts. "This is so creepy. Like the set of a horror movie. If I get turned into a werewolf, please don't let anyone shoot me."

"I'm on my way," he says, followed by rustling and him calling for the dog. "But for your information—we're team Edward in this town. So, be careful."

"That's not comforting," I mutter as he hangs up, then quickly climb back into my car.

This city might be in Bumfuck, Nowhere, but I'm not going to risk waiting outside.

There's a sudden knock on the window I see a shadow from the corner of my eyes. I shriek. Then relief washes over me when I realize it's exactly who I was waiting for. Immediately I turn to the little creature on my passenger seat and whisper, "Sorry."

"Relax," Henry says with a chuckle, and once I unlock my car, he opens the door for me. "No werewolf hunter, only me."

"I'm not sure whether to be glad or disappointed," I tease him with a wink as I climb out.

Fuck, it's good to see him. Anxiety seeps out of me as he takes charge of the situation.

"Where is the cat?" I gesture for him to come with me. He follows me so closely I can feel his warmth against my back. Even more so when he glances over my shoulder as I open the passenger door.

"Here's today's little emergency," I say and step aside, leaning down to give Jensen Ackles a proper greeting.

What an adorable little fluff face.

"Aw," Henry coos once he sees the little orange kitten. Without hesitation, he scoops her right up, talking to her in a high-pitched baby voice while Jensen and I follow him to his office diligently.

She appears even tinier in his giant hands.

I'm so distracted, I barely notice we enter the exam room, but as soon as the disinfectant hits my nostrils, I freeze. The hair on my neck stands up as memories of my last visit here race through my head. I force myself to take calm breaths as panic tugs on every corner of my mind.

Jensen gently nudging my calf pulls me out of the temporary trance, and I clear my throat, trying to relax.

"You're pale," Henry points out, worry etched into his furrowed brows as he turns to me, the cat snuggling against his shirt. "I know it's a loaded question, but are you okay?"

"Yeah," I whisper, ignoring his little jab at my rant from the last time he asked me the exact same thing. "Just … don't let her die, please?"

"I'll do my best," he says and is right next to me in two strides, gently guiding me to sit down. "I promise."

"I know you will."

My eyes are glued to him as he checks the kitten, his forehead creasing as he gently examines its leg as she keeps screaming.

Something about that tenderness and confidence has a thought hitting me with the force of a freight train: Even though I barely know him, even though everything inside me screams at me to be skeptical … I trust him.

I gulp, the realization making my fingers tremble and a heavy weight settle in my gut. I thought Jay and Marissa tore my heart to shreds, obliterated any ability I had to trust people.

Well, people aside from Lauren.

But Henry? For some reason, being close to him makes me forget about the mistrust I should have. I'm torn. He's making it incredibly easy to trust him, yet every single cell in my body is cautioning me, trying to protect me from getting my heart broken again.

On cue, my phone buzzes in my pocket, and I lift my gaze to the ceiling, blinking away tears and swallowing down my emotions. No. Not now.

I let it buzz, ignoring it. Like Henry's curious gaze in my direction.

My arms snake around my midsection as he does more tests with the cat, and all of a sudden, a knowledge settles in my gut.

I'm on my own.

Sure, there is Lauren, and she's an amazing friend, but this is … different.

There's nobody at my place who will have an opinion about me adopting this cat. Nobody who will start a fight with me about what cat food to buy or where to put which cat tree in the living room. Nobody to judge me when I spend the next few days holed up in my new home for several-day-long pity party if she doesn't make it.

Nobody will care.

The realization is a tough pill to swallow. I guess loneliness is a new emotion I'll have to get used to. Yet it's still a whole lot better than expecting Jay or any of my family members at home. Who would have thought?

"The good news is, she'll be all right." Henry's voice pulls me right out of the beginning of a self-deprecating rant. "She had a splinter in her foot. That's probably why she was so … vocal." He chuckles and runs his fingertip over the tiny creature's head. "A flea bath and some food, and she'll probably be fine."

"Probably?" I blink up at him and force myself to swallow down the panic. "What is the bad news?"

"I need you to keep an eye out if her mother comes back," he implores, and picks up the kitten, letting her gnaw on his thumb.

"It's a girl?"

"Yes, you have another lady on your hands. She's only around three weeks old, so very much still a baby. Her mom would do the best job of keeping her on track and healthy."

"I didn't see another cat," I say contemplatively. After we put her in the box, I looked under the porch again. I walked around to see if there were any other cats, but I didn't see any. "I think I have some tuna somewhere; I'll try to lure her back with it."

"Wait a second," he says and disappears into his office for a moment. "Here is some high-calorie cat food. If she is around, she'll need it with a fresh batch of kittens."

"Thank you," I say, but I don't think those words do a good job of encompassing what I mean to say. God, he's considerate.

"Are you taking her home with you?" Henry asks, and I freeze mid-movement. Right. "Because if you're not, we need to find someone to take care of her."

God, can I really care for a little creature like her? Apparently, I can barely care for myself.

"I … don't know," I whisper, swallowing down the disappointment in myself and get up, nervously pacing the room.

My phone buzzes again, and I take a deep breath, pinching the bridge of my nose and closing my eyes for a moment to collect myself. God, how I want to throw this piece of shit phone against a wall.

"Someone's important today," Henry teases with a chuckle, but I can't find any humor in this. I'm too busy spiraling.

What business do I have taking in a kitten? Evidently, I can barely manage to be a functioning human being. "What if I do it wrong?" I look at him helplessly. "What if I end up killing her?"

Chapter 7

Henry

"Listen," I say softly, walking over to her and putting my hands on her shoulders to gently guide her to sit down.

She looks so lost all of a sudden. Not at all like the woman who had been joking about werewolves with me a few minutes ago.

"She might be little and skinny, but she's not made of porcelain. Anything you do can only be better than leaving her outside to freeze." It might only be early autumn, but the nights are damn cold already. I'm keeping this to myself, but I'm not sure she'd have made it through the night if Nic hadn't found her.

"Knowing my luck, *something* is going to happen … I don't know, maybe a meteor crashing through my window right into this little cutie." She shakes her head, eyes focused on the now blissfully sleeping kitten. Her eyes dart frantically around the room, wide with panic and her breath shallow.

"I'm not even going to get into how unlikely that is," I reply with a chuckle. I crouch down in front of her and wait until her ocean-blue eyes meet mine.

Jensen Ackles, the attention-starved creature that he is, immediately trudges over to nudge his nose against my cheek, thinking I got on my knees just for him. The force of it almost makes me lose my balance. Then he lays his head on

Nic's thigh, and instinctively, her hands run through his fur, a faraway expression on her face.

Slowly but steadily, her heavy breaths even out, and she sinks back into the chair, all the tension unraveling.

"What's going on?" I ask her gently, putting my hands on her knees and drawing slow circles with my thumbs.

"I'm scared," she whispers, her eyes glistening with unshed tears through wet eyelashes as she glances at me.

"That's okay," I assure her, trying my best to convey reassurance. "And that's the exact reason I'd be okay with sending that little creature home with you."

"But—" She stops herself and keeps blinking at me, and I can almost see her thoughts racing through her mind.

I wonder why she's suddenly insecure. There are so many pet owners who shouldn't be. How come the person with the biggest heart I've met recently is too afraid?

"No more thinking. You can do it," I encourage her as I stand up. "Come on, we're giving her a flea bath, then I'll show you how to feed her."

Reluctantly, she lets me pull her up, Jensen Ackles softly protesting when his human pillow becomes unavailable.

"Come on, hold her." I hand her the kitten before she can object. As anxious as she was, she accepts her instinctively, her tense shoulders slowly sagging in relief when she realizes nothing bad is happening.

"Wait—did you say fleas?" she asks, eyes widening with concern. Immediately, she holds the cat out at arm's length, glancing anxiously between me and the furry culprit.

"You'll be fine." I chuckle and lead the two over to a sink in the corner, letting her step in front of it while I observe over her shoulder. "Now, set her down at the side and turn on the water. Check if it's a bit warmer than lukewarm."

She follows my suggestions diligently and then looks up at me expectantly. "Like this?"

"I trust your judgment." Her expression turns panicked, but I quickly continue to take her mind off the water temperature. "Here's the shampoo you'll want to use. Put some of it on your hand. The first thing you want to do is put a ring of it around her neck. Basically a soap necklace."

"Why?" She reaches for the kitten. Thankfully, she's more than happy to let Nic handle her. Not without a few weak, whiny protests when she first works the shampoo around her neck, though.

"Because the fleas will try to run to her head once you put the shampoo on her body. If you put the soap around her neck, they can't."

"Got it." She nods, slowly but surely becoming more confident in handling the cat.

"Great. Now soap her up below the neckline. Make sure to work it in thoroughly." I watch her tenderly working the product into the little kitten's fur. "You're doing great!"

"Am I?" she asks. Then she suddenly tenses when the cat protests. Damn, this cat has learned she has a voice, and she sure is making use of it. Even I have never encountered one as vocal as her. "What's going on?" she asks, her voice an octave higher and full of panic. "Why is she screaming again? Oh God, am I hurting her? Are you sure she's okay?"

I try not to laugh, but it escapes in a snort. "Everything is okay, Nic. I'm pretty sure she's just not a fan of water."

"Okay." She takes a deep breath and her shoulders start to slump as the tension leaves her body. "I get it. Right there with you, little cat. Honestly, if I'm not in a bubble bath with at least three vanilla scented bath bombs and two rubber ducks named Perry and Daisy, I'm out. And this"—she eyes the flea shampoo—"is definitely not that. Now here we go. You're all soaped up. I think. What now?" She glances at me. "Does it have to soak in?"

"Now you put her under the faucet and wash it off. Try not to get her head."

"Got it."

She flinches when the cat wriggles in her hold, trying to escape. To Nic's credit, though, she's holding the creature perfectly. Her fingers are wrapped around it in such a way that it has no way to escape.

"Now you take this sponge," I say and hand it to her, breath catching in my throat when the scent of her shampoo hits my nose. She's all vanilla and cinnamon, a cozy evening at home, and it might have become my favorite scent. Quickly, I clear my throat. "Soap it up and wash her head with it. Don't get her eyes."

"Okay." She takes a deep breath, her fingers gingerly moving around the little creature's face, quickly pulling away when she yawns.

"See, that isn't so bad now, is it?"

She shoots me a glare over her shoulder, and I grin, taking a step back. "There's a towel to your left. Dry her once you're finished, and I'll get a heating pad going."

"A heating pad?"

"Yes. Kittens that age need warmth," I mutter and turn to leave. I need a minute in another room to take a fucking breath that's not tinted with her scent.

Because it's driving me crazy.

My inability to think when she's close, the way her presence does its damnedest to override every sliver of logic in my brain—how can she hold me this captivated? I've known her for less than a week.

I mean, she could be a serial killer for all I know. A black widow who poisons her ex and tangles a web of stories about how he cheated on her with her sister.

I'm inclined to believe her, though. That level of desperation can't be faked.

Finding the heating pad on autopilot, I can't help but wonder. She appeared out of thin air, bringing a whirlwind with her … and apparently a ghost cat. Oh God.

I pinch the bridge of my nose right between my eyes and grin with a sigh.

Fuck, what the hell is she doing to me?

When I return to the exam room, I find her cradling the kitten in her hand. Nic's eyebrows are knitted together in awe, and she is softly cooing at the kitten, one of her fingers gently petting its head.

I stop and reach for my phone. Something compels me to snap a quick picture of this serene scene. Hopefully one day, when she's less panicked, she will remember today fondly and be happy about me snapping it.

Then I immediately walk backward until I disappear into the hallway again, leaning my head back against the cool wall and taking a deep breath.

I've never claimed to know what it's like to have baby fever, but I might have gotten kitten fever from watching those two. Nic-fever. Whatever it is, I could stare at the two of them for hours.

"Henry?"

I shake my head and take a deep breath when I hear her call for me in a whisper-shout.

Get it together, Henry. I haven't crushed this hard on a girl since Cindy Lawson in high school.

Rolling my shoulders, I round the corner once more to her worried gaze.

"Is everything okay?" she asks in a whisper, but hurriedly lifts her finger to her lips as I open my mouth to answer. "Wait. She's asleep. Let's enjoy this blissful silence and talk later."

"Hold her for another second," I answer, voice just as soft, as I plug in the pad and grab a box from under my table and a blanket. A second later, I've created a nest for the cat and motion for Nic to put her into it.

"Oh no," she curses, voice back to normal, when the kitten starts meowing again. "I woke her up."

"And I'm sure she'll return the favor plenty of times," I say with a chuckle. As I walk over to what I call my "food cupboard," my dog follows right along in hopes of treats.

"A baby bottle?"

"Yup." I grin, sitting down next to her. "Told you I'd show you how to feed her. And like a baby bottle, you'll want to warm up the milk to 37 to 38 degrees. Just put it in a warm water bath and test it before feeding her," I explain as I do exactly that, sensing her eyes on my every move.

"What if I mess it up?" Her wide eyes jump between the bottle and the kitten rapidly, her breaths picking up again, and I quickly reach out to give her hand a reassuring squeeze.

"You won't," I assure her. "I'm sure Chaos led you to the cat for a reason. She wouldn't have done that if she thought you'd kill her."

"Unless she's lonely and wants company in the ghost-realm. We don't know her! She could be a vengeful ghost, trying to build a paranormal army of killer cats. This could be the start of a horror movie, Henry! Just cast me as the nervous blonde girl with bad instincts and bam, new franchise."

"Or"—I can already see her wanting to protest, but I continue without letting her butt in—"hear me out. Maybe she picked you because she knew you wouldn't give up. The same way you didn't give up on her." Our eyes meet, and for a moment, it's as if the world stands still, a silent conversation happening with our eyes. Her, doubting herself as memories of her finding Chaos replay in her head, and me, trying to reassure her.

When she's still unsure, I set down the bottle and put the cat into her palm, bending her fingers into the best position to hold her.

"What—"

"You need her head slightly elevated for feeding," I explain, and put the bottle in her other hand. The longer I let her wrestle with her doubts, the more insecure she'll get; now it's time to show her she can do this. "Go on. See if she'll take it."

And as predicted, there was no need to worry, because the kitten immediately latches onto it and gulps down the liquid. "There you go."

"Oh my God, she's eating." She looks at the tiny creature with awe. Worry is still evident in her knitted eyebrows, but her expression softens with each gulp of milk the kitten takes. I just know she's going to keep her.

Jensen Ackles whines at my feet, wanting attention and I scratch his head absentmindedly as I watch her. "You're doing great."

"Am I? What if—"

"You won't." I can't help but chuckle. "Check it out—she's done. You did it. Now put her down and gently rub her belly."

I bite my lip when she puts her into the little nest, and suddenly she's so. Fucking. Close.

It takes everything in me to focus on showing her what to do, pinching my thigh to force myself to keep it together. She smells so damn good. Like a cozy afternoon buried in a book, the scents of cinnamon and vanilla radiate from her.

What the hell is going on? It's not as if we're actually in a goddamn *Twilight* movie here.

"Okay, I think I got it," she says, still sounding unsure.

"You do," I tell her confidently and take a step back. "Now do this every three to four hours until next week, and then we'll check in again."

"Every three to four …" she trails off, then groans. "Cool. Who needs sleep when you can hallucinate from exhaustion? Tell Caleb he's about to get a new favorite customer-slash-zombie. And for the love of all things caffeinated, he needs to add pumpkin spice to his menu. It's a hug in a mug, and his roast might kick my body into 'awake mode' but it's more bitter than my ex." Her eyes widen slightly, like she can't believe she joked about the very reason for the breakdown she had in here the last time.

"Careful." I chuckle, trying to lift her mood again. "Say that to his face, and he'll cut you off quicker than Netflix cancels your new favorite series." Her eyes refocus on me, and a mischievous grin tugs at her lips.

"Then I guess I'll need you to sneak me some under-the-counter cappuccino. Think of it as our first coffee-related crime together."

"First?" I lift my eyebrow at her amusedly. "You seem to have big plans for me. Do tell me more."

"It's a need-to-know basis," she whispers, shooting me a wink that makes me blush.

"Anyway—" I clear my throat nervously. "It's only until next week. If she's on track, you can adjust the interval to three times a day."

"Okay," she says with a nod and squares her shoulders. "Next week. That sounds manageable." Her eyes dart to me, and her smile finally looks relaxed instead of nervous or panicked. "Thank you, Henry."

"You're welcome," I assure her, noting an adorable blush across her cheeks. "And if you need anything, you know where to find me. You have my number now, don't hesitate to use it if you're unsure about anything. Or, you know, send me kitten pictures of this little screaming lady because she's adorable."

"I will." She smiles at me gratefully, hugging the box with the little, now dead asleep kitten to her chest.

"Thank you. Really."

There's a weight in her words I cannot place, but they wash over me like a warm shower.

"Always."

I wait at the door with Jensen Ackles until she's all situated in her car, and she waves at me when she drives off, right as my phone starts buzzing. My eyebrows wander up my forehead in confusion. How the hell did Kieran get my number?

Kieran: Hi, it's Kieran.

Kieran: This is super random, but I don't know who else to tell.

Kieran: I know where I recognize them from!!

Kieran: Are you there?

Kieran: They're actresses!

Kieran: *Bestie Goals: Actresses Nic Duncan And Lauren Kaufman Stun On The Red Carpet.*

Kieran: Helloooo?

Chapter 8

Henry

"Is it Halloween already? You're as white as a ghost!" Kieran's bashful greeting is followed by a more subdued, "Seriously, though. Are you okay, Nic?"

My head whips around when I hear her name and the worry in his voice. Jensen jumps up with a happy growl, thinking we're leaving, but I gently push him back down.

"Sorry, sorry, we're not going yet," I whisper, but my eyes are on the back of her blonde head and uncharacteristically ruffled hair.

"You sure know how to compliment a woman," Nic answers, sarcasm dripping from her voice, then playfully pushes Kieran aside. "Caleb. I need coffee. Urgently. I ran out, and I'm running on two hours of sleep. Three extra espresso shots, please."

"Are you sure that's wise?" Caleb's brow furrows, his eyes darting from her face to the window as if trying to find an escape route. But she nods and points at his coffee machine impatiently. I catch Kieran's eyes over the counter, seeing the eagerness to ask her about her job shining in them, and subtly shake my head.

I don't know why he deems it important. After all, it's only a job. He wasn't that surprised when he learned I was a vet or that Caleb owned the café.

"Two. Hours. Caleb. Chop chop, there's a kitten in my car, and I need liquid consciousness." She slaps her hand on the counter, then curses under her breath when her palm hurts. "Please."

Caleb's eyes widen, and he turns around without another word. And once Nic turns around, his reaction makes a lot of sense. I haven't seen her in the past five days. Ever since she brought that kitten that could go head-to-head with Mariah Carey at her glitteriest to me, but now she looks … unhinged. Like she's been through a bar brawl. And lost. Twice.

Her bloodshot eyes appear as though she would set the world on fire with them if she could. She's got dark bags under her eyes, and the color of her face resembles the milk Caleb is frothing up to make her espresso shots somewhat drinkable.

"Now we're leaving," I whisper to Jensen, grabbing my coffee as I get up. Caleb shoots me a glare that's probably supposed to say, "*Don't do it, man,*" but I can't help it.

I know what's keeping her awake. And there's no way I can put the life of tiny kitten into the hands of a woman who had two hours of sleep. When I became a vet, I vowed to devote my life to saving animals—I truly have an obligation to step in. It's a completely unselfish act of heroism I'm performing here.

"Yeah, you're not drinking that." I take the paper cup out of Caleb's hand as he tries to hand it to her.

"I'm asking this with all due respect, Henry, but do you want to die today?"

Her angry eyes drill into my face, but I don't relent. I put the cup down in front of Kieran, way out of her reach. Then I grab an empty one from the other side of the counter and pour my own coffee in there, and finally put both into a cup carrier.

"Do you? You're about three yawns away from becoming a cautionary tale. Let's go before you pass out mid-glare. Come on."

"Give me that coffee," she complains, but I keep it out of her reach.

"We're taking my car."

"The hell we are," she argues, almost running into the glass door.

"Nic." I step closer and lean in until my mouth is right next to her ear. "You can barely walk in a straight line. You're about to fall asleep standing up. Let me drive you home and take on kitten duty. I might not look like it, but I do know a thing or two about what I'm doing."

"But—"

"No 'but.'" I put my hand on the small of her back to guide her through the door and to my car. Jensen Ackles follows us dutifully and jumps into the trunk as soon as I open it. Nic isn't quite as obedient, but after a few more muttered curses, she's in the passenger seat, buckled in with her eyes glued to the cup carrier in my left hand.

"Do. Not. Touch. It."

"But—"

My glare makes her shut up and cross her arms in front of her chest. I can't believe she ran herself to this state for the kitten instead of asking Lauren for help or calling me. My face softens.

She seems so used to doing everything by herself, so determined to handle everything on her own.

But I won't have her head straight into a health crisis if I can prevent it. I just hope that one day, I'll have her trust—that I can be the person she turns to when she needs support. My heart warms, knowing I truly did the right thing by sending the kitten home with her. I have no doubts that the two can heal each other.

"Car keys?" Mumbling, she pulls them out of her pocket and puts them into my palm. Her car is parked right in front of mine, so I quickly collect the kitten and put the box into her lap while I climb into the driver's seat.

"Can I have some coffee now?" she asks, followed by a loud yawn.

"Just a little longer," I assure her, the way you would tell a toddler they'll get something tomorrow but actually mean never. "Why don't you close your eyes for a while?"

"I can't," she tries to argue, wiggling in her seat to sit up. Subtly, I turn on the seat heater, hoping the warmth will help her relax. "Damn. Anyone ever tell you you're hot when you're bossy?" I almost don't hear her over the sound of the engine, but when I do, I freeze. She thinks I'm hot? "I like you more when you're nice, though."

By the time we make it to her house, she can barely keep her eyes open. Her head keeps falling forward as she drifts off to sleep. Meanwhile, my thoughts circle around what she'd admitted.

"I did not fall asleep," she mumbles with a pout as she unlocks her front door. Jensen darts right past her, curious about the new place, but I don't think she minds.

"Suuure," I tease, as she rolls her eyes and turns back toward the door. She'd shoved the box with her sleeping kitten into my hands to dig for her key, and now she's taking it back, heading into the living room.

"Have you thought of a name yet?"

"No," she admits softly as she takes off her jacket and hangs it over the stair railing. "Sorry, the hook must have been offending to Chaos; she pushed it off, and I haven't gotten around to putting it back. Make yourself at home."

Nic walks off to where I assume her living room is, and I bite my lip to keep from chuckling when she almost runs into the door frame. She's not even trying to resist me being here anymore. She must be drained.

"Why?" I ask after shucking off my shoes and retrieving Jensen from the back door in her kitchen, where he was threatening bodily harm to a leaf outside.

She glances at me, but then returns to watching the kitten, her elbows propped up on the coffee table as she sits on the ground. Her head keeps dropping, and she hides a big yawn behind her hand.

"Look how cute she is," she mumbles, lips stretching into a small smile. "So tiny. So precious. So *quiet.*"

"Come on, get on the couch and I'll get her next meal ready."

"I can—"

"I got it, Nic," I say, a finality in my voice. She's a pretty independent woman, I know that much, but what I don't understand is her stubbornness accepting help. "Sit down."

Nic stares at me as if she's thinking about picking a fight, but ultimately, her shoulders relax as she gives in.

Good.

I find everything I need on the kitchen counter. When I make my way back to the living room, I freeze in the doorframe.

Nic is curled up on the couch, her head resting on my dog, who has made himself right at home on it, looking awfully comfortable. When I enter, he glances at me with an expression that says *"shut the fuck up—she's sleeping,"* before he lays his head back down and closes his eyes, too.

I spot a blanket draped over the armchair and quietly set the bottle down. When I gently tuck the blanket around her, she stirs, and I hold my breath—but thankfully, her breathing evens out again almost right away.

"Yes, yes," I whisper when the nameless kitten whimpers her complaints. "I know you're hungry. I got you, little nameless one." I lift her to my chest, smiling when she immediately latches onto the bottle. "You're a little fighter, aren't you?"

Jensen's eyes follow me as I walk to the far side of the room, softly cooing at the small animal in my hands. Thankfully, she quiets down as she's eating. "You'll be fine."

My eyes wander across her home, taking everything in. I pace her living room while I feed the kitten. It's a lovely house. It's homey yet has such a subtle luxury to it that I just know it was expensive as hell.

Her shelves are stacked with books and pictures. I step closer to one, trying to take a peek at them, before I freeze. When did I become someone who snoops while their host is asleep on the couch?

Then again, is it snooping if they're all on display? Not really, right?

The photos are beautiful—all of her, some with Lauren—but I hardly recognize them. They're almost unrecognizable: dressed in designer gowns, hair immaculately styled, their striking faces almost hidden beneath layers of makeup.

They're cuter without it.

She's cuter without it.

She doesn't seem happy in those pictures either. Her smile is forced, and it doesn't reach her eyes—and the way her eyes light up is truly my favorite thing about them.

But one thing confuses me.

All these pictures and they're only of her? She never came across that vain to me. I get she wouldn't exactly have pictures of her ex-fiancé or sister, but what about the rest of her family?

Of the pictures I have up at my own home, images I took over the years, there's barely one of me. They're of my mom and dad, of their pets, of Jensen Ackles, of nature, and of hikes we went on.

When the kitten in my arms whines in protest, I tear myself away from the pictures and quickly leave the living room so that her cries won't wake Nic.

She deserves some proper sleep.

And it's none of my business, really.

What *is* my business is the little creature right here, who I can already tell will be a menace once she's older. A cute one, but a menace nonetheless.

Chapter 9

Nic

The thing about having a ghost cat is that you stop questioning every single sound in a house. Creaking from the upper level? I bet Chaos is chasing a shadow. A glass falling in the kitchen? God damn it, Chaos, now I have to clean up glass shards that *you* can't hurt yourself on.

But the consistent sound of clanking coming from the kitchen? That doesn't sound like a ghost cat. At all. I rise from the couch with a startle, my eyes darting around the room for a weapon.

Which I don't have. There's an umbrella, a lamp, and the shovel we used to dig Chaos's grave.

Awoo-woo!

Huh? That's new.

My eyes dart back to the couch, and all the tension immediately seeps out of my shoulders. Right. Jensen. Henry. Apparently, I did not dream those two up.

"Hey, pretty boy," I coo with a happy sigh as I sink down next to him again, giggling when he almost climbs into my lap. "Did you keep me company?"

I run my hands over his soft fur, laughing when he tries to lick my face in return. God, he's adorable. And soft.

When he settles down again, I let my head drop against the couch's backrest. Maybe I should get myself a dog to heal my heart.

On the other hand, I was chosen by the cat distribution system, it appears. But cats can be … spicy. I mean, what if she hates me? She certainly likes to scream a lot, though I'm not sure all of it is in displeasure.

Then again, the same could happen with a dog.

But some unconditional love would be nice. The thought of a living, breathing being doing a happy dance when they see me when I return from a grocery trip? Riveting. I want that.

What I got is a kitten that shits in my hands and screams at me. Well, good things take time. That much even my grandma knew and ingrained in me when she was alive.

God, I miss that woman. I wish I still had her diaries, but my parents ensured none of her belongings made it to me. My sister got all her jewelry, even the simple silver necklace I begged them for. My grandma got it from my grandpa. I've lost count of how many times I've heard her joke that he stole it from a snooty rich woman to gift it to her. She knew it was a bullshit story he told, because never wanted to admit how much he paid for it.

Now that I think about it, I'm pretty sure that's the reason I never received it. I never got her picture albums either. Though I believe that was out of pure spite and pettiness on my parents' part.

"Hello there, sleeping beauty." My eyes dart to where the voice came from. Henry leans in the doorway with his shoulder against the frame and his arms crossed in front of his chest. He has the air of someone who knows exactly what he's doing—and what can I say? It's working. That stupidly perfect smirk, the rolled-up sleeves, the arms crossed as if he's completely unaware of how attractive he is. Please. He knows.

"Hey," I mumble, then I glance around, confused. "Wait. How long was I out?"

"Not that long. Two hours, maybe. I was about to wake you so that your sleep rhythm wouldn't be thrown off too much."

God, how can a man be *that* thoughtful and considerate?

"Where's—"

Just then, the little nameless cat peeks over his shoulder.

"She loves my sweater's hood," Henry snickers and walks in.

"Be careful she doesn't relieve herself in it," I warn him, but he shrugs.

"Trust me, I've found shit in worse places." A giggle falls from my lips when he grimaces.

"Thanks for that visual." I giggle and watch him curiously as he sits down in one of my armchairs.

"Sorry about before," I say, trying not to cringe. "I hate being caught mid-spiral. I swear, I'm totally normal. Just, y'know, under a very specific set of conditions involving sleep, snacks, and no screaming cats."

"Ah, what's normal?" He shrugs, fishes the cat out of his hoodie, and lets her climb over him instead. "Once in college, I pulled an all-nighter to finish a paper. The next day I ended up in the wrong lecture and sleep-deprived me thought the whole world switched to Spanish and only I missed the memo." He scratches the back of his neck and shoots me a sheepish grin. "In comparison, ordering three espresso shots and looking a little unhinged while doing so is pretty normal."

I tilt my head and stare at him. "No, I can't picture it. You seem so"—I make broad gestures at him—"put together. I don't buy it."

"Thank you, I think?" He chuckles and catches the kitten before she walks right off the armchair. "You can't fly, you little idiot," he says lovingly. Jensen shoots him a disapproving glare and then demonstratively puts his head into my lap as if he's saying, "if you replace me, I'm replacing you with her."

"I think your dog is jealous."

"He's a drama queen." The dog lets out a deep sigh. "Speaking of—" He grabs the kitten right as she is about to test her non-existent flight abilities again. "I think you should name her."

My eyes jump from Henry to the orange kitten in his hand, and I bite my lip as thoughts and worries fly through my head quicker than hummingbirds on a mission.

Can I get attached now? But what if she dies after all? What if she runs away? What if—

"Hey."

I look at Henry, who gets up, shooing Jensen off the couch, and takes his place next to me, then gently places the kitten in my lap.

"She's okay. In fact, she's doing great. There is no more chance of her ..." He clears his throat. "Disappearing than there is of lightning striking your house."

My eyes are firmly on the little creature as she turns around herself. She loses her footing on my thigh and protests with a weak *meow* when I pick her up.

"For all we know, she might outlive *you*. What if a meteor strikes you tomorrow?" My eyes narrow when he throws my words back into my face. How dare he use my logic against me? "Do you think that means she should never get attached?"

Biting my lip, I gulp past the emotions building in my throat.

"I hate that you're making sense," I whisper, feeling his body shake with stifled laughter. "You're one hundred percent sure? She's out of the woods."

"I am," he assures me. "Trust me."

I hold my breath, and all of a sudden, all the racing thoughts in my mind, all the worries, the self-doubts, they go ... silent.

Blissfully silent.

Because I do. I trust him. He might not be much more than a stranger, but my heart tells me it's okay. He's safe.

Tears form in my eyes as I exhale and watch the little creature still playing in my lap.

"Pumpkin," I whisper, the word barely making it past my lips as I choke up. "I'll call her Pumpkin."

"That's a good name," he declares. Silence settles as the sun sets over the mountains on the other side of the lake, the air thick with my emotions. The heat from Henry's arm on the backrest, his body brushing mine, surrounds me like a blanket—soft, steady, and safe. Like I can do this.

From the corner of my eye, I can see him watching me, his eyes darting over my face curiously, as if he's trying to figure something out.

I want to turn to him. I don't even know why. All I know is that I want to look at him, too. At his kind face, the small crow's-feet at the corners of his eyes, that strand of hair that keeps falling into his face—

Awoo-woo!

And in the blink of an eye, the tension is gone, and I burst into a giggle that I unsuccessfully try to hide behind my hand.

"Not now, Jensen—this is emotional," Henry scolds his dog, but leans down and scratches his head.

"It's fine," I assure him and get up, cradling the kitten in the crook of my arm. "Also, I'm starving. Can I buy you dinner as a thank you for saving me from total emotional collapse and also for not immediately mocking me for that whole 'hot' comment?" I watch him, gauging his reaction. He glances at me quickly, almost sheepishly, his fingers drumming against the couch. "Which, for the record, I still stand by."

There it is. The tiniest blush creeping into his cheeks and the corners of his mouth twitching, ever so slightly. He likes that I find him hot. That's good to know.

Before Henry can answer, Jensen butts in. *Awoo-woo!*

"Well, apparently it's decided," Henry says with a chuckle. "Jokes aside"—goosebumps rise on my skin at the way he's looking at me—"I'd love that. And for the record, I'm honored by the hot comment. Truly. I might get it engraved on something."

"Hope it's on something dramatic. Maybe a sword or a marble bust."

He rolls his eyes, but his smile certainly says he's not opposed to the idea.

"I can't believe you have emergency dog food in your car." I shake my head in awe when he enters the kitchen with the packet in hand and the sound of Jensen wolfing down his dinner coming from the hallway.

"Sometimes I get called further out—for example, if one of my cousins has issues with his farm animals," he explains, leaning against the kitchen counter. "Anyways, what are you making?"

"Pasta and tomato sauce—it's quick and easy, and the only thing my kitchen's stocked for." I shrug as if it's no big deal. "An Italian grandma taught me how to make it when I was shooting a movie in Rome," I add nonchalantly, biting back a grin when I see him freeze from the corner of my eye.

"Oh, please. Don't act as if you don't know I used to be an actress. It was written all over Kieran's face, and he doesn't seem the type who would keep that kind of information to himself."

"You're right," he admits sheepishly, and I pretend to pout. "Why did you keep it a secret?"

"I didn't." I shrug. My phone buzzes on the counter, and I subtly decline the call and push it behind some containers. I don't need a reminder of a certain someone complaining about my cooking. Or memories of him ordering takeout after I spent two hours in the kitchen for our meal flashing through my head.

"I don't exactly go around and advertise it. Lauren and I moved here for peace and quiet. Why would we introduce ourselves with, 'Hi, I'm Nic, world-famous actress, please don't call the paparazzi. And by the way, that means I'm rich, please don't rob me either, okay?'"

He tilts his head as he thinks it over, then hides a chuckle behind his hand. "So you don't need to hit me over the head with a shovel, hoping I'll get just enough amnesia to forget about it?"

"Do you *want* me to hit you over the head with a shovel?" I raise my eyebrow at him and shake my head. "Then again, I already have a ghost cat; I don't need a ghost human either. You're safe from the shovel or any other sharp or hard objects."

"Thank God."

"Anyway—" I change the topic and point toward the little orange fluff ball trying to climb Henry's jeans, a constant stream of *meows* coming from her. At least she's using her indoor voice now. "Now that it's been a while, do I need to change anything for her?"

"I can release you of the 'every few hours' feedings."

My head whips around, and I stare at him with wide eyes. "Seriously?"

"Seriously," he confirms with a nod and reaches for Pumpkin.

"That's the best news I've had in"—I take a moment to think—"at least two months!"

"Three times a day should be enough. She is a good weight, meaning you can add solids to her food now. Just mix in more and more with the milk until she eats the regular cat food and burp her after eating. Like you would a human baby, with gentle pats on her back. I also saw a litter box in the hallway—you might want to put that up. She should start using it on instinct, and if she doesn't, put her in there after she eats and reward her with treats when she uses it."

"Okay, that sounds doable." I nod and add the pasta into the now-boiling water, then squish the softened tomatoes in my pan.

"Don't get too excited too early. She's getting into her toddler phase. Meaning, she'll explore and might get stuck in places you would never expect her to be. Make sure to double-check your fridge, oven, washing machine, and microwave before using them. She'll also get more energy, meaning you might want to get her some toys and play with her a lot. A bored cat might become destructive, and your couch is pretty." He leans closer. I freeze when his face is suddenly only a breath away from mine. "Would be a shame if someone"—he suddenly holds the kitty in front of my face—"were to scratch it up."

"Right." I gulp and turn to the stove, my heart beating into my throat.

This was not part of my plan. I planned to build a life here, lick my wounds, drown in self-pity, and romanticize the hell out of my single life.

It was definitely not to fall for the hot town vet.

Chapter 10

Nic

"And then? Did you kiss?"

"What?" I stop in my tracks and stare at Lauren in disbelief. "Obviously, we didn't."

"What do you mean, 'obviously?'" she scolds me playfully and rolls her eyes.

We're strolling through the streets of Wayward Hollow, exploring our new hometown. And visiting the antique store, since Lauren needs a mirror for her hallway. Pumpkin is at home, sleeping her day away and exploring the little play pen I set up for her. She's taking well to her new food, and I sent a thank you to the heavens when she began using the litter box without any drama.

Then I sent another one for being able to leave her alone without worrying she'd stage a tiny kitten uprising the moment I stepped out of the door.

She's still a vocal little menace, but what can I say? I've gotten used to her sometimes more, sometimes less aggressive meows.

"That man took you home when you were in an exhaustion-induced delirium, made sure your cat was okay and fed, and"—she leans closer, lowering her voice to a whisper—"let me point out he never once laughed at you for the ghost cat thing. That man is boyfriend material, Nic. By the way, we're getting a coffee first, right? We can still make it before the lunch rush."

She glances at me with wide, pleading eyes, and when I nod, her lips pull into the tiniest smile.

"And I recently got out of a relationship that shattered my trust in humanity into a million little pieces," I point out and blow a strand of hair out of my face. "What makes you think I'm ready for a new boyfriend?"

"So what? Because Jay fucked up, you're punishing Henry?" She shakes her head at me, eyebrows scrunched together in disapproval.

"I'm not punishing anyone," I object and resume walking, taking a deep breath. "I just don't think jumping into dating the next guy would be good for me." Even with my family out of the picture, I can't help but jump to the worst-case scenarios. What if he's another guy who's after my money? Fool me once, shame on you, fool me twice …

"Oh, you absolutely are. Mostly yourself, though," Lauren interrupts my thoughts and falls into step with me again. "Be honest. Do you truly think Henry is the kind of man who breaks hearts?"

I bury my hands in my coat, lowering my eyes to the ground. To be fair, I never thought Jay would break my heart either, but here I am.

"How would I know?" We turn the corner and Caleb's café comes into sight. "I've known him for, like, two minutes. I don't know anything about him."

"Yet I bet you know more about his character than Jay's," she points out, nudging me with her elbow. "Would Jay have brought you home from Caleb's?"

I take a moment to think, then let my shoulders sag and softly shake my head.

"Probably not on his own and not without bitching," I finally admit with a grimace. I can almost hear his voice in my head.

"Why can't you take care of yourself? Now I have to go out of my way to get you. Do you ever think about how much trouble you cause?"

It's one of the many glimpses into my past that makes me question a lot about myself. How could I ever tolerate someone speaking to me that way?

And the only explanation I can find is that I was scared. Scared of more disapproval, scared of more rejection.

Scared of being alone.

"See?" Lauren says smugly, oblivious to the storm inside me. "Not every guy is like Jay. In fact, I think Henry's the exact opposite." She links her arm with mine and pulls me to a stop, pointing at the town square on the other side of the road. Speak of the devil.

"I mean, look at him. Everyone loves him, which *really* couldn't be said about Jay. His dog adores him, which also speaks for his character." She turns to me, while I can't stop watching Henry as he throws a stick for his dog, praising him when he brings it back. "You might think you're traumatized, but I know you, Nic. You're angry. You're scared. But please tell me with 100 percent certainty. Would you have been happy with Jay? Like, profoundly, truly happy?"

I gulp. Maybe Lauren saw more than I give her credit for.

When we first started dating, I would have said yes without hesitation. Jay made me feel so seen, so loved. He'd say all the right things, get me flowers, boast about me to his friends, and keep me firmly on cloud nine.

The changes came slowly. It was a fight here and there. His doubts increased. Which led to me letting him control more and more in an attempt to prove myself to him until I didn't have more to give.

It must have been calculated. Maybe Marissa wasn't part of the plan initially, but the rest?

Until now, I haven't allowed myself to analyze our relationship. To see how blind I was to his manipulation. But now? The realization of its extent hits me colder than bucket of ice water.

"You're seeing it?" Lauren asks cautiously, and I nod, swallowing down the emotions forming a knot in my throat. I see it clearer than ever.

"He manipulated me from the beginning?"

"That's what I suspected," she admits with a sad smile. "You sounded sadder every time we talked about him."

"Did I?" I try to think back on my conversations with Lauren, as she slowly walks to Caleb's, gently pulling me along.

She nods slowly. "Girl, your little rants when he was out of earshot were 100 percent you trying to convince yourself that's he's a good guy, trying to reason with yourself that he still loved you." She takes a deep breath. "Obviously, I can only go off what you told me, and since we barely managed to see each other in person, I never knew when to bring it up. I had an intervention planned for two days after your engagement party, though."

"You didn't!" I stare at her in disbelief and slow down.

"Yes, I did. Why did you think I had my freezer stocked with ice cream?"

We're across the street from Caleb's now, and she pulls me to a stop, taking both of my hands in hers.

"Not even I saw it coming, Nic." I try to avoid her eyes and the pity shining in them, but she won't let me. "You might be embarrassed or feel like a failure for not seeing it, but you're the one who got manipulated. You were never supposed to realize what was going on. He made sure of that. Cut yourself some slack and don't let another great opportunity at happiness slip through your fingers because of Jay. He stole enough of your years and *you*. Don't let him steal more. Don't let him win."

For a moment, we stay like this, gazing at each other in the middle of the sidewalk, until she squeezes my hands one more time. Then the emotionally charged moment ends as she drags me with her to the entrance of Caleb's. A smile washes over her face as soon as she opens the door while I'm still trying to make sense of her words.

She's not wrong. In fact, she apparently knows me better than I do.

But worry still gnaws at me, more persistent than a tick clinging to my skin.

"What if you're wrong?" I ask her in a whisper once we find a spot to sit down.

"The world will still turn, the sun will still shine, and the seasons will continue to change." She reaches over the table and squeezes my hand. "It would suck, but it wouldn't be the end of the world." Then her expression turns softer. "We can always give up and become cat ladies. And while that wouldn't be such a bad thing"—she takes a deep breath—"don't you want to try one more time? What if this is something great that will slip right through your fingers because you're too scared to hold on?"

"Maybe you're right." I nod. I hate how much sense she's making, but this whole conversation is like an emotional bomb going *boom* right inside my head. I have a lot to think about. For now, I change topics. "Do you think the cat distribution system will pick you soon?"

"I'm counting on your ghost cat, to be honest."

"Still going on about the ghost cat?" We glance up at Caleb, who appears next to our table, with his notepad in hand and his signature backward cap. Lauren's lips instantly curl into a sweet smile, and I bite my lip to keep from grinning. She might be extremely invested in me and my potential love story here in Wayward Hollow, but maybe it's time I nudge her toward her own.

"Get that amusement out of your voice," I scold him playfully. "Her name is Chaos, and she's part of the family now."

He shakes his head, but I can see his cheek dip where he bites the inside of it to keep from smiling. "What can I get you two?"

Chapter 11

Nic

As soon as we enter the antique store, a prickly, cold shiver runs down my spine—a mixture of feeling watched and like the temperature has dropped several degrees.

"Wow," Lauren whispers next to me, scooting closer. Why does it suddenly feel like we've entered a haunted maze? I half expect a fog machine to turn on and horror-clowns or discount Freddy Kruegers to jump out and yell "Boo!"

"What a vibe, right?" I whisper back and take a few steps further in. Every sound in here is muffled, quieter than trying to hear under water, as if we're suddenly cut off from the world outside. Even though the store has huge windows, barely any light makes it inside.

Furniture and paintings are stacked from the ground up to the surprisingly high ceiling. It's chaos, beautiful, and borderline cursed. Couches are stacked on tables, tangled chandeliers hang from hooks at eye level as if someone tried to weaponize home decor. Antique tea-sets are displayed in dusty cupboards decorated with the occasional spider web. The scent of lavender and dust clings to the air, and with every step, I feel more like Belle wandering the Beast's castle—vast, abandoned, but I'm more than ready to bolt.

Either we will find the most beautiful treasures in here … or die, and I'm not sure which one is more likely.

"Hello?" Lauren softly calls out, the sound echoing, practically bouncing from dusty mirror to dusty furniture.

"Ah, finally. There you are, girls." The two of us startle, a squeal escaping me at the sudden voice. "Come in, come in, you two. I made a pot of tea, just in time. Earl gray, right?"

Lauren and I glance at each other as if she'd guessed our blood type simply from this so far one-sided conversation. We're both fierce coffee girlies, but if we were damned to a world without coffee, earl gray would be our drink of choice. How did she know that?

"The cards told me you were coming. Oh, come on now, don't look so surprised." She waves us in, clearly having expected us. As if pulled by an invisible string, Lauren and I follow her.

I knew there was something about this town. First, I get a cat ghost, and now we're probably getting Hansel and Gretel'd.

When we step into an adjoining room, the woman is already seated at a table, like this is a prescheduled séance, and we kept her waiting.

The dim lighting in the store hadn't revealed much of her, but here, under a slightly brighter candle glow, we finally get a clearer view.

Unkempt curls stick out in all directions, glowing a deep, fiery red. She's wearing a dark green dress with embroidery that could have been hand-stitched by forest elves. When she motions for us to sit down, I notice countless rings adorning her fingers and hear her thick bracelets chiming against each other.

She taps a perfectly manicured nail against the top of the table—once, twice—and Lauren and I stop in place, like puppets with their strings yanked.

"The cards?" Lauren whispers in awe, the tension falling from her as she pulls me toward the table. Seriously? She didn't believe in my ghost cat, but cards talking makes sense to her?

My eyes dart around the room. We might as well have walked into a witch's coven, one that hoards antiques and souls. The entire wall behind the woman is covered in picture frames, hung so close to each other the wallpaper barely peeks through. Each frame holds a black-and-white portrait, printed or drawn on gilded paper, their expressions solemn. A few faces appear to be stretched into strange, unsettling frowns, and I swear their eyes are following us.

Is this store the Wayward Hollow version of the wardrobe to get to Narnia? I certainly feel as if we've stepped into some kind of parallel world.

"Thank you," Lauren says cheerily, accepting the cup that the woman slides across the table to her.

"I can see you're apprehensive," she says to me, and I flinch as if she caught me pocketing a cursed amulet or something. "My name is Amanda," she continues, her tone softening, "and I've been running this little antique store for … oh, nearly forty years now," she says. Her eyes go distant, her expression becoming dreamy. "A long time to be in one place. Even the walls are asking for change."

"What?" Lauren asks, surprised. "Why?"

"My body isn't what it once was. Lifting the furniture is becoming impossible." Her left hand drifts to her right shoulder subconsciously. She gives us a sentimental smile. "Times are changing. People don't appreciate the beauty of antiques anymore. The items are piling up, and the store has become untamable."

She exhales slowly.

"And, between the three of us, I'd rather run this store into the ground than have another DIYer hot-glue seashells onto a beautiful three-hundred-year-old frame."

"Oh," Lauren lets out a nervous giggle, and I bite the inside of my cheek to keep from grinning.

"Don't worry," Amanda says, leaning forward to take Lauren's hands in hers. "The mirror waiting for you is perfect as it is."

"Waiting for me?" Lauren shakes her head softly. "How do you—?"

"I know things, child." Amanda grins, revealing her perfectly straight, pearly white teeth. "Now let me show you the furniture." Her eyes flick to me, and a knowing smile curls her lips, like a ghost whispered something in her ear about us.

"I think we officially met a witch," Lauren whispers, shielding her words behind her hand, though something tells me Amanda already knows exactly what we're saying.

"I'm not sure whether to be scared or impressed," I whisper back, equally as softly. But as we turn the corner and Amanda flicks on a light switch, my breath catches.

"Holy shitballs," I mutter, staring wide-eyed at the room. I thought maybe the entrance had been decorated this packed, maybe to make a lasting first impression, but no, it turns out the entire store is committed to the chaos. Furniture is stacked high with only the tiniest paths in between to walk through, like a labyrinth of Jenga towers made of chairs, lamps, and what appear to be treasure chests.

Amanda leads us straight to the mirrors, and Lauren starts giggling beside me.

"How did she know?" she asks, eyes darting around the room, with more awe in her eyes than a child in Disneyland. "Do you really think she knew we were coming?"

I can only shrug. "It could have been an educated guess?" I offer, but the words already taste more bitter than a lie on my tongue.

Amanda has this aura about her. Honestly, if she told me that the sky was green, I'd probably nod and thank her for the enlightenment.

I trail my eyes along the closest furniture tower.

It's a shame. There must be hundreds of beautiful pieces in here—for example a picture frame near the bottom, its golden frame alive with intricately carved vines and cherubs caught mid-flight.

Do I need more furniture? Absolutely not. But if this frame mysteriously appeared in my living room, I'd hire a painter and get a portrait of Pumpkin done for it—my home's aesthetic be damned.

"Have a look around, girls." Amanda points toward a far corner. Through the legs of a probably hundred-year-old armchair I see mirrors hanging on a wall and a stack of them leaning against a cabinet. "Do me a favor though, be careful."

"Hey, Amanda," I say cautiously, eyeing the obstacle course it would take to reach them, "I hope this isn't overstepping, but … how would you feel about Lauren and me helping you tame the store a bit?"

She's right. Hiding these beauties behind hot-glued seashells, cheap paint, or rhinestones would be a crime. But my heart aches even more thinking that these amazing pieces will remain here, hidden from the world, instead of being displayed in a way they deserve. I might as well go along with this Mother Hulda kind of interaction and lean into being Goldmarie.

"Right!" Lauren jumps in eagerly, already pulling up the sleeves of her sweatshirt.

"That would be wonderful," Amanda says with a knowing smile, "but you really don't have to."

"No, no, we want to," I assure her, eyes darting around the room. "You have so many amazing pieces here that must have been incredibly hard to find. They deserve to be seen, and bought—in one piece without falling down."

"But I can't pay you girls."

"Oh, oh! Give me a card reading," Lauren says excitedly, eyes wider than a kids on Christmas morning.

"That can certainly be arranged." Amanda nods, then glances at me expectantly.

"Oh, I'm good," I tell her with a shake of my head. "Just happy to get away from my screaming cat and out of the house. Trust me, this is doing me a bigger favor than you."

"In that case …" she pats my arm as she walks past me. "Knock yourselves out, girls. Let me know if you need anything."

"Would you mind if we carry some of this stuff outside?" Lauren asks, suddenly sounding unsure, as if the weight of what we promised has hit her now that she's giving the room another once-over.

"Of course, of course. It won't rain today," Amanda mumbles, and then she's out of sight.

"For real?" I whisper, shaking my head. The clouds covering the sky while we had our coffee at Caleb's were giving me apocalypse vibes. They sure looked ready to burst into the kind of rain that makes you wish for an ark.

"Oh, come on," Lauren says, reaching for a chair to her right. "If she says it, I believe her. She's probably casting some kind of anti-rain spell right this minute. Let's do this."

"What are you girls doing?" a voice calls out, making me whirl around.

It took us a few hours, lots of cursing, and we're probably going to pay for our efforts with an epic ache in places we didn't know had muscles tomorrow, but we've managed to disassemble most of the falling hazard towers. Now, the sidewalk in front of the antique store looks like the Mad Hatter is hosting a banquet for all of Wonderland, with what must be at least thirty chairs lined up and stacked along the storefront and a long table in front of them.

"I hope you're not robbing the place," the man chuckles, clearly joking.

"No, no, of course not." I laugh, brushing a strand of hair from my sweaty cheek. "We're helping Amanda rearrange the store. Trying to eliminate the danger of getting taken out by a rogue armchair."

"Okay." His eyes shift from me to the store entrance. Lauren is waddling backward while dragging a Victorian commode behind her with both hands and an expression of grim determination. He raises an eyebrow. "Tell me how to help."

Lauren and I exchange a glance. When I turn back to him, he's already shaking his head, frowning with mock disapproval.

"In this town, we help. You girls might be strong, but with some help, everything moves faster, and God knows all of Wayward Hollow has had a near-death experience in there already. Now, what's your plan?"

"We're trying to clear most of it out, fight the spiders, and then see how we can arrange everything without falling hazards," Lauren explains. Meanwhile I stack chairs of the same make to save space and avoid blocking the entire sidewalk.

When I glance up again, a small crowd has gathered out of nowhere. The flower shop owners are among them, along with a handful of familiar faces I recognize from Caleb's.

"LA could never," I whisper to Lauren as our new helpers swarm inside eagerly, ready to pitch in.

"Right?" she says, grinning at me, cheeks flushed with a mix of exhaustion and giddiness. "Look at us, actually getting to know our neighbors."

And that's how we spend the afternoon: hauling furniture out, then back in once we've cleared space for a more organized layout, laughing, sharing stories, and getting to know the people of our new hometown.

Amanda greets every new helper with a thankful smile and keeps the tea flowing.

She doesn't even check in on us much, and when she does, all she does is watch us with a small, knowing smile playing at her lips. It's wild. We met only hours ago, yet she trusts us with her store completely.

By the time we're done, the place has transformed and is spacious, even. The furniture is finally given room to breathe. Nothing is stacked higher than eye level, and for the first time, its vibes are less 'forgotten attic' and more 'hidden gem.'

Then, suddenly, the door bursts open, and Shawna walks in, carrying a huge tray filled with mouthwatering pastries.

"Snacks on Caleb's!" she shouts, and before she even finishes the sentence, the crowd rushes toward her as if she'd offered free tickets to see Taylor Swift. Then again, Caleb's pastries are a very close second to that. The man knows his baking.

We gather around the long table we'd dubbed the centerpiece of the store, and soon it turns into a friendly interrogation. Andrea, who runs Wayward Hollow's only hotel, wants to know where we're from and if we're enjoying our new life here. Courtney, who owns the flower store with her husband, explains what we absolutely have to do in the area. Someone mentions a hiking trail only half an hour away. We learn that the man who first approached us is Dimitri, and he owns a woodworking shop a bit outside of Wayward Hollow.

By the time we step back outside, the sky is pitch-black, the streets lit by dim golden light from lanterns.

"What a day," Lauren whispers, tilting her head back and taking a deep breath of the crisp autumn air.

"A *good* day," I add with a grin, linking my arm with hers as we walk toward my car.

Chapter 12

Henry

"Anyway, I'm thinking of getting pet chickens. I will call them Chick Jagger, Cluck Norris, and Lady MacBeth."

"Hmm," I answer, but truthfully, Kieran's voice goes in one ear and out the other as my eyes trail after Nic and Lauren entering Caleb's. She seems better today, now that color has returned to her face. Well-rested and a lot less crazed than the last time I saw her at the café.

I haven't stopped thinking about our dinner a few days ago. I can't.

About her laugh when Jensen ran against her window and left a mark on the glass. Or that smile on her face as we talked over her new kitten care and watched Pumpkin try to climb out of her box. That little flinch when Pumpkin screamed particularly loud.

The way she looked at me when she thought I wouldn't notice. Those contemplative wrinkles scrunching on her forehead as she rolled over thoughts that I'm dying to know more about.

"I'm thinking of livestreaming their fights. One of them will get little boxing gloves, and I'll give the other a gun and take bets on who will win. I bet it's tough for a chicken to pull a trigger, but my money would still be on them."

"Sure." The door closes behind the two, and I shake my head as if waking up from a dream once they're out of sight. "Wait, what?"

"Ah, there you are." Kieran chuckles and even Jensen eyes me as though he's trying to say, "Dude, you're ridiculous. Pull yourself together." Kieran found me playing with Jensen in the town square and making the best of my lunch break. Though I quickly got distracted from his chatter as soon as I saw Nic and Lauren walk by.

"You want to shoot chickens?"

"Nope. I wanted to see how far I could push this without you noticing while you gawked at the town's celebs." I quickly turn my head away from Caleb's, heat creeping into my cheeks. Was I that obvious?

"On second thought, it does sound fun." I shoot him a sharp glare and lift my eyebrow, making him backpedal quickly. "Getting chickens and giving them ridiculous names, not giving them guns. Don't give me that look."

"With you, I just never know." I shake my head, half laughing as Kieran shoots me a knowing smile.

"The only thing I'm hearing is that you have a lot of faith in me," he jokes and shoots me a wink. "You know what? I'm suddenly craving coffee." Before I can stop him, he takes Jensen's leash out of my hand. And like the little traitor my dog is, he trots right alongside Kieran across the street, tail wagging and all.

"What are you—" I try to object, but he merely lifts a hand in a lazy wave and throws me a smug grin over his shoulder.

"We're going to hang out with your crush," he says in a singsong voice. I lean my head back, exhaling a deep sigh toward the sky before I follow them. That guy sure is keeping me on my toes.

Not that I'm complaining too much. I'm all for the quiet life, the expected. Maybe it's not the worst thing that Kieran shakes those things up, with a grin on his lips and mischief on his mind.

By the time I catch up, they've already crossed the street and are walking right toward Caleb's front door, held open by Mr. Peterson, who's cradling his daily afternoon pastry and paper cup containing a black coffee with an extra espresso shot.

"Thanks, Bobby," Kieran chirps, and I offer Mr. Peterson a smile as I pass. "Aw, man, what a crowd!" Kieran groans dramatically, sweeping his arm across the room like we've entered Coachella during a Lady Gaga performance. I lower my head, debating whether to pretend I don't know him. Then again, he's taken my dog hostage. There's no escape.

It's not even crowded today. There are at least two free tables. But he continues with the same amount of drama, "Where should we sit?"

"Kieran," I hiss in warning, but he's already at the girls' table, interrupting their conversation.

"Hey, ladies, mind if we join you?"

The two look up at Kieran with amused smiles as they scoot toward the window on their bench seats.

"Of course not," Lauren says, already reaching for my dog with a wide grin. "My boy Jensen is always welcome. How are you doing, you handsome, furry creature?" she coos, launching into conversation with him as he responds with a string of his signature whines. It's fair to say their adoration is mutual.

Kieran scoots onto the bench down next to Nic, shooting me a subtle wink.

"Hey," I say much more awkwardly as I take a seat beside Lauren. Nic offers a small smile, lowering her gaze to the table, but even that is enough to send the butterflies in my stomach on a mission. From the corner of my eye, I watch Lauren try unsuccessfully to bite back a grin while still cooing at Jensen.

Kieran puts his chin in his palms, leaning his elbows on the table as his eyes keep darting between Nic and Lauren, his questions all but written over his face. He might be a lot of things—a good friend, handsome—but *subtle* certainly isn't one of them.

"Just go for it, Kieran," Lauren snickers, then lifts her gaze to meet his eyes, amusement written all over her face, a mischievous glimmer in her eyes. "But for every question you ask, I get to ask one about your job, too."

"My jo—" Kieran's eyes widen, and his mouth drops when he sees her knowing grin. He catches himself quickly, then leans over the table and hisses, "How the hell do you know? Did that witch from the antique store tell you? I swear she's been looking at me funny when I see her in town."

"Please," Lauren scoffs and narrows her eyes at him. "We live in the same town with, like, one main street and five Wi-Fi signals. That and the fact that I have eyes, a fairly good memory, and Instagram. You're not as hard to recognize as you might think."

"Instagram?" Nic sounds confused, and I can only nod. What are they talking about?

"Come to think of it," I say amusedly, crossing my arms in front of my chest. "What *is* your job? I assumed it was a work from home thing."

"It has to be something that makes enough money for one of the lakeside mansions," Nic thinks aloud, narrowing her eyes at Kieran, like she's a detective who stumbled over a huge new lead. "And since you're suddenly awfully interested in the ceiling, I'm guessing it's something you don't want us to know."

"You were awfully interested in *their* jobs though," I can't help but point out. Oh, I'm enjoying this. Especially after the teasing I got about my crush on Nic. "Now I'm curious. Come on. Tell us."

"Is it porn?" Nic turns in her seat, trying to read his face better. He's biting the inside of his cheek, and avoids looking at her. "Do you sell your socks online? Spit it out, Kieran."

"Please don't spit on my floors." All four of us startle when Caleb suddenly appears next to our table, the usual grim expression on his face and two mugs in his hands. "Lattes. Here you go, ladies."

"I wasn't going to spit on your floor," Kieran mumbles, crossing his arms in front of his chest with a pout. Caleb continues staring at him without any expression. "They want to know what my job is."

"Well, I don't care. As long as you pay and tip, spare me from more gossip," Caleb says gruffly, letting out a sigh that from the sound of it must have been building since the moment he was born. Then he glances at Kieran and me expectantly. "Are you getting the usu—wait, what the hell is that?"

His eyes widen and the notepad nearly slips from his hands. A horror-stricken expression washes over his face as he stares at something behind me, as if it has personally offended his coffee-making skills.

"What?" Lauren asks with wide eyes, only the slight twitch at the corner of her mouth revealing that she knew she'd be getting a reaction out of him. "Oh, this thing?" She lifts the full liter bottle of something orange. Where did she even hide that? "This, you heathen, is pumpkin spice syrup. Says so right here." She points at the label with a smile as if she doesn't understand the problem.

"I can read, thank you very much." He closes his eyes and forces himself to take a deep breath, pinching the bridge of his nose. "What is it doing in my café?"

"I brought it for my coffee," she says sweetly and wiggles the bottle for emphasis. Oh, Lauren must have a dead wish.

Nic is hiding her giggles behind a hand while Kieran's and my gazes bounce back and forth between them faster than the ball at Wimbledon.

"Nope. Away with it. I won't tolerate this disgusting stuff in here."

"Don't discriminate." She opens the bottle and pours a healthy amount into her coffee, all while keeping eye contact with him. "Your coffee is just too strong. I need some pumpkin spice sweetness to counteract. Relax, it's not as if opening the bottle is suddenly going to make all of your coffees taste like pumpkin spice. Although you should totally consider that."

"Oh God, that hurts to see." Caleb sounds pained, and I'm fighting hard to not burst into laughter. I can see how much he's suffering, and I have to say, it's refreshing to see a break from his usual stoic poker face.

"Also, we have the mission to"—she shoots Nic a glance and both continue in unison—"romanticize the fuck out of fall." Lauren continues on her own. "And drinking pumpkin spice lattes is on the top of that romanticizing list."

Caleb stares at her with his mouth agape, before he closes his eyes resignedly.

"Anyways, Kieran's job," Nic gently redirects the conversation. Caleb wanders off, mumbling something about "damned city girls and their weakness against bitterness," and Lauren wordlessly hands the bottle to Nic, who also pours a healthy amount into her coffee.

"Can we pretend that conversation never happened?" Kieran all but begs, but my interest is piqued. "Please?"

"Nope, Pandora's box is open now. How bad can it be?" I wonder and tilt my head. "Are you selling pictures of your feet? No judgment if you do. If it gets you a house as expensive as the lakeside mansion, I might just pick it up as a side hustle."

"You're so close," Lauren giggles and Kieran grinds his teeth, before the tension falls from his body at once, and he shakes his head in resignation.

"Oh, this is going to be good. I know it." Nic takes a sip of her coffee and exhales a happy sigh.

"I'm a content creator," Kieran mumbles, shrinking into himself and clearly wishing the earth would open up and swallow him.

"That doesn't sound too bad. Or is 'content' a code word for porn?"

"Almost. He's a thirst trap," Lauren clarifies with an eyebrow wiggle, and Kieran hides his beet-red face behind his hands. "Meaning, he dances to music half-naked. And I've got to hand it to you—it's kind of hot and only a little cringe."

Nic bursts into laughter, and it's the sweetest sound I've heard all day. Which is not a hard thing to achieve when 90 percent of what I hear all day is my husky yapping.

"I loved the one where you wore that elephant slip and did the—"

"God, Lauren, please stop." I can't help but stare at Nic, feeling only a little creepy. But she's gorgeous when her eyes light up with amusement and those adorable dimples in her cheeks appear. It makes me want to learn a bunch of stupid jokes by heart, just to make her laugh.

"What's his handle?" Nic asks, but Kieran intercepts her before Lauren can hand Nic her phone.

"I'll tell you later," she whispers loudly with a wink, quickly schooling her face when Caleb is back at the table. He sets down Kieran's and my usual drink with a loud clank and glare to go along with it.

"Want some pumpkin spice syrup?" Lauren can't help but ask in a fake whisper, way too loudly to be intended as subtle.

"Don't you dare." Caleb shoots Kieran and me a hard look before he turns back around.

"You're the first person in a long time to get him to show emotion," I whisper, swallowing back a grin. "Even if it's anger."

"Good," she whispers back and smirks. "I'm going to have a lot of fun."

"That poor guy," I say with a chuckle, noting the dangerous grin on her face. Apparently, Caleb will have his hands full with this one.

"By the way," Kieran quickly changes topics. And judging by the glare Caleb shoots our way, it's the right decision. "What's with you two and the antique store? Andrea told me about you helping out that afternoon, but a little bird told me you're there pretty often."

"Oh, we help out Amanda now," Nic explains with a happy smile. "You know, setting up a website for her and all that stuff. And in exchange, she doesn't curse us. Fair deal, isn't it?"

"And I get a card reading!" Lauren adds, happily taking a sip of her coffee concoction. "I always wanted to get one!"

Nic shakes her head with a soft giggle, then glances at me. "It's fun. I get to take a break from Pumpkin's screaming and research old furniture."

"Is she still that bad?" I ask her with a grin. Of all the cats I've encountered, she's by far the most vocal one. It's funny if I only see her for a few hours, but God, I couldn't imagine hearing that twenty-four-seven, and I already have an extremely vocal dog.

"Only when she's hungry or if the day ends with Y." Nic rolls her eyes. "I'm hoping she grows out of it."

"If not, let me know. Happy to help you find a strategy to calm her down," I offer, ignoring the knowing eyebrow wiggle Lauren makes at Nic.

Chapter 13

Henry

"Mom, I'll call you back, okay? Now's not a good time."

I take a deep breath and sink deeper into one of the chairs in my waiting room, my head pounding with a threatening migraine. Good thing I listened to my gut and added comfortable chairs in here, even if they cost me twice as much.

"Are you okay, honey?" Mom sounds worried, but the question almost makes me burst into laughter.

It's the exact same question I asked Nic after Chaos had passed. Well, minus the "honey." Right now, I think I understand exactly why she reacted the way she did. Understand that sinking feeling of helplessness, a stern reminder that your own existence is temporary. As if all joy has been sucked out of the world.

"I will be," I assure her, my hand subconsciously finding Jensen's head, running my fingers through his fur. "Thanks, Mom. I'll see you on Friday."

Slowly, I lower the phone, my entire body slumping into the chair, the dull pain relentlessly throbbing behind my temples with the force of a sledgehammer.

Putting an animal to sleep is never easy. There are others that revel in the power of taking a life. I've met a psychopath or two in college who said it gave them a sense of control, with a smile that never quite reached their eyes.

But for me? It's the worst thing about my job. Even if I know it's the kind thing to do, the necessary evil to relieve them of their suffering and pain. Some days, it's hard to make peace with it. What if there was something I could have done after all? What if this animal actually had the zero-point-zero-one chance to get better?

Jensen jumps into the chair next to mine, licking my face and whining the song of his people, nudging his nose against my cheek.

"Are you trying to cheer me up?" I ask him, the corner of my mouth twitching, but not quite making it to a smile. "Thank you, Deanie-Beanie."

"Deanie-Beanie?" My eyes jump to the door when I hear Nic's amused voice. And there she is. Dressed in an oversized beige sweater and a light brown skirt, like an angel sent to rescue me from my foul mood. "I thought his name is Jensen."

Calmness washes over me, akin to a sudden warm burst of rain that washes away the exhaustion and sadness.

"It is," I answer softly, a smile coming to me easily all of a sudden. And while the self-doubt and sadness haven't suddenly disappeared, they have scooched into the background of my consciousness. "Deanie-Beanie is one of his many nicknames."

"I love it," she says with a soft grin, and that's when I notice the box in her hands. Suddenly, a flicker of worry crosses her face. "Why does he need to cheer you up, though? Did something happen?"

"It's…one of those days," I tell her and shake my head, sitting up straighter. "What's that?" I nod at the box she's holding. "Another cat?" She nods sheepishly, and I can't help but chuckle. "Nic, we have to stop meeting like this."

"Tell that to Chaos." She carefully sets the box on the counter. "But she can wait. I found her scratching at my door. She was super eager to get inside I got worried she'd scratch her way through the wood. I'm pretty sure nothing is wrong with her, but figured I'd get you to make sure anyway. What's wrong?"

"I had to put down a dog today," I whisper as she takes a seat on my other side, her worried eyes darting over my face. "You'd think I'd get used to it someday, but sometimes ..."

"I'm sorry, Henry." She reaches for my hand and pulls it into hers for a reassuring squeeze. I gulp down the emotions forming in my throat. "Tell me about it."

"It was Mrs. Thomson's Chihuahua. Rose." I let out a quiet, humorless laugh. "An annoying little creature. She barked at everything that moved, but she was Mrs. Thomson's soul animal. Her husband got her Rose as a present for their thirtieth wedding anniversary, so she'd have company when he was on business trips. That was almost twenty years ago." When I notice her crestfallen expression, I quickly add, "Mr. Thomson is fine. Alive and kicking. But watching the two of them say goodbye was just ..." I let the words hang in the air and she nods.

"I can imagine," she whispers and squeezes my hand. "I admire you, you know?"

"You do?"

She hums and offers a slight nod. "It's a form of strength to go through that again and again, knowing it's best for the animal, even if it tears you apart on the inside. I couldn't do it. The fact you became a vet despite knowing this would happen? That's brave."

I let the words sink in, forming a shield around my heart that keeps the pieces together. All I ever wanted to do was help animals, keep them healthy and pain free to live a long and happy life.

I'm not sure I'd call it brave to become a vet despite knowing a pet's ultimate fate can be out of my hands. Sometimes I'm more inclined to call it dumb. Those times I keep reminding myself of all the lives I've saved, starting with Jensen, yet that doesn't mean I don't carry their deaths with me.

"Anyway." I clear my throat and get up after giving Jensen one more pet. "It's time for something positive. Come on, show me your ghost cat's newest find."

"Are you sure?" she asks with worried eyes, and only now do I realize that she never let go of my hand. It's still there, fingers laced with mine, her warmth seeping into my cold palm.

Reluctantly, she loosens her grip, a cute blush painting her cheeks an adorable crimson. "I mean, our quota is fifty-fifty on survival. I can take her somewhere else if you need more time."

"Don't be ridiculous." I roll my shoulders and take a deep breath. "The next vet is a two-hour drive away. I got this."

"Okay, if you're sure." She opens the box and reveals a cat with the most beautiful brown fur I've ever seen.

"Oh, aren't you a beauty," I mumble and gently take her out of the box. "And you're not scratching me, which is great." I walk to the exam room, hearing the patter of four dog paws and two human feet following me. "Your ghost cat is finding you the nicest friends."

"I gave her a flea bath like you showed me." She smiles proudly. "I knew Chaos would strike again, so I got a bottle of flea shampoo. She was a much harder challenge than Pumpkin, though. She didn't appreciate water at all. Only she tried to scratch me, instead of screaming. I had to bribe her with treats. And even so, I got myself some souvenirs." She grimaces and lifts her sleeve, revealing a few superficial scratches.

"Great, you're getting the hang of it." I flash her a quick grin. "Did you name her yet?"

"Cinnamon," she says with a happy nod, her eyes shining with adoration. "Because of the little lighter freckles in her fur." I turn the cat in my hold as I inspect her for any injuries, noting the specks of brown around her chest and face. The name is fitting.

"Let's see what else Chaos has in store for me. If she keeps going at this rate, I could name a full pumpkin spice latte by the end of October." She tilts her head and taps her lips as she thinks. "Come to think of it, she would also be a great 'Coffee.' I could also call her 'Beanie' then."

"Now, don't go and steal my nicknames," I tease her and turn the cat in my hands. I gently check to see if anything is wrong, or if she is in pain. Then, I inspect her eyes, mouth, and ears. When everything appears normal, I scan for a chip. But I come up empty.

"You're right, Nic. She's as healthy as can be. I'm still going to draw some blood for testing, and then you're good to go." I set the cat on the table, and she immediately darts around to inspect everything.

"Great." I didn't realize she'd been tense until her shoulders noticeably slump in relief. "Good. That's good. Thank God. I wasn't keen on another emotional rollercoaster."

Suddenly, her phone rings and her shoulders are almost up to her ears again. "What did I *just* say?" she grumbles and declines the call.

"Who's trying to speak with you so urgently?" The words come through my lips before I can stop them. She lowers her head, biting her lip as though she's fighting with herself whether to answer or not.

"Probably my ex," she finally whispers, and I hold my breath. Her ex? My heart pounds in my ears. What could he want?

"He and my sister keep calling me from new numbers and leaving voicemails begging for forgiveness and money. It's pathetic, but I'm trying to see the upside and enjoy a little schadenfreude." She rolls her eyes and crosses her arms in front of her chest. "And my parents keep sending messages asking me to 'forgive them and move on.' Probably for similar reasons."

"No offense, Nic, but your family sounds horrible."

"Why, thank you. They are. Please feel free to be offensive all you want." She shakes her head, a cold chuckle falling from her lips. "It's okay. I've had years to make peace with that knowledge. It still stings, but being here"—she makes a vague gesture—"it helps. Wayward Hollow feels like home, and I'm determined to make it that. I won't let my past mess with that."

The last sentence hangs in the air, heavy with meaning, but I've pried enough for today.

"That's brave too, you know," I say softly, letting go of the cat to walk over to her. "Knowing what your boundaries are and following through. Starting anew here can't have been easy."

"It's not." When she glances up at me, I see tears brimming in her eyes that she quickly tries to blink away. "Sometimes I wake up and wonder if by coming here I ran away and took a coward's way out. That doesn't feel too brave." I'm about to object when she softly shakes her head.

"I know, Henry. I know it's not my fault. The same way you having to put a dog down is not your fault. But that doesn't change the fact that it *hurts*. Still, pain doesn't mean you did the wrong thing."

"It doesn't," I agree and step closer to swipe a strand of her hair that's falling into her face behind her ear. "It's their loss. You're a good person, Nic. You easily make the top five of best people I know." I run my fingertips through her soft hair, laying my palm on her cheek, and she nudges against it like a cat. "If you ever want to … talk," I start, cringing at how cliché it sounds, "I'm here. And I'm a good listener. Or shit-talker. Whatever you need."

"Thank you, Henry. And likewise." Her face softens, when a howled *awoo-woo* suddenly destroys the moment. "Aw, look at them. Cinnamon and Deanie-Beanie are friends." She nods to our right, where both are cuddled up on the floor. Apparently, Nic is not the only one finding a new home here.

Chapter 14

Nic

"Maybe you'll get to meet Chaos this time," I say with a giggle as Henry and I approach my house. The box with Cinnamon is firmly under my arm, and he's balancing a bag that contains several cans of cat food on his shoulder, with Jensen's food under the other arm.

Could I have carried it myself? Absolutely. Am I going to stop a man from showing off and carrying it for me? Hell no.

"Thanks for helping me out."

"Of course," he says with a groan as he puts the bag of cat food down on my porch while I unlock the door.

"Can you stay while I introduce Cinnamon to Pumpkin?" I give him a pleading glance. "You know, in case one wants to claw out the other's eyes. I could bribe you with dinner?" The corner of his mouth twitches in amusement.

"I'd do it without bribery, but I also won't say no to dinner."

A giggle escapes me as I push the door open. A giggle? Oh God, I've reached the giggle stage of meeting a man. Closely followed by the rambling stage.

Hopefully, I won't reveal anything too embarrassing when it begins. During Jay's and my second date, I kept going on about completely random topics, but hey, now he knows that octopuses have three hearts.

I can sense Chaos as soon as I step inside—her warm presence as she rubs against my calf, even a soft vibration of her purring against my leg. Henry seems oblivious, though.

"Let's get this over with," I mutter and walk into my living room, where Pumpkin hangs out in her little shoe box. Good thing I have enough boxes to home a zoo from my move. Two of them are coming in handy already, and who knows what else Chaos has planned for me?

Pumpkin is wide awake and trying to climb to freedom, shouting at me for daring to keep her confined. I scoop her into my arms as soon as I set down Cinnamon.

"She's exploring now and regularly gets herself into all kinds of trouble. I had to put her in box-jail while I brought Cinnamon to you," I explain, stepping out of my shoes and kicking them into a corner. "So … how do I do this? Just put them on the ground together and see what happens? How do we separate them if they try to claw each other's eyes out?"

"Let's let them have a sniff while holding them, and once we've determined they don't hate each other, we can put them down."

"Okay," I say with a solemn nod and reposition Pumpkin in my arms to get a better hold on her tiny body. Meanwhile, Henry takes Cinnamon out of her box and cradles her to his chest like a baby.

I don't think I've ever been jealous of a cat until this exact moment. Henry's arms look comfortable. And strong. I gulp. Since when do I fantasize about a guy's arms?

"Okay," Henry mumbles, gently stroking Cinnamon's head. "Yes, you're a chill little lady. I'm sure you're going to love having a little sister. Here you go." He steps closer, and I turn, letting the two cats see each other.

Then suddenly, he's *very* close. I breathe in his scent that reminds me of freshly brewed coffee and cinnamon. The warmth radiating from him sends heat into my face and makes me forget how to breathe.

And when I glance up, his face is *right there*. Right in front of me.

His broad shoulders make the cat in his arms appear tiny, his sweatshirt tight over his muscles. A lump forms in my throat and my knees turn weak; I am almost incapacitated by my overwhelming feelings.

Can I allow myself to have these feelings? These butterflies in my stomach, this soothing warmth that spreads over me like a wool blanket when he is near?

I swallow hard.

"Ahw, they're getting along," he whispers, his breath feathering over my hair, sending a shiver down my spine and butterflies racing in my stomach.

No, Nic, get a grip. This is about the cats, not the hot guy that might not even be into me. He comes even closer, and our arms touch, sending electric zings all over my skin. But we had that *moment*, that almost-kiss in his practice, at the worst timing possible.

Calm down, Nic. Deep breaths.

Pumpkin is wriggling in my hold, trying to climb into Henry's arms, and I can't blame her.

"I think we can set them down," Henry suggests, and I quickly take a step back.

"Okay." My voice is barely above a whisper, my heart beating so fast I'm afraid it's about to jump out of my ribcage. Fuck.

This wasn't planned. Romance wasn't part of the "romanticizing life" plan I made for myself. But Lauren's words keep repeating in my head, and I can't help but wonder—is that a bad thing? I mean, I had my whole life planned before, and I know how that turned out. Will doing not-planned things lead to a different outcome?

As soon as all eight paws touch the ground, the cats cautiously move toward each other. They walk in circles, trying to gauge the other. Before I know it, Cinnamon has Pumpkin in a loving headlock, grooming her while Pumpkin's eyes are closed in bliss.

"Well, that worked out perfectly," I joke with a nervous giggle, crossing my arms in front of my chest to stop them from reaching out to Henry.

"It did." I can hear the grin in his voice before I even glance at him. "Still, check on them occasionally. If one gets annoyed, separate them for a while and keep them in different rooms until they've calmed down."

"Okay," I whisper with a nod and tilt my head, a grin tugging at my lips. "What about my ghost cat, though? I can't exactly keep her out of a room."

"I don't know, maybe put salt in front of the room's door?" he jokes and reaches for Jensen's leash as he tries to approach, all of us leaving the living room. "Nope, buddy, let's give them some bonding time. Out with you."

"Aw, do you feel left out?" I ask Jensen, voice dripping with exaggerated sympathy, and he answers with a high *awoo-woo!* immediately trotting over to me when I crouch down to pet him.

"Let's go to the kitchen. I'll have bonding time with you." Once we're there, I turn around and look at Henry. "How do you feel about"—I open my fridge, grimacing when I realize it might hold a lot of food, but most of it is too complicated for my currently empty and impatient stomach—"mac and cheese?"

"Sounds perfect," he says with a chuckle. "As long as you don't judge me for going back for thirds."

"No promises." I smirk. "But I do admire a man who appreciates the finer things in life. Powdered cheese, for example."

"Right?" His grin widens. "I almost thought you were trying to seduce me with your cooking skills. My mother warned me about women like you."

"Careful, or I'll make you help stir. That's how it starts: you fall for the cook, then *boom*. You're stuck grating cheese forever."

"I'd grate cheese for you."

I clutch my heart, acting as if I'm blinking away tears. "That's the most romantic thing anyone's ever said to me."

We both break into laughter, and suddenly, an invisible curtain has lifted, the negative mood from before melting off us faster than frost on a spring morning.

While I cook, he feeds his dog. When he's done, he chops up a salad to go with the cheesy goodness, as if it's the most natural thing in the world. It's … nice. Sweet. Weirdly domestic.

The kind of too-good-to-be-true that makes you suspicious if you've ever watched one or three hundred true crime documentaries.

The future I always thought I wanted.

We eat together, but my mind won't sit still. It keeps doing mental gymnastics, flipping back to Jay.

How on earth did I ever imagine that future with him? A guy who, sure, never said it outright, but definitely had that *women belong in the kitchen* energy—wrapped in polite smiles and "Babe, you're just so good at this" excuses. How did I miss how unbalanced it all was?

And then—Henry dries the dishes. Just picks up a towel and goes for it. No need to ask nicely, no need to thank him extensively unless I want him to pout for the rest of the night.

When we head back to the living room, there's this quiet question hanging between us, more fragile than a soap bubble—do I want him to go home?

The answer is no. I don't.

"Do you want some dessert? I have some ice cream?" I offer awkwardly, wringing my hands. "I have salted caramel and pistachio. I was trying to get into this whole Dubai chocolate trend, but I don't see it. Maybe I did it wrong, though I—" *Stop, Nic. Take a deep breath.* There it is. Rambling. I grimace, one of those tight, lopsided smiles that practically screams, *well, that was too much.* "Sorry."

"I'd love pistachio ice cream," he offers with a faint smile and follows me back into the kitchen. "I don't think I ever asked, but how have you settled in here in Wayward Hollow?"

"I love it here," I quickly assure him. "I mean, after the unexpected curveballs in the beginning, I was a little skeptical, but you know what? I think everything"—I wave my hand through the air while opening my freezer with the other one—"really turned out for the best, ultimately. No offense, Chaos," I say more loudly as I close the door again, ice cream tub in hand.

"Everyone is super nice, here. I couldn't go a week in LA without getting screamed at by a director, co-star, or paparazzi. It's relaxing to be away from people who freak out after recognizing me, or the obligation to only go out with a full face of makeup and styled to the nines."

"Oh, Kieran freaked out plenty, though."

"But I don't have fans running toward me whenever I leave my home, demanding selfies," I point out. He nods in understanding, and I brush past him to get out two bowls and spoons. "I'm finally living for myself again and it's … freeing. I really needed that."

"I'm glad," he whispers as I scoop out the ice cream then take the spoon I used into my mouth and hand him his bowl. "You've got some …" He gestures to my cheek, and I instinctively reach up to wipe it away.

"Didn't get it," he says gently. "May I?"

I nod, maybe too quickly, and he immediately steps closer, brushing his thumb lightly across my skin.

Ice cream. Of course. Because nothing says *cool, calm, and collected* like dessert on your face.

Then he lifts his thumb to his mouth and licks it clean, and my eyes follow the movement on instinct, shameless and quicker than my self-control.

My cheeks heat up instantly. I'm pretty sure my heart forgets how to beat at a normal pace.

And he doesn't step back.

No, he leans in even more, a small smile tugging at his lips as his hands come up to gently cradle my face.

Everything stills. I forget how to breathe. How to think.

"I'm not imagining this, am I?" he whispers, his eyes darting over my face with an intensity as though he's trying to remember every single detail.

"Hell no. I mean, you're not." A faint giggle slips out before I can stop it, and I put my hands on his hips, the soft fabric of his sweatshirt resting under my palms. He crowds me against the kitchen island until a sheet of paper couldn't fit between the two of us.

"I don't want to rush you." His eyes dart from my lips to my eyes, searching for an answer to a question only he knows in my face. "With your ex, and—"

"Could you please not talk about my ex in a situation like this?" I press my lips together, but a grin is already creeping across my face. "I don't give a fuck about him. But I think I give one hell of a fuck about you." His hands are now on the kitchen island right behind my back, caging me in. "I can't promise being with me will be easy. I've been told I'm high maintenance, talk too much, *am* too much."

I pull back just enough to breathe, when one of his hands wanders to my waist, warm and grounding. Calming. Even if nervousness craws over my skin as if I've stepped out onto a ledge and haven't dared peeking down the abyss yet.

"I want this," I admit softly, Lauren's words echoing in my head. "I do. I *really* do. I'm just …" I exhale, trying to untangle the knot in my chest. "There's still some leftover debris. From before."

His brow furrows gently. "Debris?"

"Yeah. You know—emotional wreckage. Post-cheating storm damage. You know, trust issues with a side of flinching anytime someone's phone buzzes after midnight."

He doesn't laugh, and I'm glad. He nods, eyes steady on mine. "That makes sense."

"And I don't want to bring it into this. Into what could be an 'us.'" I shrug one shoulder, fiddling with the hem of his shirt. "But I probably will sometimes. Not on purpose. But … out of habit, maybe."

"Then we'll break the habit. Together."

God, this guy.

"I might need you to tell me more than once that you're not like him," I admit. "And I might not always believe it right away."

"I'll keep telling you anyway."

There's something in his voice—low and even, not performative. He's not trying to be a hero. He's just here. With me. Trying to assure me that he's all in. That he's got me.

I swallow hard. "Okay. So, if I completely panic out of nowhere one night and ask you weird, slightly invasive questions like 'why did your ex break up with you,' or 'who's Amanda in your phone?' you'll … what? Not run?"

"I'll probably tell you about how I put my arm up one of her cow's asses, hand you my phone, and ask if you want coffee or wine while you read through my messages. I have nothing to hide, Nic."

I huff out a laugh, eyes stinging the tiniest bit. "You're either incredibly patient or mildly unhinged."

"Maybe a bit of both," he says with a grin, then brushes his thumb along my cheek. "But mostly, I think you're worth the risk."

Silence settles over us, but not the bad kind. The kind that settles softer than a warm blanket.

"Okay," I whisper. "Then let's try. I'm in. Cautiously. Anxiously. Probably with some unnecessary commentary."

"I wouldn't expect anything less. And I'll be more than happy to shut you up like this."

He leans in again, and when our lips finally touch, it doesn't feel like falling. It feels like choosing. And I think that might be even scarier—but better.

So much better.

Chapter 15

Nic

"Now that's what I'm talking about," I whisper and sit down on my patio couch. It's a beautiful autumn morning – a crisp breeze in the air that makes me reach for the blanket I brought along and drape it around my shoulders, heavy clouds hanging over the mountains in the distance. Red and golden leaves fly past me, with the occasional drop of rain joining them.

It's the perfect morning to sit outside and start my day slowly. To have a calm morning, watch a squirrel climb up a tree while I'm drinking a piping hot pumpkin spice latte out on my porch, on my mission to romanticize the fuck out of life.

I blow on the hot liquid before I dare take a sip, the sweet taste of cinnamon and ginger hitting just the right tastebuds as I pull the blanket tighter around me and my legs up onto the couch.

I've waited years for a moment like this. A moment of calmness. Where my thoughts don't circle around worries. Just watching nature, no phone that incessantly buzzes, no people to disturb my peace. Just a moment of *being*.

At least for a while before I start my day. Reality will catch up soon enough.

"I'm nervous. Why am I nervous?" I mumble, pacing the sidewalk two houses away from Henry's clinic. I know he's in. I saw him from the other side of the street when I arrived.

Then I got overwhelmed by the butterflies trying to burst out of my stomach, and now I'm here, trying to talk myself into going inside—for once, without a feline reason to.

I mean, he kissed me. And he said I'm worth the risk. That means he more than tolerates me, right? That I can pop in randomly and unannounced, because I want to see him? Or is it too soon?

Don't be such a chicken, Nic. Take a deep breath, square your shoulders and go visit your boyfriend. Situationship.

Wait. What are we exactly? We never talked about titles. Do I *need* a title?

I shake my head at myself. What I need right now is to get a grip. I count down from ten in my head and then storm toward his clinic before I can change my mind.

"Nic!" His face breaks into a smile that melts my heart when he glances up from the computer on his reception counter.

Jensen emerges from behind it with a happy *awoo-woo* that I interpret as "So happy to see you." It makes me grin so widely that I fear my face might get stuck. God, they're both behaving like the biggest golden retrievers. Even the husky.

"Hi." I give Henry an awkward little wave, then crouch to greet his dog.

And when I get up again, he's right there. Very close. I squeal in surprise, almost losing my balance, but his arms snake around my hips and he keeps me upright, pulling me flush against him.

"No cat this time?" he asks, his eyebrow lifted in amusement and a smirk tugging at his lips.

"Pssst, don't give Chaos any ideas," I playfully scold him, letting my hands wander up his arms until I can interlace my fingers around his neck, and begin playing with his soft hair.

"It's good to see you, sweetheart." He stares at me as if we haven't seen each other in weeks instead of a day, and it's sending all kinds of emotions bubbling in my stomach.

"Sweetheart?" Now it's my turn to lift my eyebrow, biting my lip.

"Is that a 'no?'"

I tilt my head, rolling it over in my head. "It's not. I love it." I release my lip, a nervous laugh spilling out. "Now I need a nickname for you too, don't I?"

"You don't *need* one." He shrugs, but I can see him fighting a grin, telling me he's not against that idea.

"Muffin?" I think out loud, squealing when he gently pinches my hip. "Okay, okay. I'm not a fan of 'babe,' so that's out. Hmm …"

I tap my lip, pretending to think hard about it. "No, it has to come to me naturally. I'll call you 'hot stuff' until I can think of something better."

"Better than 'muffin,'" he mumbles, finally bridging the gap between us. "I'll take it," he murmurs against my lips. A happy sigh escapes me when his warm lips touch mine. The smile doesn't leaving me throughout the toe-curling kiss that's sending sparks up my spine and every rational thought out the window.

"Mmm, I'm all better now," I whisper with a soft hum when he breaks the kiss, staying close enough to count his eyelashes.

"You didn't feel good before?" Worry washes over his face. "What's going on?"

"Nothing!" I assure him quickly. "I was nervous, and then I started overthinking, and I didn't know if it was okay to stop by? Maybe you were busy. And that's such a girlfriend thing to do, and we never talked about what we are and—" He stops me by kissing me again, and I can't help but smile against his lips.

If this becomes our thing, I wouldn't be too mad at it. That means I need to ramble if I want him to kiss me, right? Maybe I'll never shut up again. Because this feeling? It's unmatched. The butterflies in my stomach, the prickling goosebumps in my neck, making me feel so light I might just lift off the ground.

"For the record, I'd love to be your boyfriend. That would make you a girlfriend," he mumbles against my lips. "Does that suit you?"

"Hell yes," I whisper back softly, and now it's my turn to lift myself onto my tiptoes and capture his lips in a messy kiss. "That sounds perfect."

"Can I take you on a coffee date later?" He lifts his hand to swipe a strand of hair behind my ear. "I want to show you off a bit."

"Uhhh, feeding the town gossip?" I wink at him, noting the blush creeping into his cheeks.

"Yeah. I want to shout to the whole world that you're my girlfriend now. But that seems excessive, so Wayward Hollow will do. For now."

God, we stand here like two idiots in a tight hug, grinning at each other wider than if we won the lotto jackpot. And I mean, who knows? This sure seems like a worthy alternative.

Awoo-woo! Jensen starts getting impatient, tip-tapping around us and nudging our thighs, not appreciating being ignored.

"Yes, yes," Henry lets go of me, and I pout at how cold I suddenly am without his arms around me. "Here's your attention, you little drama queen. You've *really* got to stop interrupting our emotional moments." He glances up at me. "By the way, sweetheart, how are the kittens doing?"

"Best friends." I shrug, trying to hide my giddiness at my new nickname. "I put them in separate rooms while I'm gone, but the only way they might kill each other is with too much love." I lower my voice. "I also think Chaos is giving them a spiritual ass-beating when they get sassy. Yesterday, Cinnamon hissed and then flinched back as if she got slapped."

"That does sound like her," he says, but I hear a tinge of sarcasm in his voice. But before I can mention it, the little bell above his door rings. Our heads turn to his front door quicker than teenagers who got caught kissing by their parents, though a lot less panicked.

"I think that's my cue to go." I grin and shoot him a subtle wink, away from his patients. "Let me know when you're done with your house call."

"Will do."

As soon as I walk out the door, my phone rings. I'm about to decline the call out of reflex when I realize for once it's not coming from an unknown or suppressed number. It's coming from my financial adviser. I take a few more steps away from Henry's clinic before I answer.

"Anna! How have you been?"

"Thanks, Nic, I'm good. Listen, I'll skip the small talk and cut to the chase—why did you open five credit cards without telling me?"

"What?" I stop in my tracks, a sudden nausea washing over me colder than a bucket of ice water. "I did no such thing. Why would I?"

"Fuck," she curses under her breath, and my blood runs cold. "That's what I thought. And feared."

"What's going on, Anna?" I ask cautiously, not sure I want to know the answer.

"After you told me about Jay, I decided to put some alerts on your credit. You know, in case he tried to pull something. And I think he did. Is." She takes a deep breath.

"Someone is blowing through your money, Nic. They opened several credit cards in your name and are spending your money on jewelry and designer clothes. They booked plane tickets to the Maldives in the last hour and a five-star hotel …"

My heart beats into my throat, but for once, it's not anxiety. It's anger. Burning hot anger.

"Jay and Marissa," I say, surprised at the venom in my voice.

"That's my suspicion, too." She sighs, and I can hear her type something into her computer.

"What do we do?" I ask, slowly starting to panic. "Those … miscreants! God, Anna, tell me how I can fucking bury them." Seriously, they didn't get my money through marriage, and now they switched to identity theft? I can't believe this. I quickly walk into an alley to find a quieter spot.

"The good news is, they've blown through so much money it's definitely a felony. That and the identity theft." She takes a deep breath. "I mean, not *good* news but a silver lining, at least." She types something before she continues.

"Okay, here's what we're going to do." I lean my back against the wall. "I'll freeze everything I can that I know to be fraudulent, including your credit. I saw Marco in the hallway a few minutes ago. I'll hand all of it to him once I've gathered evidence, and he can build his case that hopefully comes with two sweet restraining orders. We'll see what kind of proof we can find. Meanwhile, you need to go to the police and file a report—I'll send you everything you need to know." She takes a deep breath. "We'll take those fuckers down. Don't worry."

"Okay," I whisper, a sting forming in my eyes. I bite my lip to hold back my tears. They don't deserve them. Not even angry tears. "Let's destroy them."

Chapter 16

Henry

I watch my girlfriend through the window like a lovesick puppy.

My girlfriend. God, I still can't believe it.

I was hoping, but after all, we don't even know each other that well yet. I know her smile brightens a room, and I could listen to her ramble all day long, but there is so much I have no clue about. What are her hobbies, aside from collecting stray cats and arguing with ghost cats?

Counting the times I was at her home, we've had two *almost* dates. I sure was hoping I wasn't imagining the attraction between us, but this still seems too good to be true.

I mean, she's funny and gorgeous and has a big heart for animals. Her smile radiates brighter than the sun, and everyone wants to catch a ray and keep it to themselves. She's almost too perfect. Is there's a catch I've yet to be clued in on?

I've felt drawn to her since she stormed in here with Chaos cradled to her chest and pleaded with me to save her. I thought she'd hate me when there was nothing I could do. But then I met her again at Caleb's, rambling about her ghost cat. And when I got that call from her when she found Pumpkin, I knew fate would have more in store for us.

If that isn't a love story for the ages, I don't know what is.

She stops in front of the window, pulling her phone out of her bag, and I'm surprised when she answers it. Even more surprised when she suddenly tenses, and her face sets in anger as she storms off.

Huh. I'd love to know what that's about. But I'll have to wait a few hours until we meet at Caleb's.

Yet a weird unease builds in my gut suddenly, and it's neither my breakfast nor my lunch acting up.

But there's nothing I can do right now. So, I plaster a pleasant smile on my face and greet the Greens, who have their bunny in a transport box, ready for me to do a check-up.

"Hey, man." I look up, confused when a stranger enters my clinic, right as I'm grabbing my bag from the counter.

I have an hour-long drive ahead of me, and I just handed Mr. and Mrs. Thomson the ashes of Rose. I'm ready to get this day over with and meet up with Nic.

All I can think about is seeing her later and finally getting to know more about her without the elephant of "Does she feel it too?" in the room with us. I can't wait!

The guy who walked in appears nervous, but I can't see a reason why. He's all flaring nostrils and nervously moving hands. There's no animal carrier tucked under his designer suit clothed arm or pet walking with him. But there's something about him I immediately dislike. Maybe it's his nose that's up in the clouds or the "you're beneath me" way he carries himself.

He gives me the vibe of the kind of guy whose smirk arrives five seconds before he does. Whose ego probably needs its own parking space. Every brown hair is in place, probably insured. And his designer suit jacket fits as if it was stitched onto him by a tailor who hates joy, before he gained a few pounds.

His expression tells me he probably hasn't heard the word *no* since prep school. His eyes sweep the room as though he's trying to decide whether whatever he wants is worth the trouble. His jaw's sharp, his watch shinier than his personality, and his whole face radiates the smug, polished energy of someone who thinks "Why can't you take a joke?" is charisma.

"Can I help you?" I ask, ever the helpful guy.

The guy's eyes dart around the room, and he puffs himself up, lifting his chest and crossing his arms before he speaks.

"Maybe you can. I'm searching for someone."

"I think the police station would be the better place to ask," I point out, noting that I initially wanted to be out the door five minutes ago. "It's three houses down and then—"

"No," he interrupts me rudely, punching his fist on my reception table. Jensen is suddenly alert, his low growl making the stranger take a few steps back. I wrap his leash around my hand, in case he decides he wants to bite this guy's smug face off. I wouldn't blame him.

"Nicola Duncan. Where is she?"

And suddenly, I know exactly who he is.

"I have no idea who you're talking about." Now it's my turn to cross my arms in front of my chest.

"I know she's here!" he shouts, angrily pacing my reception area.

I lift an eyebrow and do a slow, deliberate sweep of the room, as if I might discover her hiding behind a potted plant.

"I don't see her," I say, deadpan.

Jensen's growl becomes louder, his entire body tense, and he's completely fixated on the guy, carefully tracking every move. He can't move his pinky without Jensen noticing at this point.

"And if you do see her," I add sweetly, "I'd strongly recommend a trip to the ER. Or maybe rehab. Or possibly an exorcism." I stare at him with fake, exaggerated worry. "Do you need me to call nine-one-one?"

"You think you're funny, don't you?" he sneers, walking right up to me and I shake my head.

"I know I am. However, I *think* you're rude and can't take a hint." I shrug and nod toward my dog. Apparently, he hasn't seen or heard Jensen yet, because he startles and takes a cautious step back.

"Now, as you can see—" I lift my bag higher and wriggle it a bit. "I was about to leave." He still doesn't make any attempts to turn around and walk out the door. "Meaning, you need to leave too."

His eyes jump from Jensen to me, his face turning red and his fingers flexing into fists before opening again. This guy wants trouble, but he'll have to find it somewhere else. Whatever his agenda is, I'm not playing along. I have better things to do than placate an ego.

"Fuck," he mutters and suddenly turns around, pulling the door open with a force that makes me fear for its hinges, and storms out.

"Well, well, well," I mumble, quickly rounding the counter and locking the door, taking a deep breath to calm down and be a good example for Jensen. "Calm down, Jensen. That fucker is gone."

But Jensen is still fixated on him, tracking his every step until he finally gets into a black Mercedes and drives out of sight. Even when he's gone, Jensen remains tense, and I swear the look he's giving me is his version of *"Why didn't you let me bite that asshat's neck?"*

"Trust me, I have no idea either. He certainly deserves it," I mumble and give him a reassuring pet once he's calmed down a bit. With a sigh, I check the time again. Twenty minutes after I initially wanted to leave. I'm officially late.

"I mean, maybe I'm lucky and the only one on the road," I tell Jensen whose only reaction is a big yawn.

Chapter 17
Henry

"*This* is your incognito getup?" I ask Nic amusedly when she slides into my booth at Caleb's. She's hiding her hair under a knitted wool hat and her eyes behind sunglasses that cover more than half her face. I fight the urge to pull them off her nose, really wanting to see her face.

"Yep." She lets out a deep sigh and dejectedly leans her head against my shoulder, her hand searching for mine under the table.

"You two are adorable," Kieran teases from the opposite side of the booth and makes a kissy mouth at us. "You are, Wayward Hollow's new dream couple. It was about time you two got your shit together."

"New?" Lauren turns and glances at Kieran, curiosity written all over her face. "Who was the old one?"

"One hundred percent the Thomsons," he answers immediately with a convinced nod. "I mean thirty years of marriage? That's dream couple material."

"We have been together for all of three minutes," I joke, glancing at Nic and giving her hand a gentle squeeze. Her mouth is set in a straight line, and I catch her eyes behind those dark glasses darting around nervously. "I don't think that qualifies us yet." In an attempt to help her relax, I lift my arm and she immediately scoots toward me, a heavy sigh falling from her lips when I pull her closer.

"God, you two are sweeter than this damned syrup," Lauren jokes and demonstratively puts the already half-empty bottle on the table.

"One of these days Caleb will kick you out and never let you back in," Kieran jokes, but Lauren only sticks out her tongue at him.

"Never. I'm his best customer at this point." She shoots him a triumphant grin.

"Very tempting thought, though." As always, Caleb appears next to us out of thin air. His arms are full of mugs and saucers, our coffee's expertly stacked along his forearms without any of us having ordered from him or Shawna.

"See? Nic and I are already regulars—he knows our orders!" Lauren jokes and happily accepts her mug with an overly sweet smile and a "Thank you!"

"You're not welcome," he tells her gruffly then his eyes dart over the rest of us. "You three are." He glances back at Lauren. "Don't bring that shit in here again." But it's missing his usual bite. He's probably given up the fight already.

And then he turns around and wanders back to his place behind the counter, wiping some imaginary stains off glasses.

"Does he ever lighten up?" Lauren wonders out loud and pours a hefty amount of the syrup into her coffee, mixing it with her spoon and humming happily when she takes a sip.

"During the autumn fair. Sometimes you can even see the hint of a smile on his face," I tell her, biting back a grin. "And throughout, the resting bitch face isn't quite as bitchy. He always pretends to hate it, but don't let him fool you. Deep down, I know he loves it."

"Autumn fair?" Nic glances at me curiously, squeezing my thigh before she starts drawing little patterns on my knee with her finger. "That sounds fun! When is it?"

"Usually the last week of October, the weekend before Halloween," I explain, only now remembering that I'm the only one at this table who has lived in Wayward Hollow for longer than a year. "The whole town comes together to decorate the town square. There are games, a crafts market, and a stage for entertainment. Then the whole thing ends with a bonfire for us townsfolk in the evening."

Nic's eyes widen with every word, her face slowly breaking into a bright smile. "That sounds lovely!"

"You're so easily excited," Lauren points out with a sigh and a soft expression.

"You're the one who said we should, let me quote, 'romanticize the fuck out of life.' How better to do that than with an autumn festival?" Nic breaks into a giggle, but it doesn't sound quite as if her heart is in it.

"Girl, that giggle was creepy as hell. Let's talk about the elephant in the room." Lauren clears her throat and pushes up her sleeves. "Jay is in town," she says and Nic immediately tenses. "Any idea what he wants?"

"Probably money." She shrugs and exhales a sigh so deep it sends a napkin flying across the table. "I mean, you can draw your own conclusions: Anna tells me *someone* is opening credit cards in my name, and a few hours after freezing them all, he turns up here? That doesn't sound coincidental to me."

I glance at her, confused. "Was that the call you took in front of the clinic?" I ask her in a whisper, and she nods slightly.

"I'll tell you everything later."

"I'll hold you to that," I whisper back, tracing reassuring patterns on her arms with my thumb. It certainly sounds like a big deal, but she appears relaxed about the whole thing. Maybe I'm overreacting.

"Surprised he had enough money for gas," Lauren mutters and rolls her eyes. The whole mood at the table has suddenly shifted, both women silently brewing while Kieran and I can only shoot each other confused looks.

"I'm sure he didn't. Fucker used my credit cards after all. I bet he had enough money withdrawn," Nic spits, crossing her arms in front of her chest.

"Doesn't he have a job?" asks Kieran, and I can only agree with a curious nod.

"Shortly after we got engaged, he was fired from his finance job," she admits with a sigh. "Supposedly because he refused to falsify data. But well." She shrugs. "Who knows if that's really true. I have no idea if he got a new job since then but judging by the way he's apparently spending my money, I doubt it."

Jensen moves under the table, and before I know it, he has his butt parked on my foot and his chin on Nic's thigh. Mindlessly, she pets him and draws little patterns over his forehead.

"Oh, I know—let's ask Amanda to place a curse on him when we're at the store tomorrow! Maybe one for him to stub his toe every hour. Or one that makes him stink to the heavens."

"I'd prefer one where he gets the hell away from here," Nic grumbles annoyed.

"Do you know for sure it's him?" Kieran wonders and Nic raises her eyebrow at him.

"Yeah, I'm pretty sure." She taps her fingers against the table nervously. "It has to be. There are no other options. Aside from my sister, but him turning up here is evidence enough for me."

"And we know for sure he's the weird guy who angered Jensen?"

"Henry's description was spot on, down to the attitude."

"Is he that bad?" Kieran tilts his head, and Lauren is already taking a deep breath to tell him all about *how* bad he is, when Nic suddenly tenses beside me.

"Speak of the devil," I whisper when the door to Caleb's opens and that same smug, punchable face walks in like he owns the place.

"You're about to find out firsthand," she whispers, straightening her back, wriggling off my arm as he approaches. I glance at her from the corner of my eye, trying not to pout that she shrugged off my arm when her ex is approaching. I'm sure she has her reasons, but damn, it stings.

Her disguise didn't work as planned, because Jay immediately makes a beeline for our table. He plants himself at its head with his chest puffed and a smarmy grin on his—indeed, very irritating—face.

"I can see it now," Kieran whispers loudly and Lauren nods.

"You're not half as hard to track down as you think, Nic," Jay sneers, and Lauren makes a gagging noise, which he ignores.

"Hello to you, too." Nic takes a sip of her coffee, trying to pretend she's not rattled. But I can see her hand trembling slightly as she sets her mug back down. "What do you want?"

"Don't use that tone. Aren't you happy to see me?"

Nic lifts her gaze slowly, clearly stunned by his audacity, while Lauren is hiding her face behind her hand, looking at him as if she doesn't know whether to laugh at him or jump at his throat.

"No. No, I can't say I am happy to see you. What do you want?" The coolness in her voice could turn our coffees into frappés, but Mr. Asshole remains unfazed.

"Listen, I know things got messy. But I've been thinking a lot about all this. We don't have to make it worse. You know, we could talk about a settlement, come to a fair agreement. We've been through too much for you to walk away without us sorting this out."

"*Settlement?*"

Lauren almost spits out her coffee.

"Oh my God, this is gold," Lauren wheezes, but I can't help but remain tense.

There is something off about his whole demeanor, how he demands her money the way a duck takes to water. Like he deserves it for the gift of his existence, like he's the one who's been wronged. He can't be serious. Right?

"We weren't married, Jay. You're not getting a settlement. I don't know where you got this idea from, but it's the most delusional shit I've ever heard."

Jay clenches his jaw, flexing his hands as if he's about to turn violent. Kieran and I shoot each other a glance, getting ready to interfere if necessary.

"This is all your fault, you know?" Jay spits. "You got me accustomed to a certain lifestyle, and it's *my right* to continue that." By now, half the café is listening in on him making an ass of himself.

"Then I suggest finding a higher paying job, or a rich lover, and going for it." Nic shrugs. "Because that lifestyle came with certain conditions you didn't meet. Like monogamy and not being an asshole."

"Don't make this so hard on me. You're putting me under a lot of stress—did all those years together mean nothing to you?"

Kieran and Lauren can't hold back anymore. They're giggling messes on the other side of the table. I'd join them if his demeanor wasn't making me want to jump up and introduce my fist to his face in a quick and abrupt manner. Repeatedly.

"Hard on *you*?" Nic climbs out of her seat, storming closer to him. "Under stress? Oh, sure. You've been 'under stress' while you were opening credit cards in my name and siphoning off money from my accounts? You're right, that sounds extremely stressful."

"I had to! We were supposed to be a team. You don't know what I'm going through. You're the one who left me, and now you're—"

"Let me try to make this clear to you." She steps closer, jabbing her finger into his chest. "We're done. That means you have no right to anything. Not me, not my money, not my fucking time. I'm done with letting you manipulate me. I'm done with being your bank and doormat, and frankly, I'm done dealing with you. Now, here's what you're going to do. You're going to walk out that door, and you're never going to contact me again. No phone calls, no emails, no attempts to get any more money from me. Ever. This is your last chance, to leave me alone and just walk away, Jay."

"But—"

"You need to leave." Caleb is suddenly there, stepping between Nic and her ex, staring him down. He's almost a head taller than him—hell, even I would be intimidated if he ever stared me down with that much venom in his eyes.

"We enjoy our town without drama. I suggest you try to blend in and shut up. I'm not in the mood to deal with dickheads, so I'm banning you from this café. You can find the door yourself within the next ten seconds, or I can assist you while making use of my right to forcibly remove you. Which will it be?"

He lifts his eyebrow, daring Jay to retort, but sadly, for once, Nic's ex is doing the smart thing.

"I'm not done, Nic," he says over his shoulder as he storms toward the door. "I will get what's rightfully mine."

"A kick in the ass?" she asks in a whisper, making the whole table burst into laughter, the tension falling from us as soon as that fucker leaves the café. "Thank you, Caleb."

"Of course," he mumbles as he stares after the guy, making sure he walks away from the café.

"Do you want to leave?" I ask her softly once she sits back down, but she shakes her head. "He's probably still lurking outside. Let's drink our coffee in peace. I'm not about to let him ruin a nice afternoon any more than he already has." She takes a deep breath and shoots Lauren a look. They hold a conversation with only their eyes. I leave them to it and scan the room, wondering if he will pop up again like a ghost, when I meet Caleb's worried stare.

Not worried because he's afraid patrons will leave because of the drama. Worried because, as little as he may talk, I know he has accepted the two of them as our own.

They're part of the Wayward Hollow family now. And there's nothing we won't do for our people.

Chapter 18

Nic

"What do you need?" Lauren asks me as we step out of Caleb's café and gives my arm a reassuring squeeze. I stare at her, not quite understanding the question. "A friend? Your boyfriend? To be left alone?" she elaborates, and that's when I get it.

"I … don't know," I tell her and let out a long, deep sigh. The moment Jay stepped out of Caleb's, exhaustion took me under with the force of a tsunami. "Right now, I need to not decide what I need, if that makes sense."

"I got her," Henry offers, and Lauren stops in front of us. Her eyes dart from Henry, who's snaking his arm around my waist, to Jensen coming to a stop in front of me, and then back to me. Suddenly, her gaze softens.

"I sure hope you do." She steps closer for a quick hug before she links her arm with Kieran's, and the two of them walk off, whispering and with a little spring in their steps.

"When did they become best friends?" I point at the two of them, confused. Henry shrugs.

"Probably somewhere between a midnight feeding for Pumpkin and finding Cinnamon," he jokes. "I think they both hang out at Caleb's a lot. Probably then."

"Huh." I take a deep breath of the cool evening air. The sun is setting, the sky a cloudless pale orange.

"Let me get you home?" Henry asks, and I glance up at him. There's a tiny wrinkle forming between his eyebrows, worry creasing his usually smooth, charming face.

Ugh. Concern looks good on him. Annoyingly good.

"I'm not about to break down," I quickly assure him, but let him lead me to his car. Good thing we shared Lauren's on the way here. "Can't say it was easy to see him, but I've had two months, a *lot* of ice cream, and shouting along to sad songs to process that cheating motherfucker. The breakdown days are behind me."

"It's still a lot for one day," he points out, and the sincerity in his voice covers me like a warm blanket, making me take a sharp breath. "It's okay not to be okay."

I gulp around the knot suddenly making itself at home in my throat and focus intently on the gazebo across the street as I try not to cry. That charming, Hallmark-movie little thing, peeking out from between the trees as if it's eavesdropping on my personal crisis.

That caught me off guard. After a lifetime of "pull yourself together" or "stop whining," someone saying *this*, in that soft, sincere tone that doesn't ask me to be strong or charming or anything other than sad for a hot second—it messes with me.

There's no epiphany, no choir of angels appearing out of nowhere. Only racing thoughts and fighting the urge to cry myself into a puddle. I'm realizing that for once, someone who's not Lauren gives a damn about me.

That little thought occupies my brain, and I hold on to it, as if it might evaporate until we arrive at my place.

"Sorry you always have to go out of your way to come here," I whisper. But before the last word passes through my lips, Henry grabs my chin and turns my face to him with a gentle, yet steady touch.

"This is not 'out of my way,'" he says firmly, voice low and resolute. His eyes are scanning mine, searching for the answer to an unspoken question. "Nic, this is the bare minimum. But you've got to let me in. Tell me what is happening, so I can help. Even if that only means being there for you while you spiral into an emotional puddle."

"I don't want to be a burden," I protest weakly, trying to avert my gaze, but he gently turns my face back to him.

"You're not."

Two words.

Two ridiculously cheesy, yet earth-tilting words. They land harder than a punch, knocking the air out of my lungs in the best way possible.

"But what if someday you wake up and I am?" I ask, my voice breaking. He lets out a breath and tilts his head, eyebrows raised, and I brace for a loving schooling.

"Does that mean you think one day I might suddenly become one?" His voice is calm but pointed. And honestly? If we weren't having such a deep moment, that eyebrow raise might be illegal levels of hot.

"No. No, of course not," I answer quickly, relieved when that pained expression melts.

"See?" he asks, now almost sounding amused. "Then why the hell would I think you would be? Come on, let's get inside."

Once inside, he makes me hang out with the animals while he prepares our dinner. When I try to check in and ask if I can help, he promptly sends me back to the living room.

But I'm restless.

I'm willing them to go away, but I keep hearing Jay's and my family's voices in my head. Their voicemails I couldn't resist listening to when I needed to remind myself why leaving and cutting them out was my only option for a life that I'm allowed to be happy in.

"You should be the bigger person."

"You're the most selfish person I know. It's not that big of a deal. You're tearing the family apart!"

"I can't believe you'd ignore your own sister over this. You need to grow up."

Pumpkin and Cinnamon are having the time of their lives, tumbling around the living room like it's their own personal bounce house. Meanwhile Jensen Ackles naps by the window, soaking up the last few rays of sunlight as though he's trying to store them for winter.

By the time Henry finishes making dinner, the three of them have migrated to the couch. Cinnamon is snoozing in my lap. Pumpkin has curled up in the pocket of my cardigan and claimed it as her new nest. Jensen is softly snoring at my feet.

I almost don't have the heart to move them. They look so peaceful, as if they're draped for a furry little family portrait. But eventually, my stomach growls louder than my conscience. So I gently shift the cats onto the couch and ease my legs out from under Jensen's warm, heavy weight and make my way to the kitchen.

We eat quietly, but it's the good kind of silence. And God, he's a ridiculously good cook. Is there anything this man *can't* do?

It's not the kind of silence I knew growing up, the kind that stung, that made me feel invisible. Back then, silence meant distance, meant I'd said the wrong thing or was better off saying nothing at all.

Every little win of mine brushed aside for something half-hearted my sister did. I was always a few steps behind in a race I never even signed up for.

But this ... this is different. This silence settles over us like a soft blanket. No tension, no pressure to fill the air. Just two people, letting the day sink in, sorting through their thoughts side by side.

It's the kind of silence that makes you want to live in it. The kind that makes you feel at home.

Until suddenly, a glass falls off the counter and makes us jump.

"What the hell was that?" Henry asks, clutching his chest and eyes darting around, confused.

"Oh, that's Chaos." I shrug and get up to put our plates into the dishwasher. "She loves to push glasses off the kitchen island. It's kind of her thing."

"You're kidding, right?" He stares at me with wide eyes and mouth agape.

"Not at all." I chuckle and pick up the glass. By some mysterious grace, it's shattered into just two pieces—instead of a mountain of sharp shards that could slice open the paw of any living animal. How considerate.

So I wipe up the spilled water and put anything made of glass further away from the edge, in case she's not done. "She always knocks stuff off counters. I'd be careful with your sunglasses over there." He immediately jumps up to scoot them to the middle of the kitchen island.

"What—" He suddenly turns, looking around frantically.

"Hah!" I point my finger at him. "You didn't believe me, but she's rubbing against your calves, isn't she?"

His eyes widen, and his mouth pops open as he gapes at me in shock. "For the record, I didn't not believe you. But how do you know?"

"Because I've been living with her for a while now," I explain with a grin and get the cat food ready for my alive pets. "I got some of your dog food in that cupboard over there."

I point to my right, and he heads over, though not without throwing a wary glance back toward the spot he's convinced Chaos is lurking in. He preps Jensen's food, and sure enough, the moment the first bag crinkles open, they all come charging into the kitchen with the force of a furry stampede on a mission.

Pumpkin is now big enough for regular cat food. And while she still loves to wake me up in the middle of the night because she *thinks* she's hungry, my living situation has become far more relaxed. No wonder my ex had to turn up now to disturb the peace I made for myself with his unpredictable ideas.

"So," he starts and turns from where he's sitting on the couch, pulling up his leg to better face me. "What was the credit card thing about?"

"Right." I take a deep breath and pinch the bridge of my nose. I wish this was some annoying dream, but I'm slowly losing hope.

"After I left your clinic, I got a call from my financial adviser. She told me that someone opened credit cards in my name and wanted to confirm it wasn't me. As soon as she knew, she froze all of them. I think that's why Jay turned up here: I shut off his money faucet. No idea how he found out where I live now, though." I roll my eyes, but anger is burning in my gut.

"After that call, I went to Erik and filed a police report. I'm also pretty sure my sister is in on it somehow, but there is no evidence yet. I hope she won't turn up here, too." I cross my arms in front of my chest. "Honestly, if she disappeared forever, I'd throw a party. Hats. Cake. Confetti. Possibly a parade. Though maybe in hindsight I'm not unthankful that she showed me who Jay really is."

I want to leave it at that, but from the corner of my eye, I see him gazing at me *intently*, so interested, that it tumbles out of me.

"You know, she was supposed to be an only child. That was made painfully clear from the start—by my parents, and honestly, by her too. Then came one reckless night, too much wine, and ... surprise! Nine months later, enter me."

He gently untangles my arms, taking my hand in his. He presses a kiss to the back of it, soft and grounding.

"I was always in the way," I say quietly. "Too loud. Too boring. Too *me.* Maybe that's why I've turned into this emotionally constipated oversharer now." I try to laugh and break the sudden heaviness in the air, but it comes out thin. He doesn't laugh—just gives my hand a firm, reassuring squeeze.

I glance down at our hands, his thumb tracing slow circles on my skin as if he's trying to calm down the storm under it.

"My happiness offended them somehow. Any glimpse of joy I had was a personal inconvenience. I thought moving out would fix that. Thought having my own life would mean I could finally breathe, finally be seen."

I swallow hard, voice trembling now. "And then the acting thing took off. It was a means to an end, something I was good at. It turned into a way to earn money and move out of that toxic household, but all of a sudden, everything turned around. Suddenly, I wasn't only tolerated, I was *impressive*. Desirable. People wanted me around. I thought maybe, just maybe, my parents would finally see me too. Maybe they'd even be proud."

I blink up fast, but the tears spill over anyway—those disloyal pricks—and I swipe at them with a little too much force. "But ultimately, friendships in show business are superficial. At some point, I became distrustful because everyone I met had some kind of hidden agenda. At some point, many people forgot that Nic Duncan is a real person and not just a means to an end."

I take a deep breath.

"Anyway, you can probably guess that my so-called family wasn't exactly an exception. They played nice, bragged about me to their friends like I managed to get where I was because of them, not despite them. They did it only long enough to keep me hopeful. And then it all blew up when I found Jay and my sister whispering their mutual dislike for me and making plans to steal my money during *what was supposed to be* our engagement party."

I pause, taking a deep, breath that seems to scrape my ribs on the way in. "Lauren got me out of there. I had a few breakdowns, then pulled my life together. Lauren found the lakeside mansions, and I moved on, moved *away.* And … well. The rest is history."

Finally, I lift my gaze. And for once, I don't feel the need to brace myself for what I might find in someone's eyes.

"I'm sorry. I bet you thought you'd get an uncomplicated girlfriend but instead, picked one with next-level self-esteem issues and a whole wagon of emotional baggage."

"And I wouldn't want it any different," he assures me and lifts his arm. Immediately, I scoot closer to him, until it lowers back over my shoulders, a reassuring weight as he pulls me to him and presses his lips against my forehead.

"What if I become too much? I'm … like a storm. I destroy everything around me."

"Then I'll be a mountain. You won't blow me away, you won't knock me down. I'll always be there."

Chapter 19

Nic

"No! Shut up, he did not say that!" Lauren exclaims, excitedly slapping my upper arm.

"Ow," I complain and rub the spot, but can't contain the grin tugging on my lips. "He did," I confirm, noticing my cheeks growing warm.

"I'm so jealous, Nic. You went right ahead and got yourself the perfect guy." A deep sigh falls from her lips, and she watches Cinnamon as she climbs into her lap, clearly in the mood to cuddle.

She's completely made herself at home here, like this house was the place she'd been waiting for all along. Her favorite spot is a bed I impulse-bought and placed right by the window. More often than not, I will find her curled up there, enjoying the sun, probably dreaming about food. Or glaring at Pumpkin when she has another of her screaming fits, though they've become significantly less frequent.

"He really is," I say dreamily, hugging a pillow to my chest. "Sometimes I'm scared he's too good to be true."

"Makes me want to find a frog too, if the prince follows that quickly," she says with a dreamy sigh. She stares with an empty expression out of my front window, probably imagining her own, probably grumpy prince charming wearing a backward cap instead of a crown. I shake my head at her.

"Trust me, you don't want that."

"I know." Her eyes jump back to me. "But come to think of it, Jay does kind of a frog-like face, doesn't he?"

I tilt my head, and suddenly, the resemblance is uncanny, and I burst into a giggle. "Now that you say it. He actually does!"

"Thank God he's left you alone since. Do you think he's gone for good?"

"Oh, no." I chuckle, but there's no amusement in it, and shake my head. "Not a chance. He's too stubborn. And I think in his delusional mind, he's convinced that he still has power over me, that he deserves my money and I need to bend to his wishes." I take a deep breath. "I fear we haven't seen the last of him."

"Can't you get a restraining order? He's harassing you!"

"Nope," I say, popping the P. "Being an asshole is not enough reason for a restraining order, I've learned. And they're still inspecting the evidence of fraud and identity theft. Erik promised to keep an eye out, though." She lifts her eyebrow, and I shrug.

Both of us have had our fair share of experiences with stalkers and know firsthand how difficult it is to get a restraining order—and how much harder to enforce it. We're both jaded by the long and mostly unsuccessful processes of trying to get away from overzealous fans who are convinced we're besties or in a relationship. And by the police's inaction until violence has been committed, pissed at how high our security budget got because we realized that *we* are the only ones who will protect ourselves.

Then again, this is a small town. Wayward Hollow might not have a ton of cops, but from what I can tell, the ones they have take their jobs seriously. Erik wrote down everything I said religiously, meticulously labeling and filing all the documents Anna sent over—much more thorough than any city cop would have been.

Sometimes I miss parts of my old life. The five-star hotels, having a stylist, and having a driver. But then I remember the downsides—the not-so-nice fans, the constant camera flashes in my face, the egos in the industry—and I'm glad to have gotten out of there.

"Anyway, it's a problem for future us. Right now, it's time for more fun activities." She puts Cinnamon on the couch and gets up. "Come on, Nic. We are baking a pumpkin pie. I keep getting spammed with recipes on my socials, and I've been dying to make one."

"You have the best ideas," I say excitedly and jump up, pulling up my sleeves. "I was just feeling snack-ish."

"Perfect. What better snack than someone's grandma's pumpkin pie?" She grabs the bag she brought with her and brings it to the kitchen. "Warm spices, flaky crust, and me dragging your innermost feelings into the open. Pure autumn magic."

"I'm okay," I assure her, rolling my eyes when I turn my back to her as I find a mixing bowl. "Honestly."

"Yeah, you keep saying that, but I don't buy it." She pulls a kitchen scale out of the bag and I hand her the bowl. "Nobody is okay after the shit you've been through over the past few months."

I take a deep breath. "Maybe I've gotten too used to it." I shrug as she weighs out flour. "My sister always got my toys, and my parents suddenly decided she deserved them more than I did. Looking back, this situation is not new, but, you know, hindsight is twenty-twenty and all that."

"Oh, wow, that's self-deprecating," she points out, then puts some flour on her palm and blows it toward me. "Away with those thoughts." I cough and take a step away from the flour cloud. "It shouldn't feel normal. You should be mad."

"I'm past being angry," I say with a sigh that makes specks of flour she blew toward me fly right back at her. "I don't have any strength for that left in me. I'm so done. Truly, irrevocably done. They've made it more than clear that they don't give a shit about me, and I'm going to return that energy from now on."

"Now that's the spirit!" She cuts some cold butter into the flour, then suddenly perks up. "No, wait, don't return anything. Pretend they don't exist."

"I meant what I said at Jay's parents' house. They're dead to me," I assure her.

"Good. Hey, by the way, Amanda sold that monstrous table yesterday. The customer said he saw it on the website you set up for her. She was so surprised!"

"I love that she's into all this paranormal, Wicca stuff, but doesn't believe in the power of the internet," I snicker. She slides the bowl toward me, and I turn around to wash my hands to knead the dough, when I see the bowl move suspiciously. "Oh, no, Chaos."

I catch the bowl at the last second and shake my head disapprovingly. "No more treats as daily night offering."

"Pfft, as if she cares," Lauren jokes. She is slowly coming around to the idea of a ghost cat, but I think she's still trying to come up with "natural" explanations for everything that's happening. Now she's keeping them to herself, though.

"Now, to come back to your concern: All of this is terrifying," I tell her, as I bury my hand in the butter-flour mixture and start squishing it. "It means I don't have anyone in this world—apart from friends and friendships can fall apart."

"One thing, Nic." She steps in front of me and grabs my elbow to make me stop kneading. "You're not getting rid of me." She flashes a smile that might be friendly or might precede a murder—hard to say, really. "I'll be the … I don't know, the pumpkin spice to your pie. Or coffee. The milk in your cappuccino. The—"

"I get it," I chuckle and flick a bit of dough her way. "And same. You're basically the sister I always wanted, you know."

"Likewise. I always wanted an annoying little sister." She grins and walks back to the other side of the counter, where a pie dish has suddenly appeared.

"What in the Mary Poppin's bag? What else do you have in there?" I ask, surprised, laughing when she starts pulling everything for the pumpkin filling out of it.

"Just about everything we need and a spoonful of sugar." She wiggles her eyebrows.

"Emotional stability?"

"I meant more along the lines of food. Pretty sure the delivery guy of Wayward Hollow already hates me. Maybe I should bake him some cookies."

"Make your snickerdoodles. They will make any man fall at your feet. Hell, *I* was ready to marry you the first time you gave them to me."

"Is that so?" she asks, gazing out of my kitchen window contemplatively. "You know what? I just might. After Thanksgiving though. They're Christmas cookies. I can't bake them before Thanksgiving. Pretty sure there's some kind of divine rule that would make me burst into flames."

"That makes sense." I nod with a grin and set down the bowl, giving the dough a few more kneads on the marble countertop. "Here you go."

"Speaking of—" She greases the pie dish, then puts the dough in there and pushes it toward the edges until she's happy with how it's turning out. "Be a darling and preheat the oven?" I turn around and do exactly that as she continues. "We're spending Thanksgiving together, right?"

"Erm ... I haven't thought about it yet, but I kind of assumed we would?" I shoot her a look over my shoulder as I set the temperature. "Why? Do you have other plans?"

"Only with me, myself, and I. What do you think about making a Friendsgiving out of it? If you're fine hosting because my place is still a mess, and I don't see that clearing up anytime soon," she says as she puts parchment paper and pie weights onto the dough.

"Sure. As long as nobody is allergic to cats."

"We could invite Kieran. He mentioned he's not too close to his family either. No cat allergy."

"What about Caleb?" From the corner of my eye, I see her blush and avert her gaze. "If we invite Kieran, we have to ask at least—don't you think?"

"I mean, if *you* say so. Sure." She tries to shrug nonchalantly, but the smile on her face gives her away. "What about Henry? Is he spending Thanksgiving with his family?"

"No idea." Now it's my turn to shrug. "Thanksgiving hasn't come up yet, but I'll ask him." I put the dish with the dough and pie weights into the oven and open my cupboards and drawers, trying to find a hand mixer. "He's coming over later today."

"And he's gonna stay the night?" She wiggles her eyebrows at me and that grin is just screaming indecent thoughts so I shake my head at her. But not without grinning myself.

"Nope, just a good old movie and dinner date," I point out, feeling my cheeks fill with heat. I can't wait to see him.

"Aw, you have that smile on your face again!" She rounds the kitchen island again and puts her floury, buttery hands on my cheeks. "I'm so happy for you!"

"Thank you, Lauren." I giggle and join her in her little happy dance. "I don't think I've ever been this giddy about a man before."

"Like your whole body is tingling?"

"No. I don't know how to describe it. It's … like pumpkin spice! Okay, no. Maybe that's a crappy comparison."

"Try me." She lifts her eyebrow, clearly ready for the challenge that is keeping up with my brain and weird comparisons.

"You wait all year for pumpkin spice," I say as I carry the empty dough bowl to the sink. "And then it shows up, and suddenly … you're happier. It's not something you *need*, but drinking it, tasting it—it brings this little spark of joy. It makes life warmer, brighter. Even if it's only for a season."

"I was with you until it turned self-deprecating again." She pinches my arm, and I swat her hands away. "Henry isn't only for a season. Pay attention to the way he looks at you."

"How does he look at me?"

"As if you're the sun." She giggles, getting a dreamy look on her face. "And he'll never let you go. Like he would punch Jay, your sister, and your parents in the face if it meant you'd cheer up. And you know what?"

"What?"

"You kind of look at him like that too."

Chapter 20

Henry

"Have fun at work, hot stuff. May you have a day with cute, fluffy patients and no cow behinds," Nic jokes, then lifts herself to her tiptoes to press her lips against mine.

"Thanks, sweetheart."

She returns my smile, and I tear myself away from her. Something is off. The spark in her eyes has dulled, and her smile doesn't quite reach her eyes, her thoughts everywhere but in the present.

No wonder. With her history, an ex showing up would probably throw me for a loop too.

An angry voice in my head scolds me to stay and be there for her, but I have appointments today, and animal health is not exactly something I can reschedule. The only thing I can do is pop over when I can, whether that's on a detour on my way to work, or after to spend the evenings with her. Right now, though, I can only watch her close her front door, heart dropping and anxiety twisting my stomach into knots.

Walking to my car, I can't help but glance over my shoulder. Through the narrow, frosted glass sidelights next to her door, I catch her shadow. At first, she's leaning against the door, back pressed to it. But by the time I reach the car, she's slid down to the floor and sits on the floor.

She's still there, motionless, even after Jensen climbs into the passenger seat, and still when I get behind the wheel.

Everything in me screams, fighting the urge to jump out and run back inside. To hug her to me tightly and not let her go until she tells me what's going on in that complicated, beautiful mind of hers.

Yet a more rational part of me knows it's more likely to push her away.

It sucks. All I can do is sit by her when her thoughts are miles away, tighten my hug, and be there for her if she ever decides to talk about it. This thing between us is still fragile, still trying to find its footing, more unsteady than Bambi learning to walk. It will take more time until I can read her and know what she wants without asking.

We're getting there. She doesn't often open up about her emotional turmoil about her ex anymore. And I get it. It's an awkward topic to talk about with a new boyfriend. Yet I treasure each and every time she does, hoping she'll soon understand that I'm here to stay and nothing she says could drive me away.

Until that happens, life goes on as usual: With me getting coffee from Caleb's and Jensen getting his daily treat from his favorite uncle. And later we'll go on a walk so I can try out the new lense for my camera.

Business as always.

"Henry!" I glance up to see Lauren waving at me from her seat at the counter, an excited grin on her face.

"Morning, Lauren," I greet her, not quite as enthusiastically, and lift my hand for a quick wave to Caleb. He's never been a man of many words and is even less so in the morning.

"You don't seem as happy as you should be." She narrows her eyes at me, trying to read me like a goddamn book. "What's going on?" she asks carefully, absentmindedly petting Jensen when he puts his paws on the edge of her chair, subtly keeping him away from her coffee on the counter.

"I don't know," I admit with a deep sigh, leaning against the counter next to her with both my elbows. "I wish I knew. Nic seemed so at peace after you guys began helping out in the antique store, but now she's drawing back, and I'm not sure what to do. She's like … water, slipping through my fingers. Do you have any ideas?"

She tilts her head and studies the array of mugs on the other side of the bar while she thinks. "Did she tell you why?"

"No." I shake my head and take a deep breath. "I thought everything was going great." I clear my throat. "I first noticed it right after Jay appeared, but it has gotten worse over the past few days."

"I can think of a reason, but a word of caution, I can't read her mind," Lauren says and gives me a hard stare. "Which I think is for the better, but … please keep that in mind?"

"Okay," I say, climbing into one of the bar stools beside her. "Tell me."

Her fingers tap the wooden countertop nervously, causing small waves in her coffee as she tries to think of the right words.

"You know, after Nic broke up with Jay, she stormed forward right away. I mean, after a few days of crying and getting out preliminary sadness and anger. From the beginning, she was determined to bury the whole thing, pretend her family didn't exist anymore and that the whole debacle didn't happen. Now, for the record, there is no way she would *ever* return to Jay." She quickly points out and I nod.

"That's the one thing I have zero doubts about," I assure her and she nods.

"I think what's currently catching up to her is the rest of it." She makes a vague gesture with her hand. "Her sister's backstabbing. Her parents' betrayal. That whole black-sheep versus golden-child dynamic." She takes a sip of her coffee, just as Caleb places my to-go cup in front of me.

"Nic has always yearned for a warm family. She wouldn't admit it—hell, I'm not sure if she even *knows* it—but the more you watch her, the more obvious it becomes. Instead, she has a bunch of ice blocks with spikes who she shares her genes with. Yet ever since I've known her, she's held onto those spikes as hard as she could. Even if that meant getting frostbite on her fingertips and only receiving pain in return. Now she finally, *finally* let go and she never got the chance to properly grieve what could have been." Lauren shoots me a knowing look. "She might have all of us, but it's not the same. She's scared."

"Right." I gulp, many of my jumbled thoughts and worries falling into place.

"There's no security net," Lauren continues, and I subtly nod along. "She even told me she thinks friendships can fall apart quickly. The only person she dares to count on is herself."

"I don't know what to say," I whisper, my heart aching for Nic. Lauren shakes her head as she continues.

"You should have seen them." Her voice is barely above a whisper. "I've never seen that much venom in someone's expression. So much hate in their words, and they directed them at their *child*. They scolded her for causing drama—can you imagine?"

"Better if I never meet them, then." I take a sip of my coffee, sliding Caleb's money over the counter as he walks by. He grabs it without even glancing at me, rounding the counter. Jensen immediately runs over to him, playing his part in their everyday ritual, and almost makes Lauren lose her balance on the thin bar stool.

"Trust me. It is." Her eyes follow Caleb on the ground as he plays with Jensen. Their daily morning ritual that always, without a fail, ends with a treat for my dog.

"Nic likes you. *Really* likes you," Lauren points out softly. "Give her some time to open up. There's a lot she needs to figure out by herself first."

"Do you think it would help if I introduced her to my parents?"

"Wow, aren't you moving fast?" Lauren chuckles and slowly shakes her head. "I don't think it would help. I imagine it's still too raw. But then again, I'm not her. The only one who will know when she's ready for that is Nic. Maybe let her find her balance on her own two feet before throwing your parents at her, though."

"Okay." I take a deep breath and straighten my back. "God, I'm a fish out of water here." I rub my chest right over my hurting heart. It's been years since I last went on a date. My last relationship broke apart when I decided to move back to Wayward Hollow and had to spend all of my time building up my clinic. But this is where I always saw myself living and growing old.

"Let me tell you a secret, lover boy. We all are." Lauren looks at me amusedly. "Being here is new to Nic, and being with her is new to you. It will take some time for you two to find your balance. Take it slow or you'll be two people trying to sprint across a slackline and will drop and fall faster than stones. Nic is honest—if she needs space, she'll tell you. If she's quiet, that's usually a good sign. She's like a cat that way." Lauren chuckles, and I can't help but join her.

"There are certain parallels."

"Right? And I mean, you're a vet. You know how to handle cats. It was meant to be." She shoots me a wink and jumps up from her seat. "Now, if you'll excuse me. I have some bookshelves to build." She makes a funny handyman pose before walking off, leaving me alone in the café with Caleb and my dog.

"Got your daily serotonin in?" I ask Caleb jokingly and he nods. I swear I even see the ghost of a smile on his lips.

"Thanks," he grumbles and throws Jensen his treat.

"Don't stop on my account." I grimace and take a deep breath. "I'll have to examine some horses today, I'm taking all the procrastination and delays I can get." I shudder. Cows are fine, but for some reason, horses give me the heebie-jeebies. They're big. And fast. And really fucking strong.

"No can do." Caleb shakes his head. But right as I'm about to leave, he stops me with a hand on my upper arm.

"Don't mess it up," he says softly, and my eyes widen in surprise.

I don't need him to spell it out to know that he's not talking about the horses.

"Those two"—he nods to the front door that Lauren walked out of—"they are special. I just know. So please …" his eyes dart around as he's trying to find his words hidden in his café's decor but comes up empty. "Don't fuck it up, Henry."

"I'm doing my best," I assure him and clasp his shoulder. "And you make sure you don't scare them away with your natural enthusiasm."

"Lauren will give me a heart attack before that happens," he grumbles, returning to his counter.

I shake my head at him and call for Jensen. With that pep talk in mind, I feel a lot better than on my way here. I only hope that whatever is weighing on Nic will resolve itself soon.

Chapter 21

Nic

"So, the autumn fair. I think the three of us should get involved, being the newbies and all, don't you think?" Lauren asks and takes a hearty sip of her pumpkin-spice primped coffee. Caleb is shooting us a glare, but he has given up on trying to make Lauren keep the syrup out of his café.

"What exactly do you think we should do? Do we *have* to?" Kieran wonders, then buries his face in his hands. "I'm too introverted for this stuff."

"You? Introverted?" I ask, amused, biting my lip to keep from grinning at his misery.

"Why do you think I chose a job that doesn't involve talking to people?" He sighs, glancing up from his hands. "Through a screen I can do, but real life? I'd rather not."

"Fair point." Lauren leans back in her seat, hands in front of her chest as she thinks. I'm only listening with half an ear, my thoughts circling around Henry. I know he's aware of my mood. I didn't exactly try to hide that I'm not feeling my best, and thankfully, he didn't pry. I wish I could shake this feeling off—those gnawing thoughts that I don't deserve him, that I'm not good enough.

One day I'll get there.

"Earth to Nic!" Lauren waves a hand in front of my face. "Stop with that sad face."

"Right? Are you seriously letting your asshole ex tear your mood down?" Kieran narrows his eyes at me.

"I'm trying not to," I say with a groan and take a deep breath. "But shockingly, there's not exactly an off switch for 'haunted by my unhinged ex' in my settings menu. Trust me, I checked. Twice."

The two of them shoot each other knowing glances, and Lauren quickly changes the topic back to the autumn fair, pretending my past never came up. Which I prefer if I'm being honest. I need normalcy in order to build distance from it. To build a wall that I can safely bury the painful memories behind, only to be seen again from a safe distance.

"Oh, hey, Caleb." Kieran waves at Caleb, who has once more mysteriously appeared right next to our table. "Henry told us about the autumn fair. What's it about? Is there anything we can do to help?"

Caleb peers at the three of us, skepticism written all over his face.

"You three can volunteer to decorate," he finally grumbles, turning the page on his notebook that he uses to write down orders. "Make the damn thing presentable for once."

"You're not a fan, I take it?" Lauren asks sweetly and Caleb's eyes and the disgust shining in them speak volumes. I hide a grin behind my hand as he continues.

"It's loud. It's annoying. It blocks the whole damn town center. Some of us have better shit to do," he mumbles and walks past us to another table.

"To be fair, Henry mentioned that Caleb pretends to hate it," Kieran points out, voice shaking as he tries not to laugh, and I nod slowly.

Caleb doesn't seem interested in any kind of festivity. He's the type who wouldn't even dress up as the Grinch for Christmas. Who acts as if their birthday is a day like any other and will glare you into the ground if you dare to congratulate him.

Who are happy with a boring existence. But hey, to each their own. He probably has his reasons, but I'm excited to see if he'll actually warm up for the autumn fair.

"I wonder why," Lauren says softly, tapping her fingers against the table. "Maybe there's some town lore we don't know yet."

"Or maybe it's the charm of his grumpy personality." Kieran lifts his shoulder in a lazy half-shrug and Lauren shoots him a glare.

But before she can answer, my phone buzzes on the table, and Taylor Swift's "You Need to Calm Down" blares through Caleb's like it's trying to make a point. Everyone here turns to see where the song suddenly comes from. Not awkward at all.

"Say hi to Joel for me," Lauren says with a wink as I get up and rush outside to take the call. If Joel's calling, something's probably on fire—figuratively or otherwise. He's my former manager-slash-publicist and should know better than to bother me with anything less than an actual emergency now that I'm retired. I'd threatened to bite his head off enough times during my first week off to make that perfectly clear after he kept bothering me and asking me to reconsider.

"I swear to God, Joel, if this is another attempt to get me back to acting—" I talk myself into rage as soon as the door to Caleb's closes behind me, but he quickly interrupts me.

"Calm down. It's good to hear from you too, Nic."

"What do you mean 'too?' If you're calling, I know it isn't good news." I walk away from the entrance, leaning against the cool brick wall, letting the back of my head fall against it. "Please, spit it out."

"Someone is shopping around for magazines or paparazzi who want to know your new address. Or so a little birdie told me."

My heart beats into my throat, my blood suddenly turning into ice. I let my head fall forward and pinch the bridge of my nose.

"No. No, no, no." I curse, kicking a pebble away from me.

"The good news: You're yesterday's news." He sounds truly happy about it, but I can't see the same silver lining. "I mean, I say that with love. With you retiring from acting, there are bigger fish to catch, but I think at some point, someone is bound to pay up."

"Oh, God." I exhale a sigh so deep I fear it will take my soul right along with it and close my eyes.

"Do you know who it is?" Joel asks, sounding eager to spring into action. "Can we pay him off?"

"Oh, Joel." I take a deep breath. "I can only imagine that it's Jay. And I'd rather pose for a horde of paparazzi than give that sorry excuse for a man even a cent." I gulp and hug myself with my free arm, my fingers tapping against my hip as I try to think rationally.

What do I do now? I love this life here. How calm it is, how I'm only another girl in town. That I'm not *Nicola Duncan, award-winning actress* here, but Nic. Just Nic. I don't want that dynamic to change.

"Maybe he's dumb enough to blackmail you?" Joel offers, drawing an unamused chuckle from me.

"That would make everything too easy, Joel." I take a deep breath, trying to collect my thoughts. Then again, Jay hasn't exactly proven to be very bright. "Thanks for warning me. I'll keep an eye out."

"Take care of yourself, Nic. And if you ever want to come back, you have my number. Hope we won't need to talk again soon, but I'll let you know if I hear anything else."

Before I can return that sentiment, he hangs up. And I'm left in the streets of Wayward Hollow, a cold weight on my chest and tears forming behind my eyes.

Everything continues to pile on. What did I do to deserve this? Didn't Jay make me suffer enough already? Now he wants to sell me out to paparazzi?

I want all of this to be over.

All I want is to enjoy my calm new life here in Wayward Hollow, instead of continuously looking over my shoulder, fearing being photographed or that Jay will be around the next corner for another attempt to get money from me.

The fact he's ruining what I'm trying to build for myself is low. Then again, he fucked my sister during our engagement party. What did I expect?

Once upon a time, I thought he loved me.

And even with all his manipulative ways visible in hindsight, I thought there was at least a time he *respected* me. Saw me as a partner instead of a piggy bank, an object he could own.

I was wrong. And now all I can do is wait for the justice system to do its thing. Sit on my ass until I hopefully get a restraining order and can at least call the cops on him if he gets too close.

But who knows how long that will take? Or if it even goes through? What else is he planning to make me miserable in the meantime?

I watch Lauren and Kieran through the window. They're joking, grimacing at Caleb, trying to draw a reaction from him. Not a care in the world, while I'm emotionally tumbling like someone pulled the ground from under my feet.

I'm so fucking angry.

Even though a piece of bread has more empathy than the people who created me, my heart still yearns for a mom to rage with. A dad who would pull up his sleeves and go to war for me.

I'll never have that.

It doesn't matter. I take a deep breath and square my shoulders. I don't need anyone but my cats, the people in Caleb's café, and Henry. Well, and his dog.

I'll be all right. But it still really. Fucking. Hurts.

Chapter 22

Henry

"It looks like Jay finally left," Nic tells me, sounding as if a weight got lifted off her shoulders. "Nobody has seen him around town, but I'm pretty sure he'll be back at some point."

We're taking a walk along the lake, hand in hand, talking about nothing and everything at the same time. There is a lot I still want to know about her, and so many questions she has for me. The sky is hidden behind heavy clouds, darkness coming from the mountains. I'm not sure whether it comes from the heavy rain clouds or the fact that it's already late afternoon.

Jensen darts along the shoreline at full speed, bouncing between the beach and the grass, always circling back, never straying too far.

"Why, though?" I lift my eyebrow at her, confused. I was hoping he'd run off with his tail tucked between his legs.

"Because he's a narcissist who doesn't understand the word 'no,'" she explains, lifting one of her shoulders in a half-shrug. "You were there at Caleb's. He loathes not getting to have the last word."

"Right," I say, furrowing my eyebrows. "Just let me know if Jensen should have a bite of his calves," I joke, trying to lift the mood and pull her closer by her hand until I can snake my arm around her waist.

"I can handle him," she promises and snakes her arm around me too, giving my hip a reassuring little pat. "And you have nothing to worry about."

"Who said I was worried?" I try to joke, but yes, the truth is, I am worried. She was so distraught when she appeared at my vet clinic with Chaos. Thinking that she loved him so much, that his betrayal hurt her that deeply?

It's hard to remember that and not feel concerned. Whether she wants to admit it or not, he has an effect on her. And I admire her for her loyalty, how she loves with her whole heart. I can see it in the way she loves Pumpkin and Cinnamon, in her friendship with Lauren. When she loves, she loves hard. It gnaws at my thoughts that her asshole ex once had that, an ever-present reminder that once upon a time, she picked him. That she trusted him in a way she doesn't trust me yet.

"You keep asking about him." She lets out a deep sigh. "And you try to pretend he doesn't infuriate you. You don't need to say it out loud. And you better leave the acting to me," she quips, and I notice my shoulders relax.

"I promise you, he's not even a topic anymore. I left my past, and him, behind. I have no intention whatsoever of going back." She comes to a stop, making me halt as well. "You're my future."

She shifts in my arms, sliding her hands up to cradle my cheeks, gently guiding my face down until we're eye to eye. "You're the person I want to be with. The only one I want to kiss." She softly presses her lips against mine, and I feel hers stretching into a small smile. "And the one I'd love to wake up next to." When I open my eyes again, she shoots me a wink. "Don't give him any power. I might be a bit bummed, but I'm not letting him ruin us, and neither should you."

"Okay," I whisper, burying my hand in her hair while pulling her flush against me with the other one against the small of her back. "I believe you. I trust you, Nic."

She nudges her cheek into my hand like a cat as her hands wander down my arms until they come to a stop at my hips. They dig into my jacket as she's holding on for dear life as I lean in and kiss her.

It's the kind of kiss that makes me forget everything around us. It consumes me to the point I don't even realize it has started pouring until she draws back, and we gaze at each other with heavy breaths and disbelieving smiles.

"Do that again," she whispers, biting her lip really fucking seductively.

I pause, smirking. "Careful. I'm, like, one kiss away from carving our names into one of these trees."

She giggles, eyes twinkling. "Wow. Full teenage love energy. Should I expect matching couple's hoodies next?"

"Only if you promise to wear mine to make it smell of you."

She tilts her head, tapping her lip as she considers it. "Hmm. Do I get a say in the font you use for the tree carving?"

"No. It's cursive or nothing. I have standards."

"Oh, well, as long as it's classy vandalism and doesn't hurt the tree."

"The classiest," I whisper and lean in, tugging her lip from its cage between her teeth. My heart thunders against my chest as the wind whips her hair around us, the scent of her vanilla shampoo ever-present, and that sweet taste that is so unmistakably hers on my tongue.

She is all my senses, all I can see, all I can hear. Every single cell of my body is tuned in to her, *yearning* for her.

"We should get inside," I whisper against her lips, and she answers me with a vehement nod. Her cheeks are flushed with heat, her eyes are glossy, and I can't help but press my lips against hers once more in a quick kiss. Then I take her hand and pull her after me, with an urgency I don't recognize from myself, back to her house.

One shrill whistle and Jensen follows suit.

"He's all wet. Let me—" I say as we step inside, but Nic shakes her head and tugs me with her.

"I don't give a damn if you don't," she whispers hoarsely and shoots me a seductive grin over her shoulder, and I mean, who am I to object? I still can't completely help myself, and one handedly throw a blanket over him as I follow her.

I let her tug me up her stairs and down the hallway, giving zero fucks about the wet trail of rain we're leaving behind us. Her grip is firm and certain, as if letting go isn't even a possibility. I kind of love it.

She's trouble. But the good kind. Beautiful, smart-mouthed trouble with a smile that makes me feel like I've been handed a prize from the universe. That makes me see nothing but her.

Once we're in her bedroom, she kicks the door closed behind us, then crowds me against the cool wood, wet hair plastered to her face and a mischievous glint in her eyes.

"You keep looking at me that seductively," I murmur, my pulse quickening as her hands wander up my body to lock around my neck, "and I can't guarantee anything."

She doesn't respond with words. Instead, she lifts herself on her tiptoes, and her lips crash into mine, hungry and determined, our tongues fighting to take the lead of this little dance.

She kisses like she's been left waiting for too long. Our kiss outside was deep, all-consuming, but this one? This one is messy, urgent, a promise of what's to come. She tastes of rain and trouble, clouding my senses, making everything but her disappear from my mind.

I grip her waist, pulling her flush against me, and she moans into the kiss, sending a jolt of electricity through my whole body and right to my cock.

"You want me to stop?" I ask, my voice rough, my eyes drawn to her plump lips, silently praying for her to not deny me. My brain is about to short-circuit, and I want to give in badly. Let instinct take over and have her.

"Are you insane?" Her voice is barely above a breathless whisper. "Don't you fucking dare stop."

I grin at her, a low chuckle escaping me as I slide my hands down her back, giving her ass a squeeze that makes her giggle as I pull her in closer.

A happy sigh falls from my lips when her body melts against mine like we were made for each other. She kisses me with a hunger I can feel in my bones, her hands wandering under my soaking wet shirt, her hot hands drawing patterns over my freezing skin.

"Fuck. You don't know what you do to me, sweetheart," I growl into the kiss, my hands sliding down her sides, tracing the curve of her waist as my knee slides between her legs. She shivers when I squeeze her ass, her hands wandering to my front to hurriedly push my jacket off my shoulders.

"Then show me," she murmurs, her voice laced with need, and it shoots blood straight to my cock.

I groan, my heart thundering in my ribcage as I pull her into another kiss, rougher, more desperate. I need to have her. I can't get her close quick enough. Not breaking the kiss, I pull off her jacket and mindlessly throw it into a corner, my hands immediately finding the hem of her shirt.

We break the kiss, blinking at each other breathlessly, with flushed faces and desire so intense that for a moment, we both freeze.

But then her face breaks into a grin. I catch her lips in another heated kiss as I walk her backward to the bed, unclasping her bra as the back of her knees nudge against the bedframe.

She lets out a small gasp when I break the kiss, my fingertips dancing over her skin. I'm trying to remember every curve, every dip, trying to memorize every sound falling from her lips.

I drag my mouth along her neck, her soft, breathy moans sending shivers down my spine, urging me on and making me crave more of those sounds.

"You're fucking beautiful," I murmur, kissing the soft skin along her collarbone. I continue down, drawing a wet line between her breasts with my tongue, while my hands find her panties, fingers trembling as I pull them off, shaking with restraint.

"You're not so bad yourself," she whispers breathlessly, her fingers running through my hair.

I pull away for a second and sit up, breathless, taking a moment to look at her. Her hair is a mess, spread over her pillow in a tangled halo. Her chest heaves with every breath as she stares back at me through hooded eyes, that lip between her teeth not doing a good job at hiding her seductive grin.

"What are you thinking about?" she asks in a whisper, and I tear my eyes away from that tortured lip and back to her eyes.

"Thinking about how you're mine," I whisper, my lips tugging into a smile as that knowledge settles in my gut. *She's mine.* My hands wander up the back of her thighs. I pull her legs around my waist, grinning when it elicits a soft shriek as I pull her down the bed a bit. "How I'm never going to let you go, ever."

Fuck, she's so wet already. My fingers glide through her wet folds, my cock hardening more with every soft moan falling from her lips when I sink a finger inside her.

Before I can react, she suddenly frees her legs, sits up and turns us around, pushing my back onto the mattress and straddling me. Her hands slide down my chest, then free my cock from my briefs. I let out a sigh when she palms it, giving it a few wavering strokes.

Her lips press against mine, then kiss a trail along my chin as she twists her wrist and lets her thumb glide over my head, drawing a groan from my lips.

"You want me?" she whispers against my ear, her voice thick and raspy with desire.

"Always," I admit with a growl, gripping her hips tightly. "Need you, Nic."

She shivers, a soft laugh making her body tremble before she presses her lips against mine for a deep kiss. Her hands draw patterns over my chest, while mine find her ass, pulling her core tightly against mine, and I swallow her moan.

"Fucking beautiful," I whisper when I sink a finger into her, finding her clit with my thumb. She bucks her hips and throws back her head in pleasure. "Take what you need, sweetheart."

"I need *you*," she whispers. Her admission makes my heart jump, my cock straining with the need to claim her finally. "Inside me, Henry. Now."

I'm about to line myself up with her entrance when it hits me.

"Are we … good?" I ask her softly, and her eyes jump to mine, surprise written all over her face. "Are you on birth control?"

"Yes." She nods vehemently. "And I got tested before I moved here."

"Same. All good." I whisper, adding a second finger. She throws her head back again, her wet hair cascading over her naked skin like a waterfall as she lets out a deep moan when I crook my fingers the tiniest bit, hitting just the right spot.

"Oh fuck, yes. Right there," she says breathlessly, and I make a mental note as I remove my fingers and line myself up with her entrance. She sinks down on my cock, bit by bit, and I reach up to palm her breast.

"God, the way you take me—" I can't take my eyes off where we're now joined. "Like you were made for me." She moans and takes another inch of me. "That's it, sweetheart. Just like that."

Once she's taken all of me, she stills, getting used to my cock. "You feel so good, sweetheart."

"I aim to please," she says, her voice strained, and shoots me a wink. Fuck, this woman.

And when she starts moving, all I can see are fireworks behind my eyes. Every time she takes me again, I swear she's bringing me closer to heaven.

"Fuck, sweetheart," I curse, making her giggle. "You feel so fucking good I can't think straight."

"That's kind of the point," she murmurs and goes for it in earnest, the sound of skin slapping against skin obscenely loud in this otherwise silent room.

"If you keep this up, I'm proposing by breakfast."

She laughs, her breath hitching. "Nice. I love my coffee with commitment."

"Done," I groan when she chuckles yet again, tightening around me. "Let me get a ring and pumpkin spice syrup to sweeten the deal."

"Already pretty dang sweet if you ask me."

I find her clit, circling it while she rides me, trying to bring her higher. Her moans turning desperate, breathier, and suddenly, I can't take it anymore. I grip her hips, meeting her thrusts with vigor.

"God, you don't know what you do to me," I say through gritted teeth as I fuck her from below.

"Almost there," she moans and before I know it, her walls tighten around my cock, her whole body trembling as her release washes over her.

"Henry!" Hell, my name has never sounded sweeter from her lips.

And that's all it takes. Her moaning my name, her walls tightening around me, and the knowledge she's mine. They combine forces to form an orgasm more intense than I could have imagined. And when she collapses on me, heavy breath feathering against my wet skin, I hold on to her as if I might wake up from a dream, and she might slip away.

"You're stunning like this," I tell her with a grin, once I catch my breath, swiping a strand of wet hair behind her ear. "So messy. So mine."

"All yours," she whispers and presses her lips against mine. "So fucking yours. Don't you forget it."

"Never," I whisper and drop a kiss on her forehead. She's never getting rid of me.

Chapter 23

Nic

"I can't believe you're taking your cat on a walk." Lauren nods at my bag with a giggle, but I shrug.

"Cinnamon lived outside before she came to me." My hand finds the little creature's head for a quick pet. "I can't just suddenly deprive her of it."

"Wouldn't she walk then?"

"What can I say?" I say, chuckling and hugging the bag with Cinnamon to my chest. "I tried to get her to, but she's a lazy little lady."

Cinnamon has turned into the biggest cuddle bug. When I unlock my door, she's already waiting behind it, meowing incessantly with a look that says, "How dare you leave me alone with the child for this long?" She immediately rubs herself against my legs until I've shimmied out of my shoes without losing my balance and scoop her up and cradle her to my chest.

Pumpkin couldn't care less. She's happy whether I'm there or not. Some days, I'm not sure she even knows the difference. Her gaze is always so vacant. I wouldn't be surprised if she forgot about my existence when I'm not in the same room as her for more than ten minutes.

"Lazy and calm," Lauren points out. "She's really imprinted on you, hasn't she?"

"Wherever I go, she follows. When I leave or close the door on her, she voices her displeasure. Loudly. Preferably right into my ear in the middle of the night when she has somehow managed to pry the door to my bedroom open. I'm sure a certain cheeky ghost cat is more than happy to assist her with that. I'm only thankful I wasn't blessed with two cats that have the pipes of Adele. Little Cinnamon's voice here is more of a Billie Eilish, her meow's are a lot softer, but higher-pitched."

The three of them have turned into a mischievous trio that keeps me on my toes. "The other day, I'm 90 percent sure Chaos opened the door to the cat food container for them. I found them munching away on it in the kitchen."

"She wants to be close because she loves you!" Lauren leans over to give Cinnamon a kiss on her head. "Such a cute little admirer. Not quite as cute as the human one, though."

"Right," I say, sensing my face turn red.

"Oh, there's a story there." Lauren immediately gets into Sherlock Holmes mode. Her stare burns into my skin while I do my best to keep my eyes forward with the best poker face I can muster. "Oh my God, you did it!"

"What?" I try to sound surprised, but internally, I'm panicking. Oh my God, what gave it away? Do I have "freshly fucked" written on my forehead? Because I feel like I do.

"Don't try to lie—you've got a hickey on your neck." Instinctively, I lift my hand to hide it, but Lauren bursts into laughter. "Relax. You don't. I just wanted confirmation."

"You're … evil. And a genius." I narrow my eyes at her.

"You may call me Einstein."

"I'll call you 'Dr. Drakken,' though your skin is a healthier color," I say with an eye roll and nudge her with my elbow. "Let's go to the town square park. Maybe Cinnamon will walk on her leash in the grass there."

The town has become extinct, even though it's a few minutes after noon. There are no humans on the streets, no cars driving by. Hell, I can't even see anyone through any shop windows.

"Where is everyone?" I ask and glance around curiously. The antique shop and flower store have their big closed signs out, indicating their lunch break, but this is giving me zombie apocalypse vibes. I'm not surprised though; Amanda appreciates her lunch time. According to her, card readings on an empty stomach lead to erroneous results.

"Probably still at Caleb's," Lauren says overly nonchalantly, and I suddenly stop, narrowing my eyes at her.

"You've got a crush on the town grump!" I don't know why I haven't voiced it yet, but the way she said it, with a tinge of sadness and apprehension, tells me there's something going on.

"I do, captain obvious." She giggles and averts her eyes, an unreadable expression flickering before she schools her face.

"What are you going to do about it?"

She rolls her eyes. "I'm going to—ALARM!"

Suddenly, she grabs my arm and pulls me after her, ducking and motioning for me to do the same. We hurry past the gazebo and hide behind a bunch of bushes.

"What the fuck, Lauren?" I ask, but she puts her finger over her lips and shushes.

"What's going on?" I ask more quietly, voice barely above a whisper.

"Enemy approaching," she says cryptically, stretching her neck to peek over the shrubbery. "I swear I saw Jay and Marissa."

My blood runs cold, and my heart beats into my throat. "What? Are you serious?"

"They just got out of the car." She gets back into a crouch and gives me a strange look. "Maybe we should have them admitted to a mental health facility. That level of delusion can't be healthy if they still think they can get anything out of you."

"Please. They are hopeless. Jail would be better," I whisper back and shake my head. "Fuck. What do I do, Lauren?"

"Run at them, bat swinging?"

"Where would I get a bat from?"

"I don't know." She shrugs and takes another peek at what's going on. "Can you launch Cinnamon at them like a Poké-mon?"

"What'cha doing down there?" Both of us startle when a voice suddenly appears behind us. Lauren throws her hand over my mouth before I can squeal in surprise.

"Get down here," she hisses at Kieran and when he doesn't react, she reaches for his shirt and abruptly pulls him down to our eye level.

"Why are you two hiding? And, Nic, why are you glowing? You're radiating. I saw it from all the way over there." He points somewhere behind us, and I shoot him a stare that's supposed to convey *really?*

"Oh." The penny drops. "Ohhhh. Damn, girl. Congrats." I sigh and pinch the bridge of my nose. Apparently, I do have "freshly fucked" written all over my forehead, after all. That's not embarrassing at all.

"I swear, she's been annoyingly happy all day," Lauren chimes in, and I can't help but rib her.

"Jealous?" I lift my eyebrow at them, lips stretching into a smile.

"Hell yes," Lauren hisses with a pout and Kieran bursts into laughter. "Don't laugh," she scolds him. "Do you seriously want to tell us you've never had any problems that couldn't be solved with a good fuck."

"Can't say I have," he presses out, still chuckling. "In fact, my best fucks have only gotten me into trouble."

"I will need those stories sometime," Lauren says, curiosity written all over her face as she crosses her arms in front of her chest.

"Ohhh, you have a cat here." Kieran suddenly notices and makes grabby hands toward Cinnamon with the brightest smile on his face, and I let him pull her out of the bag. She meows in a weak protest that quickly dissolves when he cuddles her to his warm chest and tucks her into his jacket. "Who are you, cutie?"

"That's Cinnamon," I introduce her with a grin and watch him instantly fall in love with her. "Cinnamon, that's Kieran."

"Okay, okay, now with the introductions out of the way, we need to do something." Lauren's eyes dart between me and Kieran. "Her ex and her sister are in town." She narrows her eyes at him. I guess she must have filled him in on everything at one point. "Are you up for a secret mission?"

"Always." He gives us a terrible salute and hands Cinnamon back to me. "Tell me what to do, ma'am."

"I like that." Lauren grins before her face suddenly turns serious. "They're at Caleb's. Go in there and try to find out what they want. We'll make a run for it while you distract them. Make sure they don't see us run for our lives. When you have the intel, we meet at Nic's house." She narrows her eyes at him even further. "Bring cat treats. And coffee."

"And one of those marzipan thingies, please. I'm hungry," I add.

"Make that two."

"I accept the mission." He gives the two of us a serious nod. He stretches his neck to check our surroundings and all but jumps up, patting the dirt from his jeans, while trying to seem inconspicuous. "Give me three minutes after entering." He shoots the two of us a dramatic look. "May fate be ever in your favor." And then he runs off.

"Do you actually think he'll find anything out?" I ask her, but she shakes her head, staring at her wristwatch and counting down the minutes until we make a run for her car.

"Let's be honest, we both know why they're here," she explains, then gets ready to bolt. "But if he gets them distracted, that's all we need. Now, let's go."

Then she takes my hand, and we run faster than I've run in years as I hug the bag with Cinnamon to my chest.

"That was boring." That's how Kieran greets me when I open the door for him. He walks in, immediately handing me a tray with three coffees and a bag of baked treats for us humans, then another one with treats for my cats.

Cinnamon immediately trots over, and he scoops her up to cuddle her to his chest, kissing her tiny head.

"You're such a pretty girl. We'll be best friends," he coos at her while making his way to my living room like he owns the place.

"Oh. Hi, Lauren," he greets her offhandedly before sitting on my couch and petting Cinnamon with a mischievous grin that would rival a James Bond villain.

"What happened?" Lauren asks, turning around with Pumpkin cuddled into her hood, her small face popping up between her hair. "Tell us everything."

"Oh my God, there's another one?" Kieran's eyes widen.

"Right, I forgot you haven't met them yet." I point out. "That's Pumpkin. She has as many brain cells as one, and she screams so loudly I fear for my windows every day."

"God, she's adorable." He gazes at her dazed as he mindlessly pets Cinnamon, then shakes his head as if he's waking up from a trance. "But anyway, nothing happened. I stalled them for a few minutes, but ultimately Caleb kicked them out because of the ruckus your ex caused the last time. Didn't give a fuck about your sister's crocodile tears. She couldn't believe it. Honestly, it was glorious to watch."

"I wish I could have seen that," I mumble and sit on the couch too.

Immediately, both cats decide to not give a fuck about their respective humans anymore and make their way to me.

"Are you the cat whisperer?" Kieran asks, voice full of awe, and I chuckle.

"Nope, I'm just the favorite." I grin and Kieran gets up to distribute the coffees I put on my coffee table. I hope Marissa and Jay will go back to wherever they came from if they can't find me here.

And there are worse things than cozying up with my cats for a few days and keeping a low profile.

Chapter 24

Nic

"We wish you a merry autumn," Lauren sings to the tune of "We Wish You a Merry Christmas" as we trudge through town, a swing in her step and a bright smile on her face.

It's the first time I've been back in town since Jay and Marissa appeared. Amanda vowed to keep an eye on her website inquiries herself. Meanwhile Lauren and I had a grand time hanging out with my cats, baking more autumn treats, and rewatching *Gilmore Girls*. Although Lauren always bid her farewell when Henry came over to visit because, as she said, "You two are too sweet. I'll get cavities."

But Kieran assured me he hasn't seen either of them in town for the past few days, and now here we are.

A part of me wonders if he only said that because he's sick of bringing me coffee, instead of having all of us meet up at Caleb's. But whenever he complained about it, either Lauren or I put a cat in his lap. That never failed to make him forget about his dissatisfaction at having to be our personal coffee-bringer.

Caleb's coffee might have been too strong for Lauren and me when we first drank it, but now? We can't imagine life without it.

And now we're back in town, coffee in hand, because Kieran told us today is the autumn fair meet up, and he ordered us here to help.

"The decorations definitely need a female touch, so I signed you up," he'd said, which didn't really leave any option to say no. And despite the questionable work distribution, Lauren and I decided to put our all into it.

Over the past few days, we put our heads together, checked what kind of decorations were available and could be quickly delivered, then made a list of everything we wanted to buy.

Both of us were more than ready to buy them ourselves and declare the decoration a contribution to the community. But whichever committee organizes the autumn fair decided to wave them through as expenses.

Which didn't stop us from making a trip to the nearest store to buy even more ourselves. Once we started, there was no limit—whatever we found cute went into the cart. And whatever we don't use for the autumn fair will get put up at one of our houses.

I'm pretty sure by the time we're done, Wayward Hollow will look like an autumn wonderland. Visitors will have no choice but to give in to the autumn vibes. It's going to be awesome.

"Do you think they really got the scarecrows?" I ask Lauren, but she only answers with a giggle and points to the other side of the street where a whole army of scarecrows is awaiting us.

"They weren't kidding," she laughs and links her arm with mine to cross the street. "We could stage a famous battle with those."

"Or Caesar's assassination?" I think aloud, tapping my chin. "'Et tu, Brute' strangely fits my life."

"God, I love that you can joke about it already," Lauren says, relieved, and gives my arm squeeze. "I have no idea what I would do if you were one of those people who didn't deal with trauma through humor."

"Nic! Lauren!" Kieran waves at us from afar. He's wearing a red and black lumberjack shirt and has a small hay bale flung over his shoulder. Romanticizing this fall was Lauren's and my mission, but he's definitely a step ahead of us, at least outfit wise.

"Am I tripping or is that kind of hot?" Lauren whispers while we wave back at him and I can't help but laugh.

"I think you're tripping, but then again, you also think that black-and-white fish from *Finding Nemo* is hot."

"And many others share that opinion. Don't discriminate," she playfully scolds me, and we make our way to Kieran.

We barely take two steps when I suddenly hear the sharp click of heels on asphalt behind me, and my blood freezes in my veins.

Because I know who it is. I don't even need to turn around. There is only one person who would wear fucking heels in a town like Wayward Hollow, and sadly, we share genetics. God damn it.

"Nicola! Oh my God, there you are!"

I freeze. That sugary sweet voice she uses when strangers are around drips down my spine, like scalding hot caramel. Fuck. I thought she was gone.

Lauren tightens her arm around mine, shooting me a worried glance, and I give her a reassuring smile. I take a deep breath, then square my shoulders and turn around slowly.

There she is.

Marissa. Dressed as if she jumped out of a damned autumn fashion magazine. Every single hair of her blonde bob lies perfectly, and there's not one wrinkle in her designer outfit. She's completely out of place here, where everyone is dressed for manual labor. She's wearing that overly friendly, disingenuous smile that has gotten her everything in life—the one I've dreamed about wiping off her face for years.

"Wow," she says, walking up to me as though nothing ever happened between us. The way she smiles, you'd think we were the best of friends who hadn't seen each other in a while and just ran into each other by chance. "I mean, look at you.

Small-town life becomes you. I almost didn't recognize you at first. You"—she makes a broad gesture at me—"look so relaxed. You really stopped trying, and it totally works on you."

Lauren builds herself up next to me, clearing her throat, but I beat her to an answer. It's one of the more harmless backhanded compliments she's given me, and over the years, I've learned that ignoring her jabs will rile her up more than any reply could.

"What do you want, Marissa?"

Her perfectly lined eyes, framed with fake lashes, widen in mock surprise and she clutches her chest dramatically.

"Well, that's not very welcoming. I thought only nice people lived in this town. I only wanted to come visit my baby sister!"

"Is it money?" I lift my eyebrow, then glance at Lauren, our eyes speaking volumes without a word being exchanged. "I bet it's money."

"Come on, you're overreacting again. I think it's time we bury the hatchet!"

"You what?" I can't help myself—I burst into laughter, and I'm not sure whether it's because Marissa is being fucking ridiculous or if it's hysterical. "*Bury the hatchet?* Oh my God, that's funny. You planning to bury it in my back again, or twist the one you left there?"

For a moment, only one split second, her mask falters. Her nostrils flare, and her jaw clenches, but she quickly catches herself.

"Oh, Nic, you're still too dramatic. You and Jay were never a good match to begin with. You must have realized that. You need to let it go. Let the past be the past."

"No, thank you." I shake my head. Marissa's face tightens and Lauren tenses, and I gently squeeze her forearm. Marissa's not worth catching a charge for violence. "I'm doing fine without you. In fact, I'm doing great. Way better than I ever did." I let go of Lauren and step closer to Marissa, plastering my own overly sweet smile on my face. "And I meant what I said. You're dead to me. Now, how about you turn around and get the fuck out of my life?"

Marissa's smile doesn't waver, but the belittling amusement leaves her eyes, making room for pure hatred. She takes one small, deliberate step forward, heels crunching leaves under them.

"You know"—her voice dips low, until only I can hear her—"I'd hoped you'd come to your senses, but I guess not. You're still nothing more than a circus monkey, making a fool of yourself and hoping to find people who might actually love you." Her head tips slightly as she gives me a once-over.

I'm not going to lie, it stings. Not 'a thousand needles prickling my skin' sting, the way it did on the evening I caught them. It's a dull pain, like someone flicking the same spot thousands of times.

"And I thought you might actually get it through your thick skull that you will never get a penny from me." I curl my lips into an emotionless smile. "Guess not," I quote her mockingly and cross my arms in front of my chest. And then I decide to rub it in.

"Who needs a loving family when I've got money to live the life I always wanted? The fact I get to live it without you butting in? An added bonus. Now, let me be as clear as I can possibly be and spell it out for your goldfish brain: I never want to see you again. You will never, in any universe, *ever* see a penny from me. And trust me, Marissa, after that stunt you pulled, I am willing to go to great lengths to ensure that."

She holds my gaze for a second. Then another. The facade crumbles as her smile slowly drops.

"For once, Mom and Dad can't come to your rescue," I continue, my voice sharp. I take a step forward, making her walk backward. "Because their opinion matters even less than yours. I'm done. With all of you."

She catches herself, coming to a halt and plastering a fake smile back on her face, accompanied by a glare that could kill.

"You've always been so dramatic. Honestly, it's exhausting." She turns to Lauren and adds with a bright smile, "I don't know how you put up with her. You're a saint."

Lauren's about to open her mouth—probably to say something unrepeatable—but I shake my head. Not here. Not for her.

This is my fight. Not Lauren's.

"Enjoy your little fantasy, Nic," Marissa says as she backs away, her heels echoing across the street. "But remember—fairy tales always end. Usually right after someone angers the wrong witch."

"God, your threats are laughable." I roll my eyes. "What are you going to do? Run to Mom and Dad the way you did when you were ten? News flash, Marissa, the times where they could tell me to share my toys are over."

She gives me a hard stare, her lips quivering, then spins on her heel and storms off, appearing completely unbothered to the unknowing eye.

But I know her.

I can see the anger in the way she flexes her fingers as she pulls out her phone, no doubt preparing to unleash whatever venom she didn't get to pour out in person.

"A fault confessed is half redressed?" Lauren says with her eyebrow raised high, but I shake my head.

"You'll never catch her admitting fault. Not even to herself. That notion doesn't exist in her mind." I take a deep breath. "Whatever. I'm ready."

Chapter 25
Henry

"They've been hanging around town, more insistent than Scientologists on a recruitment mission," Caleb mutters as he slides my coffee over the counter, exhaling an annoyed sigh. He nods toward the window, where Nic's ex and her sister are leaning against their car, sneering at everyone passing by them more arrogantly than unimpressed judges at a talent show.

"About time we're finally getting some entertainment here," Mr. Peterson jokes, his eyes firmly on the unwelcome guests of Wayward Hollow. "Shame we don't hunt people out of town with torches and pitchforks anymore."

"Bobby!" Caleb gives him a mock stern glare, and I laugh quietly. He doesn't seem the type to keep his pitchfork ready—not at all.

Mr. Peterson is your idea of a small-town dad personified—the one everyone loves, who gives advice when he knows you need it and stops to help you change a tire. He's all grey hair, kind smile and deep laughing lines. Jensen also loves him, always making a beeline for him and falling asleep at his feet and today is no exception.

I don't think I've ever met someone he talked badly about until Jay and Marissa came to town. Hell, he's so nice he even got Caleb to warm up to him. I'm used to calling him by his last name—I addressed him as "Mr. Peterson" since I was a child, and similarly to all my teachers, switching to his first name felt wrong.

"Give it three more weeks," I tell him amusedly and lean my elbows on the counter. "They might still make enough ... *friends* for that to happen. I already know five people who would love to volunteer."

"Make that six," Caleb adds gruffly, and I lean over the counter, narrowing my eyes at him.

"Why? What do you know?"

"That's what I'm saying, boys—finally some proper gossip in this town." Mr. Peterson leans in curiously too. "Come on now, tell us. Don't be shy."

Caleb's eyes dart between me and Mr. Peterson, his resolve to stay out of gossip clearly struggling to prevail against his dislike for Jay and Marissa. Finally, his shoulders sag and he curses softly under his breath before he tells us.

"I heard Andrea kicked them out of her hotel yesterday," Caleb whispers, eyes darting around the room to make sure nobody is listening in, wiping the already spotless counter with a cloth.

"She said they were screaming at each other the whole night, and when they started throwing vases at each other, she had to call in Erik. They wouldn't leave, so he had the pleasure of escorting them and their stuff outside."

"Please tell me he brought them straight to a jail cell?" Mr. Peterson asks, eyes twinkling with glee. "Bet that would beat some sense into them." But Caleb shakes his head, and I swear a flash of disappointment crosses his face.

"Erik's too nice for his own good." I sigh and take a sip of my coffee. "I wish he'd send them off." My eyes dart to the door when I hear the little chime announcing new guests, waiting until they're seated at a table out of earshot. "Hey, has anyone else noticed that Erik's acting kind of weird?"

"Not really," Mr. Peterson says gruffly and takes a sip of his coffee. "He's probably not used to anything of worth happening here. That boy has probably had to comb through his handbook to know what he needs to be doing." His hearty chuckle tells me that he's not saying it maliciously.

"How is Nic dealing with all this?" Caleb asks, and I do my best not to show my surprise. It's not every day that he expresses curiosity about what's going on in the city, much less about anyone's emotions. "I saw her fighting with her sister a few days ago. For a moment, I got worried it would turn into a brawl."

"She's, you know, dealing with it her way, which means she's quietly brooding about it." I shrug and stir my coffee with the little spoon that came with it for a lack of something to do with my hands. "She's angry at them, frustrated they won't leave her alone, and annoyed that the whole town knows what happened. But what unnerves her the most is that there's nothing Erik can do about them yet."

"I wouldn't be surprised if the pitchforks emerged sooner or later. Tell her to hang tight." Mr. Peterson sighs and gets up, apologizing to Jensen when he wakes up. "If you'll excuse me, lads, I'll have to go sharpen mine. You know, just in case." He winks at us and walks off, his cane clicking on the ground. He holds the door open for Nic, who was about to enter. Her eyes are focused forward as the town's unwelcome guests try to accost her like some skeezy salespeople.

Jay and Marissa try to follow her inside, already babbling over each other about their "right" to her money and how she should "let the past be the past." But one hard stare from Caleb, and they suddenly remember that they're not welcome in his café.

"Hey," she greets me with a tired grin and takes Mr. Peterson's place. "I'd greet you with a kiss, but I fear that might make you a target." She nods to the unwelcome guests, still outside, glaring at Caleb, who couldn't give less of a fuck about their anger. "And trust me, you don't want that."

"I really want that kiss, though," I say and purse my lips in a pout.

"I know," she says sadly and releases a deep sigh. "But trust me. They're not above lacing dog treats with rat poison. They would do a lot to get to me." She waves at Caleb, who acknowledges her with a nod and turns to his coffee machine to make her latte macchiato.

"When I was little, I used to beg my parents to get me a hamster. It took me years until they finally gave in and let me have one. I was elated. Honestly, my eleven-year-old heart was on cloud nine. I called him Mr. Snuggles because he was the softest and cutest hamster ever." A sad smile stretches her lips.

"Every evening, I'd spend an hour talking to him. I did everything—cleaned his cage, fed him, changed his water, and then one day …" She gulps, emotions tugging on her face. "She gave him chocolate. Put a whole damn bar in his cage. By the time I saw, he had suffered a slow and painful death." Her eyes dart down to Jensen Ackles, who glances up as if to say *What's that got to do with me?*

"Jensen might have the best caretaker in the world, but I'm not putting him in danger by letting them know we're together. It would mean the target on my back extends to you both, and I kind of like you two too much for that."

"Wow, your sister is a psychopath," Caleb grumbles, and I nod in agreement. How horrible.

The more I learn about her relationship with her sister, the more I loathe her family. How could her parents let Marissa get away with that? Therapy should have been the minimum course of action.

"Don't I know it?" She sighs again and plays with the rim of her to-go cup. "She can have the sweetest demeanor when others are around though. In this case, she shed some crocodile tears and told our parents it was an accident—she had no idea chocolate was poisonous to hamsters, even though I put a laminated list of no-no foods right over the cage so *I* wouldn't mess up." She shrugs and shakes her head, and I need to fight the urge to snake my arm around her and hold her tight.

"She's a witch," she continues in a rough whisper that tugs at my heart. "And she sure put a spell on my parents to make sure they'd always see her as that innocent little girl who deserves the world."

"Let karma do its thing, honey." Shawna suddenly appears with her tray and puts an order together behind the counter. "I'm sure they'll get taught their lesson sooner or later."

"I've been hoping for that for about half my life, Shawna," she says with a deep sigh and tucks a strand of her hair behind her ear. "Your word in the universe's ear."

"Anyway"—she turns to me, a newfound spark in her eyes—"they don't matter. But you do. How about you come to my place later?" she asks, pulling her lip between her teeth and fluttering her eyelashes at me. "And you can have all the kisses you desire."

My eyes are locked on her lips, the teasing edge in her voice sending a shiver down my spine. I shift in my seat, uncomfortable now that my cock has clearly taken notice too.

"It's a deal," I press out and the little giggle that falls from her lips sounds like heaven.

"Perfect," she purrs, and her tongue flicks out to wet her lips. "I'll be waiting."

She puts the money for her coffee on the counter and walks away with hips swinging, her to-go cup firmly in her hand. However, her posture changes once she steps outside and her sister talks to her. Instead of listening, she demonstratively puts on some over-ear headphones and confidently goes on her merry way with her chin high.

"I have a bad feeling about this," I admit to Caleb and he nods. It's an uncomfortable grumble in my stomach, the uneasy sensation you get in a haunted house when a monster can pop up around any corner.

"You're not the only one."

Chapter 26

Nic

"Oh, not again," I groan and pinch the bridge of my nose when I see Jay leaning against a tree only a few yards away. He wears a long, dark green coat with gold accents he could hop on a runway with and holds a bottle of fancy-brand water in his hand. Which I assume is solely because Caleb won't serve him in his café. I can't remember him ever drinking anything but coffee or maybe tea. "Lauren. Incoming asshat."

She follows my gaze, her expression immediately darkening, and her hands tighten around the small pumpkin she's holding. We just had a little competition on who of us can build the highest decorative pumpkin tower – which I was about to lose.

"Do you want me to throw a pumpkin at him?" She throws the fist-sized one into the air to demonstrate. "Say the word. I'll do it. With pleasure. I'll try to make it look like an accident."

"Don't tempt me," I whisper.

"You could run?" She suggests in a hiss, but I subtly shake my head. I'm not going to give him what he wants, and if I run away, it will only confirm whatever opinion he already has of me.

The autumn festival is this weekend, and Lauren and I were summoned to put up the final batch of fresh decorations, like hay and pumpkins.

The second pumpkin delivery arrived an hour ago. We've already spent the whole morning placing the first one along storefronts, in the gazebo, and throughout the park, playing around with all the different sizes and colors until we're satisfied with how they're styled.

God, I never knew how many kinds of pumpkins actually existed. Half of them barely seem real.

And it's taking forever.

Lauren and I are trying to make a good impression on everyone in town we haven't gotten to know yet, and we want it all to be perfect. Considering my ex and my sister are a thorn in everyone's side and only here because of me, I feel twice as obligated to make these autumn fair decorations a success.

"What do you think it would take for them to leave?" Lauren asks, annoyance clouding her voice as she steps up next to me, shoulders tall and arms crossed in front of her chest. She reminds me of a Chihuahua trying to protect their owner with their aggressive aura alone.

I'd hoped they'd go away. Hell, I even researched if there was any way to get Chaos to haunt them. Maybe some ghostly taunting would drive them away, but no such luck, since I wasn't about to kill an innocent frog to make the questionable spell I found work. Maybe Amanda has a better idea. I'll need to ask her about it the next time we're at the store.

Yes. Apparently, I now believe in ghosts *and* witchcraft. Although, maybe I'm only hoping the latter is real so I can get Jay's hair to fall out or something.

But they're still here, acting like they own the town and showing no intention of leaving.

Erik assured me the investigation is in full swing, but I'm losing hope. I'm not sure what else he needs evidence for. After all, Anna sent him all the proof she could gather, and Lauren even provided her recording of the scene he caused at the café that I never even realized she took. I don't understand what else needs to happen for him to file it as harassment and finally arrest those two.

"I'm working on it," he said. To his credit, he completely understood my frustration. And then he hit me with, "Would you rather I rush this and have my mistake let them walk free?" And I'm afraid he's got a point.

And now Jay is here. Again. All arrogance and sleaziness and completely unaware that half the town would love to bury him under those hay bales.

He never was quite able to read a room.

"Karma will get him. Karma will get him," I whisper to myself with closed eyes. Then I square my shoulders and prepare myself to listen to more bullshit as he gets closer.

"Nic," he says in a slippery smooth voice once he's in earshot, pretending this is a charming meet-cute and not a karmic punishment for me. "You've been avoiding me. Us."

"You don't say." I roll my eyes at him as Lauren tries to cover her laughter with a cough.

"Don't be a smartass."

I scoff. "If you don't like it, feel free to walk away. In fact, *please* do."

He smiles—the kind that once meant I was home. That made my heart beat faster and butterflies run amok in my belly. Now it makes me fear to get eaten by the big, bad wolf and evokes the urge to throw up on his polished designer shoes.

It's a good thing I'm not holding a pumpkin. The temptation to throw it at his face would be too great to resist.

"Relax. I just wanted to talk. You're so tense. Is this place getting to you?"

I don't answer. Lauren is standing next to us, and I have no doubt that she's recording every word he's speaking, letting him dig an even deeper hole. And who knows? Maybe his brain has conjured up some more helpful nuggets for Erik's investigation that will finally push it along.

So, I let him talk.

He takes a slow sip of the overpriced water bottle in his hand. "You know, when you left, I really worried about you. Everyone did. You were … almost spiraling, weren't you?"

My jaw tightens. "I wasn't spiraling. I broke up with you, and you're throwing a fit about that. Big difference."

"Right," he says gently, with a tone that tells me he's only humoring me. "That's how you remember it."

I blink. "Excuse me?"

"You were under so much pressure the past few years. Overwhelmingly stressed when your career was taking off. Remember how you said some extremely unkind things about your coworkers, Nic? I took some interesting screenshots and recordings of voice notes you sent me over the years—of course, I never would use those against you," he adds quickly, his voice slimy with fake reassurance, "but, you know. Just in case something happened."

I lift my eyebrow at him, unimpressed. He's not trying to use them against me but uses "just in case" less than ten seconds later? I glance at Lauren, who appears to be just as dumfounded as I am. We both know I'm the kind of person who bitches about coworkers in person while sipping a cocktail.

God, I would love to learn more about how his brain works. That level of delusion and unrecognized hypocrisy would make life a lot easier. Who cares about facts?

He steps closer, dropping his voice and from the corner of my eye, I see Lauren subtly step closer too. I have no idea how he doesn't see the phone in her hand, but I'm not questioning it. And when she slips it into my hand, I hide it in my sleeve and subtly bring it up higher to catch every word leaving his mouth.

We would make a good spy team at this point.

"But if the public sees those messages now? Or those late-night voice notes? They're not going to think, 'Oh, she was under pressure.' They're going to think you're unwell.

Maybe even dangerous. And if someone tells them our relationship broke because of cheating, you *know* how fast the internet turns on people."

"You're twisting everything," I say with an annoyed sigh and roll my eyes. "Then again, that's nothing new. Now your plan is what? To get former coworkers to hate me? To get me under a conservatorship?" I can't help but giggle. "Please, Jay. That's a dumb plan, even for you."

"Come on, Nic," he says softly—almost pitying—and a wave of disgust washes over me. "I'm trying to stop you from making things worse for yourself. If you walk away from this? Drop the charges? We both move on. No damage done."

"No damage?" I echo, incredulous, trying my hardest to not break into hysterical laughter. Does he seriously think I'm going to let this go?

"You lied to me. You used me. You and Marissa planned to scam me, and when that didn't work, you stole my identity and committed fraud. That's not a misunderstanding, Jay. That's a crime."

He sighs, casting himself as the wronged one, who's exhausted by my antics. "See? This is what I mean. You keep rewriting things in your head. You need someone to blame. It's easier than facing what's really going on with you."

He leans in, brushing imaginary lint from my shoulder, and it's taking every ounce of my willpower to not flinch when he touches me.

"Let's keep this quiet. Let it all go. Pay what's fair. You don't need a headline calling you hysterical and a cheater, along with pictures of your new friends. I don't think they'd appreciate being in magazines all over the country. Or hordes of paparazzi running all over your little town here, trying to get interviews."

I stay where I am, lifting my chin and giving him the most pitying look I can muster. Every nerve in my body is screaming, and my hand is tingling with the urge to slap him, but my voice comes out steady.

"Your bluffs don't work on me anymore," I say as calmly as I can. "But honestly, if this is the one thing you see through, I'd be surprised. You couldn't manage to do the same with a job. Or a relationship. Go ahead. Leak what you want. Make your threats. I don't care. I know you're lying and who do you think people will believe? A vindictive ex or the person they've worked with?" I subtly glance over at Lauren, who's giving me an equally subtle thumbs-up. "Next time you try to blackmail someone in their former industry, don't pick the person who still knows all the right people. This isn't going to go how you think."

Jay stares at me for a beat. Then smiles. A cruel smile that sends a shiver down my spine.

"You always did have a flair for drama."

"And you always underestimated me," I shoot back, then turn around and walk away, with my heart pounding and my mouth dry.

Lauren is right with me, linking her arm with mine, and I hand her back her phone. I force myself to take deep breaths, willing my thoughts to stop running at a mile a minute, and try to repeat the same thought over and over again as I remind myself to breathe.

Everything will be okay.

It has to.

Chapter 27

Nic

As soon as Jay is out of sight, I sink onto the upper step of the gazebo. All the fight leaves me at once.

My thoughts run wild, showing me all the worst-case scenarios, making my blood freeze in my veins and my heart pound in my chest. What if the paparazzi come here? Will my lake house become a prison, with each step outside of its safe four walls published in tabloids?

I never even noticed the crowd forming around us, but now, their curious and worried stares prickle into my skin like a thousand needles. I pull my knees to my chest and sink further into myself.

"Hey."

Lauren crouches down in front of me, trying to catch my gaze, but I nervously shake my head at her, still trying to remember how to breathe. It's not even the fact he tried to blackmail me—I don't give a damn if he tries to taint my name. Those whose opinions matter to me know that I would never do that.

But I'm exhausted. How much longer does this have to go on?

"Henry?" she shouts for him loudly. Before I know it, he trades places with her, kneeling before me while Lauren shoos everyone away from this little spectacle.

"Hey, sweetheart," he says softly, and the worry in his voice is almost enough to make me break into the tears I've been trying to hold back. "What's going on in that pretty head of yours? Talk to me."

I try to hide my face in my palms, but he catches them before I can, holding them in his big, warm hands. Jensen is suddenly beside us, trying to make sense of what's happening, tip-tapping around us and nudging me with his nose nervously.

"Sweetheart," Henry mumbles again, swiping a strand of hair behind my ear and keeping his warm palm against my cheek.

"Talk to me. What's going on?"

"Everything," I admit in a broken whisper, finally ready to meet his eyes. "I'm frustrated. And angry that those two keep appearing like some annoying pop-up ad from my past saying, 'Remember, you're unlovable.' And the next second, I'm sad because they were the people who were supposed to love me."

I swallow past the knot in my throat, trying to push my emotions down with it.

"They were supposed to take me for who I am. To build me up, to celebrate my wins, to mourn my losses. But now the only loss I'm mourning is them. And it's unfair. Why do I have to care if they don't give a damn? Why can't I switch those fucking emotions off for good?"

I glance around helplessly because I don't know where to look. And that makes me angry again. With trembling fingers, I wipe away a tear and lower my voice even further.

"And some days, most days, I know they're wrong. I'm awesome. A fucking delight to be around." A sobbing laugh escapes me. "But then the days creep in when I believe them, you know? What if I'm not? What if I deserve it, after all?"

"Oh, sweetheart," he says, wiping another tear away from my cheek. "Listen to me closely. You are the strongest woman I know. You are radiant. You light up every room you walk into. And I know it's easy for me to say and much harder for you to believe."

He lifts my hand and presses a kiss into my palm.

"But I'll keep reminding you. Every single day that you let me. You deserve love. You *are* loved."

At this point, the tears keep streaming down my face, sobs breaking out of me.

"And they are idiots not to have seen it. Now come on, sweetheart. Breathe with me."

He puts my hands against his chest, taking slow and deep breaths that I'm trying to imitate.

When I finally get it, I nod. And then I see his lips curl into a small, proud smile, though the amusement doesn't quite reach his eyes.

"Should I take you home, sweetheart?" he whispers and lifts my hand to press a kiss into my palm, the tingle from his scruff distracting me. "I think you need a break."

I quickly shake my head, glancing up at him through wet eyelashes.

"If I go home now, I'll keep thinking about it," I whisper and force myself to take a deep breath, swallowing past the ball of emotions in my throat. "I want to stay. I want to help." Determination makes my voice stronger as I blink up at Lauren. "I want to romanticize the fuck out of life."

A proud grin slowly tugs at Lauren's lips, and her hunched shoulders sink as the worry leaves her.

"And I've been really looking forward to this," I add, eyes darting around the town square. Most of the stands are built and ready for the fair. There's barely a square foot without a pumpkin on it.

"We still have a bunch of garlands and knickknacks we need to put up. And all of this—" I make a vague gesture around us. "It's coming together so nicely," I point out with a pout, then lower my voice. "I had such a fun time before he opened his mouth."

"I'm coming with you later though," he decides and gets up, extending his hand to pull me to a stand.

His voice lowers as he keeps me close to him, his hand snaking from my waist to the small of my back, like it belongs there. It's a movement already so deeply ingrained in his mind, he probably can't help himself.

"The threats might've been empty, but the fact he's bold enough to say them worries me," he mumbles, and I nod. Is he reading my mind?

Lauren gets closer, talking in a hushed voice as well, her eyes darting around, fearing Jay might jump out from behind one of the pumpkins.

"I've already sent the recording to Erik and you. Make sure to forward it to your lawyer as soon as you can, all right?"

"Will do," I say with a small, sad smile. "I don't know if I'll ever be able to thank you enough, Lauren."

"Oh, please," she waves it off like it's nothing.

But I mean it.

"No, seriously." I slip out of Henry's half-hug and grab her gently by the arm.

"You're saving my butt here. Just take the compliment."

"Well, in that case, please keep them coming by all means," she quips, and the joke lifts the mood, just a little. "Now come on. We've still got a mountain of garlands to hang."

"I'm sorry," I tell Henry later in the peaceful quiet of my living room, limbs tangled as we cuddle under a warm blanket

He made good on his promise. After making a quick stop at his house to load up on clothes and dog necessities, he drove right over to my place, arriving at the exact same time as the pizza he ordered for us. The empty boxes are on the coffee table, with Pumpkin cuddled up on one of them. It must have still been warm when I put it there.

"What are you sorry for, sweetheart?"

His hand is absentmindedly drawing patterns over my shoulder, sending a tingle all over my skin. I could stay here forever. With my head against his chest, listening to his heartbeat, Cinnamon curled up in my lap, and Jensen Ackles asleep on the couch next to Henry.

Chaos is somewhere on the couch pillow behind my neck, finding her spot halfway on my shoulder and halfway on the back of the couch. Her soft purr vibrates against my shoulder.

The silence is only broken by an old cartoon softly playing on my TV. I stopped paying attention to it a while ago, though, my thoughts somewhere else entirely.

"I bring trouble wherever I go," I explain in a low voice, distractedly playing with his fingers, gently tracing them with my fingertips before interlacing them with mine.

"I mean, first Chaos died. Then I got my ex and sister to ruin the whole town's mood. I'm just …" I exhale a deep sigh and close my eyes. "I don't know what to do anymore."

He presses a kiss against my temple and pulls me tighter against him.

"I don't care," he whispers into my ear and squeezes me to him. "I mean, I probably would care if the trouble you brought with yourself was … I don't know, a biker gang out to get you. Or the Mafia, trying to marry you off to their boss. Or clowns. I hate clowns." He quirks an eyebrow at me. "I'd still protect you from them, but I'd probably scream louder than a five-year-old-girl in a haunted house."

My lips curl into the faintest smile.

"But this?" He shakes his head. "You had an error of judgment. It can happen to anyone," he assures me. "I've had my fair share of those too. Why do you think I chose to work with animals?"

"Really?" I glance up at him curiously. "That's hard to imagine." He's so … put together. He's got a handle on his life; an old soul, wise way beyond his years, the one you go to when you need advice from an *actual* adult.

"Really," he reiterates and takes a deep breath. "I used to have a buddy in college, Ryan. We became best friends in the first week of high school and grew up together. Naturally, when we ended up at the same university, we decided to rent a flat together. Worst mistake of my life."

I glance at him, curiosity eating me from the inside, but I wait for him to continue.

"He almost got us kicked out of the flat several times, because he spent the money I gave him for rent. Then, one day, he got caught with drugs in his car and tried to blame me."

"What the fuck?" I turn fully to look at him, as Chaos gets up and jumps down onto the couch pillow.

"That's what I said," he chuckles. "That little accusation could have cost me my job and my entire future. Thankfully, the cops already thought he was full of shit, and when they came up empty after searching my room, I was cleared."

"Thank God," I whisper, drawing a pattern over his shirt with my finger.

"What I'm trying to say is 'I don't mind' would be an overstatement. Jay and Marissa are not your responsibility. Whatever they're doing, whether it's beef with people from our town or bringing down your mood, it's not your fault," he continues, and every word hits closer to home. When he calls Wayward Hollow "our" town, I'm one breath away from bursting into tears again.

"It's just so unfair," I mumble, cuddling against his side. "I know I keep saying that, and life isn't fair, but everyone always talks about karma and …" I take a deep, shaky breath. "Right now, it feels like they will never get their comeuppance. They get to be shit people their whole life, and it only benefits them. Now they are parading around town with this we-can-do-whatever-the-fuck-we-want attitude, because they *know* there won't be consequences. There have never been any. And I'm sick of it."

I glance up at him, gnawing on my lip as I carefully choose my next words. "All my life, I'd hoped Marissa would get knocked off her high horse and land in the mud."

His curious stare drills into the side of my face, and I pretend to watch TV while I continue.

"God, that makes me sound mean. But, you know, I thought if she finally got consequences, it would force our parents to finally open their eyes and realize what kind of person they raised." Cinnamon moves in my lap and I run my fingers through her soft fur, smiling when I hear her purr.

"To be fair, I'd hoped it was in her best interest, but it was also my own chance at schadenfreude."

He chuckles and I grin when he presses a kiss to my temple.

"You want to know what happened to my buddy after the drug incident?" he asks softly and I nod.

"He caught a grip. A few months after I moved out, he messaged me and apologized for being a shitty friend and roommate. I think he's some kind of computer hotshot nowadays, but it took the police, a few nights in county jail, and rehab for him to realize how badly he'd messed up."

"The difference is I'm pretty sure neither Marissa nor Jay will ever reach that point," I say, and take a deep, frustrated breath.

"Marissa has her head so high up her own ass, she's basically wearing herself as a crown. In her mind, she is the main character. The only person in the whole wide world who matters.

Nothing can happen to her. Nobody ever tells her no. And if they do, she'll just pretend they didn't. Because there won't be consequences."

I pinch the bridge of my nose.

"Maybe you're underestimating Erik," Henry mumbles, and I nod against his shoulder.

"I sure hope so," I admit, softly tracing a subtle line of different colored fur on Cinnamon's back. "But all I can do is wait. And I hate waiting and not being able to do anything. It makes me feel helpless."

I sigh as he tightens his arm around my shoulders, pressing another kiss to my head.

"Their time will come," he assures me. "Mr. Peterson already volunteered to run them out of the city with torches and pitchforks."

I shoot him an amused smile. Paired with Lauren's offer of playing one-sided dodgeball with Jay, Marissa and some pumpkins, it makes for a very amusing picture in my mind.

"I'm just saying it could be a highlight of the autumn fair," I say with a giggle and cuddle further into him. "Can we chant the song from *Beauty and the Beast* while we do it? 'Kill the Beast' seems fitting."

"I'll be in the first row," he assures me. "Just have to get my pitchfork out of the basement."

He pulls me into his lap, much to Cinnamon's dismay.

"We got this, Nic. Whatever happens." He whispers against my temple, and I exhale all the tension and doubt that have been building over the day.

God, I'm so lucky Chaos brought me to him.

Chapter 28

Henry

"Aww, there's our grandchild," my mom coos as soon as she opens the door for Jensen and me, her gaze immediately dropping to my dog. She's in her usual weekend getup—a soft sweater, reading glasses still perched on her head, and that warm smile that somehow takes me right back to being six years old.

Jensen immediately barrels inside their house, tail wagging so furiously he's about to lift off the ground, and singing the song of his people. His excited tippy-taps echo through the hallway as he zigzags indecisively—torn between saying hi to my mom or my dad first.

"No, Jensen, down," I say sternly when he decides to greet my mom first and jumps at her. My mom has owned dogs all her life too and doesn't give him any attention until he sits at her feet calmly, only his wagging tail to show how excited he is.

"Such a good boy," she says in a high baby voice and gives him a treat, now finally greeting him with some pets and kisses—way more enthusiastically than she greeted me, I might add.

"Go to the living room. Food's almost ready." Mom waves me through, and I chuckle as I close the door behind me.

"Good to see you too, Mother," I can't help but point out dryly and shake my head at her with faux disapproval.

"Yes, yes." She kneels on the ground, letting Jensen lick her face and answering his whines. "Your owner is grumpy today!"

I hear another set of paws approaching and my gaze darts to the living room with a grin. "There you are, Nala."

My parents' golden retriever might be old already, but in her heart, she's still a puppy. She greets me excitedly, zig-zagging around the hallway as she follows me to the living room.

Dad is in the kitchen, putting the finishing touches on the food. He's wearing one of his well-worn flannel shirts, sleeves rolled up, and his reading glasses perched on the tip of his nose as he studies the food like it might try to escape.

Nala gets a distracted pat from him when she brushes against his leg. He's completely in his element, humming something under his breath and perfectly content.

"Son," he greets me with a quick hug and a strong shoulder clasp.

"Ooh, mashed potatoes," I say happily and quickly swipe my finger through it, cursing when it's way hotter than I expected, and promptly lick it off. "It's delicious, Dad."

"Thank you, thank you," he says prouder than an Oscars winner and grins, not even pretending to disapprove of me taste-testing anymore. He lost that fight twenty years ago. "Help me set the table."

"Sure." I take the plates out of the cupboard and bring them to the dinner table, setting them at the same spots we've sat at ever since I can remember.

"Did she ever love me as much as she loves Jensen?" I ask amusedly, watching my mom entertaining her grandchild.

"I wouldn't be sure," my dad jokes as he hands me the cutlery. "Then again, remember, she had to raise you—tantrums, shitting in flower vases and whatnot—not just love you the way she does your dog. She's stricter with Nala too."

"Fair point," I admit with a chuckle and put the forks and knives next to each plate.

"Though I won't ever complain about a human grandchild," Mom says pointedly, sending a sharp glance my way with her eyebrow raised to her hairline, which makes me roll my eyes.

I don't even dignify that little dig with an answer and continue setting the table.

"Hey, by the way, are we still doing a late Thanksgiving?" I ask as I pour us all drinks, giving Nala a pet as she gets into her *"Please sir, may I have some food?"* position right next to my chair.

What can I say? Mom might spoil my dog and sneak him food, but I do the same with theirs to get even.

"Yeah." Mom and Dad nod, confused. "Why wouldn't we?"

"No reason," I explain with a shrug. "It's just that Nic and Lauren asked if I wanted to join them for a Friendsgiving. I wanted to double-check with you that your cruise is still on, and it won't impose on our plans."

"It is very much still on." Mom walks over to dad, who immediately snakes a protective arm around her while she kisses his cheek. God, those two are still disgustingly in love. I want that one day.

"We have a wedding anniversary to celebrate."

"Damn right we do." Dad grins and presses another kiss against the side of her head.

"Remember to invite Caleb, Honey. But speaking of Nic and Lauren ..." She wiggles her eyebrows and motions for me to sit down while the two of them carry the pots to the table, and I groan. I know exactly what's coming.

They might live three towns over, but gossip travels fast in this area.

"We heard about strange people hanging out in Wayward Hollow." Mom glances at me, worried, and reaches for my hand. "Is everything okay? Are they dangerous?"

"I don't think so," I say and squeeze her hand back, then let go to put a good amount of mashed potatoes on my plate.

Jensen is, of course, lying down right next to the table, shooting me a glare that says, *"Go ahead, enjoy your food. I'm only starving here, but fine,"* that I've learned to ignore over the past months.

"Who are they?" Dad asks, confused. "Nobody quite knows."

I glance up, surprised. Seriously? That part didn't make it into the gossip?

I chuckle and scoop up some potatoes with my fork, blowing on it to cool it down. My still slightly burning finger reminding me of the lesson I learned during my quality control earlier.

"They are Nic's ex-fiancé and her sister." The two of them shoot each other a confused glance before they turn to me again.

"That's … not what we were expecting. Karen said they're some kind of hooligans."

I give them the rundown of everything that's happened, and with each detail, my mom's expression shifts further into shock. Even my dad's usually solid poker face cracks, especially when I get to the part about her parents not only knowing about their scheme all along but encouraging it.

"Her fiancé? And her sister?" Dad asks, shocked, and I nod slowly.

"That poor thing," Mom finally whispers, tears shimmering in her eyes. "Oh God, I can't imagine. How are you two dealing with all of this?"

"She's dealing with it … somehow. Sometimes I catch her on her back porch, staring at nothing, and know she's still mourning the family she wanted to have. I don't know how to help her," I say, pushing my food around the plate, suddenly losing my appetite. "I can't exactly wipe away her emotions."

I take a deep breath, putting down my fork.

"She's suffering, but that encourages them. They enjoy putting salt in her wounds and watching her be in pain, and there's nothing I can do aside from being there for her."

"I mean, you could give them a proper ass-whooping," Dad points out, but I shake my head, and Mom shoots him a disapproving glare.

"He will do no such thing," she scolds him then shoots me a sharp glance. "Tell me you won't."

"Scout's honor."

"Good. Honey, from my understanding, what those two want is a reaction. It's a tale as old as time, the true motivation for any regular old bully. They don't care what kind, but if you give them a reaction, they know they can get to you. They've accomplished their mission. As much as I'm sure most people in Wayward Hollow would appreciate you breaking his nose, and as much as I'm sure Erik will coincidentally turn the other way and not see a thing, I don't think it would be wise to give them what they want."

Mom frowns, putting down her cutlery. "I'm sure their comeuppance will come. And until then, the best you can do is ignore them. Maybe that will make them go away by themselves."

"I'm not that optimistic, but we don't exactly have a choice," I say, my appetite slowly returning, probably because of that nice buttery smell from the potatoes that makes me salivate. "And if not … who knows? Maybe the pitchforks will actually come out."

"I do expect a call in that case," Dad says with a mischievous grin. "Last witch hunt was when we were in high school."

"Honey, you realize that wasn't real, right? Just some event they organized to build some neighborly spirit."

"And it worked," Dad laughs, and I shake my head at them.

"Oh, plenty is happening, though. Did you know that Jacob's cow gave birth a few days ago?"

"No way," Mom says, full of excitement, her eyes shining happily. She adores baby cows. "You know, I wanted to visit your aunt soon anyway."

"Suuure you did," I say and shake my head amusedly.

If she could, she'd have half a farm here, but then again, she wouldn't be able to go on that cruise. They might allow dogs, but I'm not sure about cows.

And while the two of them bicker about when to visit my dad's sister, I can't help but watch them. The way they look at each other. How acutely aware my dad is of every single move my mom makes, putting his hand over the table's edge when she picks something up off the ground, to prevent her from banging her head on her way back up.

That is the kind of love I want to have when I'm their age.

And I think I might know who I want to have that with.

Chapter 29

Henry

Lauren: Come to Caleb's. NOW.

"Fuck," I mumble, lowering my camera and quickly slipping the lens cap back on before tucking it into my bag. I whistle sharply for Jensen Ackles, who immediately comes running to me.

It was time for another long hike, somewhere far enough from civilization for him to run wild and free without spooking other dogs or cows. And by that, I mean a whole twenty minutes outside of Wayward Hollow, a spot with vast grassland and beautiful hills as far as we can see. I love this spot, especially in spring when the entire scenery is a giant flower ocean.

Though it's not any less photogenic in fall, with trees turning orange in the distance and leaves in all kinds of autumn colors flying around us.

Jensen yawns, clearly exhausted from running around as he trots beside me, ready for a warm, soft spot to take a nap in. Good thing it's only a few more minutes to where I parked the car, where he can do exactly that.

As I walk, I can't stop thinking about Lauren's text. What's going on? With the state things are in and how little information Lauren messaged me, this could be about anything. Did

Jay and Marissa pick another fight with Nic? Did Mr. Peterson actually bring out the pitchforks? Maybe Chaos brought another cat to Nic. What if I get into Wayward Hollow and the whole town is on fire?

I pick up my pace as we make our way back to the car: I drive to Caleb's at what must be record speed for me. Curiosity and a sense of impending doom weigh on my shoulders, as worry about Nic gnaws at my conscience.

My car comes to a screeching halt in front of Caleb's, and my eyes flick around, confused. There's nobody around, which is not surprising for Wayward Hollow on a late Sunday afternoon. The windows are dark, and I can't see movement inside. Is it closed?

Right. It's Sunday. He's usually closed today, but why would Lauren order me here then? Did she get it wrong?

I'm about to call her when I see her head pop out the door, quickly waving at Jensen and motioning for us to hurry inside.

"What's going on?" I ask her once the door closes behind us, somehow compelled to whisper.

"It's a town meeting," she answers just as softly with a mischievous grin, though her eyes dart around nervously.

"What the—?" It's packed at Caleb's. Jensen immediately wants to race off to meet his favorite people. I hand the leash to the first person who falls victim to his charm, knowing full well I'll get him back by the end of whatever the hell is happening here.

I can't remember the last time anyone called a town meeting. And when they did, we met up in the town square.

"Is the whole town here?" I ask, surprised when I internally tally up who I see.

"Henry." Lauren gives me a hard stare. "I'm new here. How would I know?"

"You've got a good point," I admit. Bewildered, I make my way through the crowd over to Caleb and find Nic leaning against the counter, her face breaking into a smile as I get closer. Lauren stays where she is, eyes darting around the room uneasily.

"Hey, sweetheart," I greet Nic with a quick kiss and put my arm around her shoulder.

"Hey, hot stuff," she whispers with a grin and snakes her arm around my middle. I glance over her head at Caleb, who isn't impressed at all.

I am, though. I never would have guessed that the café could host the whole damned town if it had to. "What in the ever-loving fuck is going on here?"

"Trust me, I'd love to know too." His arms are crossed over his chest, and he shakes his head at someone trying to place an order. "Apparently, I'm hosting, but all I got was a message from Harry telling me to show up, and then boom, he ambushed me into opening the place for a town meeting." He mutters a curse under his breath.

"I didn't even get a heads-up. And don't give me those puppy eyes. I'm not firing up the coffee machines. They take forever to heat, then forever to clean, and at this point, it's about the principle. They can't warn me, nobody gets coffee." He curses more about how that would fuck with his inventory when suddenly a loud voice booms over the confused murmur.

"Can I have everyone's attention, please?"

Harry has climbed onto one of the tables, swaying dangerously, and I can see Caleb's face turning red with anger as he quickly scans the countertop for something to throw. I bet that right about now, he wishes he had opened up and had a mug handy.

"Get down from there, Harry! I got no insurance if you fall on your damned face because you decided to play Tarzan in my coffee shop!"

Caleb has never been Harry's biggest fan as is. In fact, he loathes the man who always reminds me of the horse from

Tangled. Not because he has a long face, but because he can get that same unhinged, wide-eyed look in his eyes. He's the head of our town's council and when Caleb first opened up the café, they had some run-ins that left a sour taste in his mouth.

There was the time Harry demanded he painted the sign for his café green—not for any particular reason, but because he thought it would match the town's aesthetic better.

But despite his HOA comparable pettiness, overall, Harry is all right. Now that he finally has grandchildren, he complains much less about small details.

"All right, all right," Harry mutters and climbs down, the town collectively gasping when he sways as if he loses his balance. Instead, he motions for everyone else to sit down and only continues once they do.

"I am sorry for this impromptu meeting, but there is something urgent we need to talk about collectively, as a town, regarding the autumn fair this weekend."

Everyone quiets down, not even a whisper in the room, anxiety turning the air into thick syrup.

"What's going on?" Mr. Peterson asks, swinging his cane.

"Somebody is trying to sabotage Wayward Hollow's beloved autumn festival." The whole crowd gasps, shocked. Nic suddenly tenses in my hold, and I press my lips to her temple.

"There have been complaints filed for"—Harry checks a list in his hands—"improper food handling. The setup being against code. Fire hazards. Noise." He shakes his head, listing off a few more items that sound more and more ridiculous.

"It's them," Nic whispers and lets her head fall against my shoulder. "It has to be."

"If they wanted to anger the whole town, they certainly achieved that," I murmur and take a deep breath.

"Now, I assure you that everything has the proper permits, and the setup has been double checked by the county's fire department. The health department will be here tomorrow for another inspection, but I see no issues arising. Everyone, please know that it's our highest priority to provide you a safe and fun autumn fair, as we have done every year."

Harry scans the room. "And I do not appreciate someone trying to interfere with this festival that has been a staple in Wayward Hollow ever since the town was founded. If anyone has anything to say, please do so now."

"I bet it's that weird homeless couple!" Courtney exclaims, her husband nodding along vehemently as she earns a murmur of agreement from the rest of the town.

Nic's eyes widen before her whole body starts shaking with laughter.

"Homeless couple," she whispers, hiding her face behind her hand. "God, that's golden."

"Can't we kick them out of town?" Andrea asks loudly, shaking her head. "Those two almost destroyed one of my hotel rooms. They're bad news."

"They always drive too fast too!" someone else speaks up. "They almost swiped my car. Three times!"

"I'm afraid 'almost' isn't quite enough of a reason to run them out of town," Harry says, not too happy with that assessment himself. "For now, we are fully cooperating with any departments that receive complaints because we are up to code. We have nothing to hide. But if any of you run into more issues with those two"—he takes a good look around the room—"tell me. I'll see what's possible. And no, 'almost' doing something doesn't count."

"Aw, man," Lauren pouts, and I startle. When did she get over here? The rest of the room breaks into mumbles about their dissatisfaction as well until Harry claps his hands so loudly it makes Nic flinch.

"That's all!" Harry states, and everyone streams out of Caleb's, until its name giver, Lauren, Kieran, Nic, Jensen Ackles, and I are the only people left inside, silent anger brewing in all of us.

"Oh, thank God, I was getting claustrophobic," Lauren whispers, still a little pale. Caleb slides a glass of water over the counter wordlessly, and she offers him a small smile before taking a tiny sip.

"We need a plan," Lauren announces, determined, and takes a seat on one of the bar stools, the rest of us following suit. Apart from Caleb, who stays in his usual spot behind it, arms crossed in front of his chest and his signature unreadable expression on his face. "They can't stay here."

"You don't say." Nic rolls her eyes at her best friend. "But what can we do? Harry was right, 'almost' doesn't quite cut it."

"I've heard people mention pitchforks," Lauren points out, and I laugh when I see the glee in Kieran's eyes. "I vote that!"

"It's sounds tempting," Nic concedes with a shrug. "I can't say I'd be opposed."

Suddenly, Lauren's phone buzzes, and she excuses herself, walking to the other end of the room to take the call.

"They did what?"

All of our heads whip around. Lauren stands as still as a statue, all of our eyes on her back as she listens to whatever the person on the other end tells her.

"Okay, thanks for letting me know. I'll tell her."

She turns around slowly, her face set in stone and jaw grinding ever so slightly. With an annoyed sigh, she lifts her hand to rub her forehead, probably wondering if she's surrounded by idiots and is about to burst into a song about world domination.

"I have good news, and I have bad news," Lauren says and looks at Nic, who is squeezing my hand as if it's her personal stress toy.

"Bad news first," she whispers, and Lauren nods.

"That was Massimo, wondering if I also got a weird message from someone claiming to be 'looking out' for them"—she uses air quotations and rolls her eyes as she says it—"or sent screenshots of conversations you allegedly had about me."

"Those fuckers," I mutter, but Nic squeezes my hand again.

"And the good news?"

"He knows it's bullshit." Lauren shrugs, and the corner of her lip twitches. "And everyone else he's talked to also knows this is a setup. He says 'hi' and hopes you're well, and if you need a witness statement from him or anything, let him know."

"That's good. Right?" Kieran asks, eyes darting between Lauren and Nic.

"I can't believe they went ahead with it," Nic whispers. Her face turns from hurt to angry within moments. "You mentioned pitchforks?"

"Let's try a nonviolent way to get rid of them first," Lauren suggests, glancing at all of us with determination in her eyes.

"That smile scares me," Nic points out, but then leans closer. "I'm all ears."

"We need to be one step ahead," Lauren starts, and cracks her knuckles. "So. I think it's fair to say they're planning something for the fair. Knowing them, it's something that would embarrass Nic and what they perceive would ruin her reputation. Maybe they will call paparazzi, or maybe they will drive their car into a booth—we need to be prepared, friends!"

"I don't think they'd drive their car into anything," Nic says contemplatively. "Jay is too proud of that ugly thing to risk scratching it."

"The paparazzi sound likely though," I point out. "Maybe they'll crash one of the evening performances?"

"It does sound more likely," Nic admits, worry etching a crease between her eyebrows.

"Then we'll turn the tables on them." Lauren might as well have a light bulb over her head. "Here's what we'll do ..."

Chapter 30

Nic

"God, I feel like a teenager on a date," I joke, staring lovingly up at Henry.

We're walking over to the autumn fair hand in hand, and I have to say—it is way more adorable than I thought it would be. Lauren and I might have lent a hand with the decorations, but what makes the atmosphere are the vendors showing off their crafts and goods, and the people.

I'm eating a still-warm churro with cinnamon, while Henry is sticking to a caramel apple. Jensen curiously trots beside us, eyes darting everywhere, overwhelmed about what to focus on first.

"Come to think of it," he says with a lovestruck grin playing on his lips, "this is our first real date, sweetheart."

"Oh my God, you're right." I come to a halt. "I didn't even think about that!"

I'm more than content with our staying-in-and-cuddling dates. Cinnamon gets angry with me if I'm away too often, and Pumpkin is gnaws on furniture—and I love spending time with Henry no matter what we're doing. I never needed big dates or gestures—being with him is all I need.

"Want me to shoot you a plush toy?" he grins, nodding to our left.

I turn to follow his gaze, and my eyes widen when I spot the stand. It's tucked between a booth selling homemade pumpkin pies and one with spiced apple cider, all adorned in warm autumn colors. Wooden signs hang above it with hand-painted prices, and strings of little felt leaves and fairy lights frame the edges of the canopy.

Plush pumpkins, owls, and foxes with goofy faces dangle from clothespins, waiting for someone to take them home. And that someone could be me, apparently.

Lauren and I haven't been back here since we set up decorations, so we completely missed the vendors moving in and claiming their spots. Seeing it all finished is like walking into a little pocket of autumn, much more magical than I thought this would turn out.

"Are you trying to woo me with your shooting skills?" I try to sound nonchalant as I glance back at him, cheeks flushed with heat. I might not be one for clichés, but him winning me a toy would honestly make my day.

"If it works, I'll clear the whole booth." He grins, throwing the core of his apple in the bin as we make our way to the stand. "It might take a while, though. I don't have the best aim."

"Then it's a good thing my affection can be bought for the low, low price of one low-quality stuffed animal." I pat his back playfully, then step aside to let him do his thing, taking Jensen's leash out of his hand.

I can't say I'm overly fond of guns. Do I still have one because I'm a woman who lives alone in the middle of nowhere? Obviously. But I've never considered them hot.

Yet there's something about the way he handles the little plastic shotgun—the way he braces it against his shoulder, that little crease between his eyebrows as he focuses, the way he squints his eyes in concentration as he aims it … it's sexy as hell.

Fuck, I'm such a goner for this man. It's not even funny anymore.

There's something about him that settles me. As if my heart finally knows how to beat in the right rhythm when he's around. His hugs are home, more cozy than fleece blankets and soft music on a rainy autumn afternoon. And every time he looks at me as if I'm something special, my stomach flips so fast it's giving Olympic gymnasts a run for their medals. His kisses? As addictive as that first swirl of pumpkin spice syrup in my coffee: comforting, exciting, a little bit magic.

I used to think I knew what love was. But wow, I was way off.

Love isn't sticking it out for the sake of it. It's looking into someone's eyes and thinking—*yeah, that's home.*

The exact way he makes me feel.

His focused face breaks into a wide smile when he hits the target.

"Oh my God, well done you."

I bite my lip, shooting him a grin as he picks out a teddy bear for me. The poor thing is worn out as if it has already survived a war. But somehow, that makes him even more lovable.

He hands it to me with a proud little grin and holds out his hand, expecting me to take it so we can keep walking. Instead, I bypass it entirely and slip my arm around his waist, cuddling the battle-worn bear against my side as if it's the most natural thing in the world.

"Thank you," I whisper and stretch my neck, lips pursed for a kiss. He happily obliges, his lips sending a jolt of buzzing electricity through my whole body. The smile he shoots me afterward makes my face burn.

God, I think I love this man.

The air cackles between us as our eyes lock, his hold around my waist tightening, when suddenly Lauren appears from behind a pumpkin tower.

"Nic, Nic, Nic!" she whisper-shouts with worry in her eyes and quickly pushes the three of us past a wall of hay bales behind a craft stand.

"Lauren, Lauren, Lauren!" I whisper-shout back, confused, but she shakes her head quickly, her expression almost panicked.

"They're here," she says ominously, glancing over her shoulder, scared we're being followed, and I lift my eyebrow at her. Jensen is relaxed though, so I doubt Jay is around.

"Who are 'they?'" Henry asks, and I shrug, equally confused.

"What are you talking about, Lauren? We knew Jay and Marissa would be here," I point out, but she shushes me, carefully peeking around the hay.

"I'm not talking about Jay and Marissa. I'm talking about your parents."

The words hit me harder than a punch to the sternum. My heart falters, and I turn to stare at Lauren. Suddenly, the air is molasses, and my lungs are tight, as if the air is too heavy to breathe.

My mouth opens, but my brain can't form a single word. Something sharp presses into my chest, a weight I thought I'd left behind creeping back in. I blink, trying to steady myself, but all I manage is a quiet, shaken stare.

"What?" Henry asks, and I nod. That's exactly what I'd love to know, too. What the actual fuck?

"Marissa must have told them." Lauren starts pacing, nibbling at her thumbnail.

"Great," I say and pinch the bridge of my nose. "Then again, I can't even be surprised," I mumble, making the two of them turn to me, eyes wide with surprise.

"Jay knew how hard I fought for their approval," I tell them with a nonchalant shrug, trying to hide how badly he hit a spot that still hurts much more than I want to admit. "He witnessed it firsthand, listened to all my self-doubts. If they want to hit me where it hurts, why wouldn't they involve my parents?" I lay my head back, gazing at the clear autumn sky for a moment. "God, I hate them."

Henry gives my hand a reassuring squeeze.

"Their presence doesn't change anything about our plan," Lauren says decidedly and crosses her arms in front of her chest. "Remember, Nic. They're air. They're nothing to you. And you are so much more than your birth givers' approval."

"Thanks, Lauren," I say with a small smile. "This came from left field, but thank you for warning me. I'm 95 percent sure the rest will happen exactly as we think. This is only a small, unwelcome surprise."

"Well then, until their little plan turns into action"—her eyes dart from Henry to me. When they land on the teddy bear in my hand and his arm around my hip, her expression softens—"have a fun date."

"We will," I assure her, and the smile on my face finally turns genuine.

Henry's arm is a protective reminder around my shoulders as we continue to walk through the autumn fair. With each step, I understand better and better why Wayward Hollow prides themselves on it.

It's fun. There's barely anyone without a smile on their face. The vendors are chatting with customers, handing out warm drinks and sweet treats.

Visitors wander from stand to stand, holding cider or cotton candy, while kids run around with painted faces and sticky fingers. The air smells of cinnamon, warm apples and roasted nuts, and there's soft music playing from a speaker somewhere. Everything is warm and alive, like the whole town showed up just to be happy for a while, resembling a small-town Disneyland.

"We should carve a pumpkin," Henry suggests with a chuckle as we walk past the tables where children are throwing pumpkin seeds at each other. He holds Jensen's leash tighter as he perks up at the scent of potential food.

"Later," I say with a grin, nodding toward the sticky residue on the benches and where a girl is massaging pumpkin gunk into a boy's hair. "I don't think I can be trusted with a knife right now."

"Fair point," he admits and pulls me past it, when I suddenly see a familiar face.

"Ralph?"

"Nic! It's great to see you." The familiar middle-aged man's face turns into the same bright smile he always had on his face when we ran into each other. His temples have grayed a bit since I last saw him, and he's gotten tanner, but he's still the annoying-because-of-his-job-but-actually-a-nice-guy I've gotten to know over the years.

"Were you on vacation?" I ask him, and he breaks into a grin.

"I mean, yeah. Now that I can't photograph you anymore, the job is only half as fun. Might as well reap some rewards from my hard work." I shake my head at his blatant flattery.

"Henry, this is Ralph, one of the paparazzi I've become acquainted with over the years. Ralph, this is Henry, my boyfriend."

God, saying it aloud makes me giddy. Some days I still fear that I will wake up and it turns out he was too perfect after all and only a product of my imagination. Henry extends his hand with a pleasant smile to greet Ralph, and when they shake hands, they nod at each other with some kind of quiet understanding.

"It's good to meet you," Henry says, sounding a little stiff. No wonder. He might be used to being around me, but paparazzi? That can be scary stuff. Ralph is one of the good ones, though, the kind who waits at a respectful distance and wouldn't kneel to try to get a shot of my panties. He'd say hi instead of barking orders to pose at me.

"Hey, would you mind if I—" He motions between Henry and me, and I glimpse up at my boyfriend. Ah, I'll never get enough of calling him that in my head. Boyfriend.

"Is it okay?" I whisper. "You don't have to."

"Sure," he agrees then leans closer to my ear. "Did you really think I'd oppose claiming you in front of the whole world?" I glance up at him, my face flushed. "You're mine. And everyone can know that." He winks at me.

"You can't say that kind of cute stuff. Now I'll look like I'm auditioning to be the face of sunburn awareness month," I complain playfully and pat my cheeks, hoping the redness will go down while we find a spot in front of some of the decorations and coordinate a cute little pose.

"Three, two, one, smile," Ralph counts us down until his flashlight instantly blinds me. "Oops, sorry. My bad!" He takes another one without it and lowers his camera.

"Send me a pretty version," I tell him with a wink, and he gives me a thumbs-up.

"Of course, Nic."

"I'm curious, though," I say, trying to act completely innocent, noting Henry hiding a grin behind his hand beside me. "It's lovely to see you and all that, but what brings you here?"

"You know, there's a tip going around that this is the place to be. They didn't even want any money for it. Not sure what it's about, but I thought I'd take a chance. And now I met you, so I guess the tip wasn't half bad."

"I take it you're not the only one, then?" I lift my eyebrow, and he quickly nods.

"I think I saw about five of us about. Welcome back to the spotlight, I guess," he says with a chuckle, and I exhale a deep sigh.

I talked to my former PR company, and while they can't predict the future either, they are confident I can ride out any kind of public attention by continuing to live a normal and, as the woman I talked to called it, "extremely boring" life.

She predicted that when the paparazzi couldn't find me doing anything interesting, they'd leave me alone, and even my new relationship would become old news at some point.

And I guess I have to find out the hard way if that's true. Henry and I shoot each other a look. It means our plan is working, though, and we didn't even have to do anything yet.

But then something else catches my eye.

"Oh no," I whisper, my stomach dropping as I glance past Ralph and spot my egg and seed donors. They've got a familiar expression on their faces: smug, polished, and dripping with condescension. They stroll past the stalls as if they're too good to even breathe the same air as everyone else—their noses tilted sky-high, probably ranting about how the scent of warm apple cider personally offends them. Their tense body language screams *we don't belong here.*

"Ralph, we need to go," I say, already tugging on Henry's sleeve. "I'll see you around."

Henry pulls me and Jensen around a stall, pressing my back against the solid wood while Jensen curiously sniffs around in the grass.

"You know I'm starting to dig this whole hide-and-seek vibe," he whispers, his face only a breath away from mine.

"Thank you," I whisper and interlace my fingers around his neck. "Having you here makes all of this a whole lot easier to handle."

"I aim to please," he mumbles and when his lips find mine, I forget all about the shitshow happening in my periphery. All I can think about is the taste of caramel on his tongue, and his cinnamon scent mixing with the smell of caramel in the air. About the way his hands roam my body and pull me closer to him, and the way he takes my damned breath away.

Before I know it, the sun slips behind the trees, and Harry switches on the string lights Lauren and I spent the last week hanging. They flicker to life one by one, casting a soft glow over the fair. I can't help the small smile that forms as I take it all in.

"It's beautiful," I whisper, my eyes drifting over the entire scene: the pumpkins carved by kids and attendees, stacked on hay bales and glowing softly as the daylight fades. Laughter carries through the air, mingling with the warm scent of every fall treat you could imagine.

I wish I could bottle this moment, keep it tucked away to revisit whenever I need it.

I take a deep breath. I've found my last piece. Now it's time to put it in its final place.

"You know what this feels like?" I whisper and gulp, trying to fight against the tears forming in my eyes.

"What?" Henry asks curiously, and I choke up as I answer.

"Home."

He presses a kiss to my temple, and I close my eyes, trying to savor this moment, the realization that I'm exactly where I've always wanted to be. Surrounded by people who love me, in a place that feels like home.

But suddenly, the shrill feedback of a microphone makes everyone jump and turn their heads to the little stage Kieran helped set up right in the middle of the town square.

Henry gives my hand a quick squeeze, and his whole body goes rigid with tension. This is it. The moment we figured would come.

"Are you sure about this?" he whispers, giving me the chance to back out. "We could still run off and ignore that this is happening."

"No," I object gently, taking a deep breath and squaring my shoulders. "I've had enough. I'm dealing with this today. For good."

"Okay," he says, with a proud smile playing on his lips. "I'll be right here, every step of the way."

"I know," I assure him then turn back to watch Marissa, who is now on the stage, her face distorted in a sugary, *I'll melt your face off*, grin.

Chapter 31

Nic

"May I please have your attention?" Marissa taps against the microphone, even though all eyes are already on her. She smiles brighter than as if she's about to give a toast at my wedding. I cross my arms in front of my chest, trying to brace myself for whatever she's cooked up.

I know what she's about to say will be attempts to tear me down, disguised as backhanded compliments. Even though that's how she's spoken to me all my life, and even though her opinions shouldn't matter, I know this is about to sting nonetheless.

"What the hell is going on?" Andrea whispers beside me, and Henry untangles my arms, grabbing my hand to pull me closer to the stage, the murmurs around us getting louder with every step.

"I want to thank you all for being so welcoming during our stay," she declares sweetly, putting her hand on her chest and pretending to blink away tears.

But from the way the mood shifts from carefree and happy to grim and *what the fuck does she want?* it's not giving her quite the reaction she was hoping for. Instead of cheers, there's whispering. Instead of hospitality, there are crossed arms and glares in her direction. Which is already making me feel a whole lot better. She can only thank herself for that. She didn't exactly become a town favorite over the past few days.

"And because you are all so nice, I think it is my duty to tell you who the new addition to your wonderful town really is."

We are still making our way to the front of the crowd, but I can't quite bring myself to lift my gaze from the ground. Shame weighs heavily on my shoulders for being the reason she's here, that she's disturbing the autumn fair for her own petty agenda. God, I wish the ground would open up to swallow me. Or her. I'm not picky.

"It means the world to us. Especially to me. Seeing my little sister surrounded by so many … kind, *trusting* people." She smiles wider, like she's tasting something bitter but trying to sell it as honey.

"I know she's made a big impression on this town," she continues dramatically. "She always does. That's kind of her thing, showing up somewhere new, pretending to be a different person. I used to think it was brave, honestly. Starting over, pretending none of the wreckage she leaves behind matters."

A murmur goes through the crowd and flashes from cameras light up the approaching night, making my heart beat into my throat and my hands clammy with anxiety. Henry gives my hand a reassuring squeeze, and when I look up at him, it's to a reassuring smile.

"And because you've all been kind, it's only fair to tell you more about the person you've embraced so wholeheartedly. In her last relationship," she says with a sorrowful shake of her head, "Nicola was … not faithful. She cheated on her fiancé only days before the wedding. We were all devastated. He was, *is*, a good man. And now he's heartbroken after getting so utterly humiliated."

I can't help but nervously giggle when she dabs beneath her dry eyes with a tissue she clearly brought up there only for this moment.

Damn, they've really dramatized and rewritten their version of events. It's almost funny.

She wipes another nonexistent tear off her face before she continues. "And then she disappeared. Walked away without a care in the world. No explanation. No apology. She left everyone who loves her behind. Especially me."

She takes a fake shaky breath right into the microphone for the full effect, while I straighten my shoulders and finally lift my chin.

When she catches my eye, I can see her almost breaking into a triumphant grin, but she catches herself at the last moment. At this point, the only thing I can do is let her dig a deeper hole, waiting for the perfect moment to push her into it.

"She left her poor fiancé with nothing and ran to be with *him*." She points at the two of us, and it's taking everything inside me to not burst into laughter when the crowd's murmur turns from confused to angry.

She might have had a chance if she'd only attacked me. But to pull Henry into this, a man who's lived here all his life, who everyone here has watched grow up into the wonderful man that he is today—that's when she completely loses the crowd.

"I came here thinking maybe we could reconnect as sisters. But watching her pretend nothing happened? Making herself the victim? It's not only dishonest. It's dangerous. And if it saves even one person here from falling into the same trap we all did … then maybe it's worth speaking up." She clutches her chest, trying her best to sound sincere.

I don't think she realizes yet that there is not a single person in this crowd left who believes her. Courtney and Phil are shaking their head with amusement, while Mr. Peterson is inspecting his cane, probably wondering how to best use it as a weapon. Hell, even Amanda's jaw is set in anger, and she's basically the queen of being unbothered.

I motion to Lauren, who has been waiting at an angle where Marissa couldn't see her, and she hands me a microphone, motioning for Kieran to cut the one on stage.

"You know, I have a slightly different version of events," I say into the microphone as I climb up the stairs to the stage, taking out my phone. She tries to cut in, her eyes narrowing at me when she realizes her microphone is dead.

Lauren has spent the past day cutting up all the incriminating recordings that we had of her and Jay. Initially, Lauren wanted to cut the videos into a music video and edit them into dancing clowns, but the rest of us agreed that would be overkill. In the end we settled on only using sound. All I need to do is hold my phone against the microphone and press play.

Now it's my turn to play the victim part—and I'm the, albeit former, sister that *actually* got paid and won awards for her acting.

I watch Marissa pale when she hears first Jay's then her own voice coming from the speakers, listening to snippets of the conversation they had during what was supposed to be my engagement party.

"Once the papers are signed and the period for an annulment is over, I'll divorce her, take half of her money, and we can be together. We talked about this, baby. I'm doing this for us."

"I hate having that bitch between us."

The whole crowd gasps, and I bite my lip to keep from grinning, as all of them turn to glare at Marissa. She is slowly but surely sinking into herself, probably wishing right about now for the ground to swallow her whole.

"Me too, babe. But I'll make sure she sets us up for life. We're going to take all the vacations we talked about—on her dime. Just imagine, the two of us on a beach in Hawaii, cocktail in hand, laughing at her miserable life."

The murmur grows louder, and I notice several people in the audience pulling out their phones to film the spectacle.

"People like her are meant to be used. She's always been a joke. Way too emotional and way too stingy with her money."

The camera flashes become crazier with every word coming from the speakers.

I'm sure we make an interesting image. Me the victim, blinking incessantly as I pretend to try not to cry, and Marissa next to me, utterly humiliated, paling until she could give the town ghosts Amanda keeps telling Lauren and me about a run for their money.

Once the recording ends, I lower my phone and bring the microphone back to my trembling lips.

"I used to love you dearly, Marissa, but I can't let you lie to all of these wonderful people," I say and clutch my heart. "You said it. They deserve the truth!"

She opens and closes her mouth, floundering harder than a fish on dry land as she tries to figure out how to come back from that. But before she can, Erik climbs the stage in his uniform, handcuffs shining in his hand.

"You're under arrest," he says dryly, opening them and Marissa stares at him with wide eyes, panic washing over her face.

"What?"

"You're under arrest," he repeats. "For identity theft, credit card fraud, disrupting what was so far a calm and nice event, defamation, and harassment. Please turn around and put your hands on your back."

"You can't do that," she protests, trying to wiggle out of his grasp, but he's got her locked up. "Do you know who I am?"

"Yes, I do, remember? I saw your ID when I escorted you out of the hotel," Erik chuckles, and a weight falls off my chest when I hear the *click* of the handcuffs locking. "You have the right to remain silent, and I recommend you make use of that."

"You can't do this!" Marissa shouts.

A sudden commotion breaks out in the back of the crowd, and I spot two of Erik's uniformed coworkers, snapping handcuffs onto Jay's wrists. He's trying to resist, but he's got no chance against the two men.

Before I can even fully process it, Henry is right beside me, his hand steady and warm on my shoulder. I lean into him without thinking, letting the weight of it all settle, knowing he's got me.

"This is the best moment of my life," I whisper, noticing him shake with silent laughter. "I hope Lauren is filming this."

"You did great," he murmurs proudly and kisses the side of my head, to a few *awwws* from the crowd that make me blush.

"You must stop them!" Suddenly my egg and sperm donors appear in front of the stage, faces distraught as they watch their golden-child daughter be escorted away by police.

"Excuse me, do I know you?" I lift my eyebrow at them.

Funny. It doesn't hurt as much as I thought it would. I spent the past few days, ever since Lauren came up with the plan, agonizing over how this would go.

But now that it's here? It's cathartic.

Sure. Seeing the people I used to call my parents still stings. There is still an underlying voice in my head, but instead of a constant scream of *why don't they love me?* there is only a whisper. It is there, and I fear it will always be there.

But the voice reminding me of all the wonderful people who have my back is much louder now.

"How dare you talk to us that way? We are your parents!" my mother curses, and my sperm donor, face red with anger, remains silent—probably fearing that he'll incriminate himself if he opens his mouth.

"Parents?" I stare at them, pretending to be confused, then amusedly glance at Lauren and burst into a giggle. "Lauren, these people claim to be my 'parents.'"

Lauren hurries over immediately, face scrunching in anger as she quickly positions herself between them and me.

"Really?" she asks, pretending to be as astonished as I did. "I mean, parents are supposed to love their children unconditionally, aren't they?" Her eyes jump between me and them. "I'm sorry, but you must have the wrong person."

"You dare do this to us after all we did? Is that your thanks for us raising you?" my father grits out between clenched teeth, and I shake my head.

"You did the bare minimum. You don't get to claim a favor from me for it now," I say with an overly sweet smile on my face. "And I'm not going to do shit. Marissa has committed fraud and theft on a felony level. For once, not even you can get her out of this. My lawyers will throw the whole extent of the law at her, and there is not a single thing you can do to stop it. And you know what? I will be able to sleep better at night for doing so."

My heart pounds loudly, and I can't help but let out the nervous laughter that's been bubbling in my belly. "And just so you know, if you ever talk to me again, ever try to contact me again, I have my lawyers on speed dial and will record any attempts."

"You are such an ungrateful—" my dad talks himself into rage, but I demonstratively lift my phone and shake my head at him with a sneer when he immediately shuts up.

"I'm done being a doormat," I say exhaustedly. "Fuck you. Have the life you deserve, far away from me."

"How dare you!" my mother jumps in, trying to walk toward me and climb onto the stage, but my father holds her back.

I don't waste one more breath on them and turn around, letting Henry lead me off the stage. As soon as we are out of sight from the crowd, I break into the biggest grin and Lauren lifts her hand for a huge high five.

"God, I feel so free," I say, letting my head fall back and releasing the tension I'd held on to since Marissa noticed her own voice coming from the speakers.

"I'm so proud of you," Henry mumbles and presses his lips against the top of my head, which immediately makes the tears finally overflow. God, I don't know what to feel. Anxiety falls off me, but there's still that numb sting, still sadness and anger but also pride and relief, all coming together at once.

"We all are," Lauren assures me and reaches for my hand. "You were amazing."

Kieran runs over to us and throws his arms around all three of us in a chaotic hug.

"Caleb's at the front, but even he was impressed. I think I even saw a smile on his face," he tells us excitedly then breaks into laughter.

"That's like the highest badge of honor," Henry whispers, and I can't help but grin, even though tears are still streaming down my cheeks.

"I fucking did it," I whisper.

"It's over," Lauren says, and I shoot her a smile.

If only this didn't seem too good to be true.

Chapter 32

Henry

"It's time to celebrate!" Kieran shouts in the distance, holding up two bottles of what I assume is hard liquor. Laughing and stumbling in a way that makes me worry about the alcohol he's holding, he makes his way to our group.

The rest of the autumn fair had gone on without a hitch. A few paparazzi attached themselves to Nic and me, photographing our every move, which lead to us leaving with Lauren shortly after the whole Marissa ordeal. Kieran stayed behind and reported of some whispers, but overall, the fair apparently went back to business as usual quickly.

I have no doubts our faces will be plastered over gossip magazines for the next few days. But hey, it's free advertisement for my vet clinic, at least, and I'm not going to complain about that.

Lauren and Nic quickly got the idea to get everyone together to celebrate our plan working, and now we're here, sitting by the water. The lake is calm and dark under the night sky, as we huddle around a campfire since the big one in town is likely still riddled with paparazzi. Jensen is in Nic's home, keeping an eye on the cats.

The mountains in the distance are only faint shapes now, their edges soft against the stars. Chaos's last resting place is not too far off, which I find fitting, considering how Nic's and my story began with her.

A small bonfire crackles gently between us, casting a warm glow over the circle, and for a moment, it's just easy. Quiet. Comfortable.

"How are you feeling, superstar?" Kieran asks Nic, happily accepting one of the beers Caleb is handing him and cracking it open.

"Light as a feather," Nic answers him with a wide grin. Nothing has been able to wipe it off her face since we arrived at her house and the realization that Jay and Marissa actually got arrested settled.

"I feel amazing." She leans her head against my shoulder, and I put my arm around hers.

"You look like you do," Kieran grins and sets down his beer. "Ooh, Caleb, you going all caveman here? That's kind of hot."

Caleb only grunts in response. He went over to Nic's house to get more wood for our bonfire, carrying a bunch of it over his shoulder, subtly showing Kieran his middle finger.

Lauren chuckles, and reaches for one of the bottles Kieran brought, squinting her eyes as she's trying to decipher the label in the flickering firelight.

"Do we already know how it played out?" Kieran wonders, glancing around our circle curiously.

"Couldn't bring myself to Google my own name," Nic explains and looks up at me, squeezing my knee. "So Henry checked."

"Ooh, understandable," Kieran and Lauren say in unison, and I shake my head at them with a chuckle.

"And I'm happy to report, it worked out exactly as we hoped," I declare and cough when the fire suddenly goes out right as the soft wind changes and blows the smoke right in my face. "All the headlines are along the lines of, 'Jealous sister tries to humiliate superstar,' or along those lines," I explain with air quotations, making Nic and Lauren giggle. Caleb is ignoring us, though I'm sure he's listening in as he tries to relight the fire.

"There are even some videos, and the comments are tearing Marissa to *pieces*."

"Hell yes," Lauren punches her fist in the air, then gives in to Kieran's high five. "Ah, I love winning."

"And also, I now have a lot of cute pictures of Nic and me at the autumn fair." I grin and press a kiss to the side of her head. "So, who really won here?" I already know exactly where to hang one of them. It was taken when I won the plush for her, right as I leveled the little plastic gun, with Nic and Jensen behind me.

But what makes me want to print a wall-sized version out and plaster it all over my home is not Jensen, or the fact that I'm really damn handsome when I'm trying to aim with a plastic gun. No, it's the way she's looking at me, with that smile in her eyes, a certain softness in her expression.

It's already my phone background until I can shoot a better picture of her.

"Stop it, you two!" Lauren throws the cap of her beer toward us, and I grin before picking it up and putting it into my pocket.

"I'm not going to apologize for that," I point out, laughing, and take a sip of my beer. "Also, my phone has been going off with people who want Nic's new boyfriend to shove his arm up their cow's ass. I'm taking today as a win."

"Who would've thought the two of them would end up doing you a favor?" Kieran says with a chuckle, suddenly cheering when Caleb finally manages to relight the fire. "There you go, boss man! Great job!"

"We knew you could do it," Lauren adds with a grin. "Never had a doubt."

"Suuure," Caleb mumbles and rolls his eyes, before he sits down next to her, and I could swear her cheeks turn a darker shade. Though it's hard to say if it's because of Caleb, or because the fire is so hot.

"What's going on with those two?" I whisper to Nic, and she shoots me an amused smile, leaning closer to whisper right into my ear.

"She has a crush on him. What about Caleb?"

I watch Caleb for a moment. He's as quiet as always, but his face has gotten softer. I can't see the usual crease between his eyebrows or that perpetual frown on his forehead. He seems almost content, and then I see his eyes darting over to Lauren.

It only lasts for the faintest moment, and immediately after, he resumes staring at the fire, a faraway expression on his face.

"I think he's crushing too," I whisper back, and gently nip her earlobe, making her giggle.

There have been enough pictures and camera flashes today, but I still can't help myself and keep my phone ready—this mood, this carefree celebration, deserves to be remembered. And judging by how tipsy Lauren and Kieran are, I'm not so sure their brains will keep up.

"Get a room, you two!" Kieran shouts from the other side of the fire, and we bring a bit of space between us. It's hard to keep my hands off her when I'm sober, but give me a few beers, and I'm probably never letting her go again.

"By the way, who's going to clean up the autumn festival stuff?" he asks curiously. "Do other people volunteer afterward?"

To my surprise, Caleb jumps in to answer. "They hire people for that."

"Really?" Lauren asks, eyebrows furrowed as she tilts her head in surprise. "They have the budget for that and new decorations? You townspeople put a lot of money into this."

"Oh, that's where the proceeds from it go," I point out, making Lauren even more confused.

"Harry made it a nonnegotiable part of the budget," Caleb explains gruffly. "In previous years the decorating volunteers had to spend half a week with detangling everything the clean-up-volunteers only threw in boxes. So now he hires a company to do it."

"After the autumn fair, no one could be bothered to pack the decorations away properly," I tell add. "Though that might also have been because Harry insisted on taking down the decorations the next day already, when half of the town was still hungover. He tried waiting a few more weeks, but nobody would volunteer then. So, yeah, he hires a crew to put everything away neatly. Now we can get right to decorating without destroying half the garlands during the detangling process. It always lead to delays."

"This town is so strange," Nic says, kind of in awe. "But I enjoy this strange," she quickly adds, and Lauren nods in agreement.

"It fits our strange," she says, shooting a grin at Kieran in silent solidarity.

"Oh, absolutely," he agrees and takes a sip of his beer. "I don't think we could have picked a better place to move to."

The night goes on, and we stay huddled around the campfire. Caleb somehow ends up as the self-appointed fire warden, fetching more wood whenever the flames slowly die down and making sure we have flames, not only a glow.

And when it hits two in the morning, and yawns start replacing real conversation, he's the one who heads down to the lake for water, dousing the fire and covering the whole pit with sand. Just to make sure we're not accidentally starting a forest fire.

"Look at you," Lauren slurs, then breaks into a giggle-fit, clearly drunk. "Responsible!"

We made the bonfire between Nic's and Lauren's homes, and if it were still light out, we could also see Kieran's further down the lake shore.

"Damn, it's dark," Kieran also sounds less than sober. I think I hear him fall off the log he sat on, as my eyes get used to the dark.

I've got a good of a buzz going, but nothing compared to the three city folks in our group. Caleb watches them with quiet amusement, the same way a kindergarten teacher would watch their children badly explain their parent's job.

Nic is curled up against my side, trying to stifle a yawn into my jacket. Meanwhile Lauren can't be more than one blink away from also slipping off the log she's perched on.

"Will you two be all right?" I ask as I stand up, pulling Nic with me, shaking my head when she whispers a complaint.

"Hey, sweetheart, open your eyes."

She does, not willingly, but grinning lazily when she sees my face. "You're so pretty," she says and lifts her hand to poke my cheek. But her aim is terrible, and she almost pokes my eye, so I catch her hand and keep it in mine.

"We're fine," Lauren mumbles, and tries to get up, almost immediately losing her balance and stumbling right into Kieran's arms.

"That's okay. I got you," he says lazily and bursts into a giggle. He then tries to get up, still holding onto Lauren, which is not working out too well.

"I'll get the two of them home," Caleb says, and I give him a worried glance.

"Are you sure? Let me get Nic inside, and I can help you."

"I got this," he assures me.

"Are you okay to drive?" I tilt my head and narrow my eyes at him until he nods.

"I had one beer, Henry. I'm good."

"Really? Because Nic has a guest room," I point out, but he shakes his head. "I knew you were scared of the ghost cat." He answers by scratching his cheek with his middle finger, right before readjusting his cap. "Okay. If you end up needing a place to crash after all, you've got my number."

I pull Nic flush against me, the same way we walk around town: With her arm around my waist and mine around her back. Taking a few cautious steps, I almost carry her along. It works though.

Meanwhile, Caleb's eyes dart between Kieran and Lauren, both of whom are smiling lazily at him.

"How strong is your stomach?" he asks Lauren, and she quickly shakes her head, still grinning.

"Not strong at all. Why?"

"You?" he asks Kieran, ignoring her.

Kieran puffs his chest and quickly proclaims, "Stronger than steel," and without any further ado, Caleb steps closer to him and leans down. Then he throws Kieran over his shoulder like he weighs nothing.

"Don't you dare throw up on me."

"Oh my God!" Kieran exclaims, arms flailing. "Why is the world upside down?"

"Damn, that's sexy," Lauren says, with wide eyes and mouth agape.

"Hold on to my arm," Caleb demands roughly, and she skips over to his side with a wide grin, hugging his arm tightly to her chest.

"Take your phone flashlight and make some light," he directs her, and she does as he says. Meanwhile, I'm wondering where he learned to manage drunk people this well.

"One day, you're going to make an amazing dad," I tell him with a grin, and he shoots me a glare.

"Goodnight, everyone," I say and give them a wave, slowly maneuvering Nic up to her house.

"Night, night!" Lauren singsongs, while Kieran shoots us a grin and an upside-down wave.

I'm not saying Wayward Hollow was boring before the three of them moved here, but it's gotten one hell of a lot more entertaining since they did.

Chapter 33

Nic

"Your house is cute!" I say as I walk in. Thanks to Cinnamon and Pumpkin, our hangouts have been happening mainly at my place—they're not quite as easy to take along and are not nearly as happy about it as Jensen, so it made the most sense.

A house is the best reflection of a person, and I was more than curious about Henry's. And what can I say? It's very close to what I expected. A simple, modern cabin style with solid wood furniture and a lovely, light ambience.

"Thank you," he says with a sheepish smile, his hand rubbing the back of his neck, and I can't help but grin. He's nervous about having me here.

He's adorable when he's nervous.

He leads me to his living room. It's so cozy. So homey. So … *him.* It has an effortless kind of comfort—as if every single part of it was chosen carefully, picked intentionally over time.

It is all warm wood tones, and one entire wall is made of glass, somewhat similar to my living room, only his faces the forest instead of a lake. Golden light spills through the trees, and I can see a movement in one of the forests bushes a few feet away from his window front—maybe the wind, maybe a bunny, maybe a killer. Who knows?

"Oh God. Just imagine you look out there and suddenly see glowing yellow eyes," I shudder and Henry bursts into laughter.

"The same could happen at your place."

"Nope," I tease him, lifting my chin and glance up at him with fake defiance. "I've got a free view of the lake. No animals can sneak up to my home without me seeing. But this here"—I make a vague motion to his glass wall—"is basically an invitation for the big bad wolf."

"Good thing Jensen will protect me," Henry chuckles, and I lean against him happily as we watch the sun set. Through the window's reflection, my eyes scan the rest of his living room, too curious to focus on nature's daily spectacle.

There is a stone fireplace and shelves lining the other walls stuffed with books on animal anatomy and photography. There's a gallery wall opposite it, with all kinds of images framed in simple wooden and a few golden-painted frames.

Curiously, I step out of his arms, walking closer to get a clearer view.

The first one that catches my eye is a portrait of Jensen. Golden light makes him radiate like an angel, his eyes closed with bliss, and I could swear he's smiling. It screams *serenity*, the perfect image to show how at peace Jensen is with Henry.

The second one is of him and Jensen. They're posing in front of a mountain backdrop in the distance. Henry's kind face contains a bright smile as he kneels next to his dog, who's gazing up at him like he hung the moon.

The third one is of a mountainscape that seems familiar. But the trees are covered in snow, reflecting light off the rising sun and painting the whole scenery a lovely pink.

"Did you take all of these?" I ask, completely in awe. I think I could spend all day staring at them.

"Yes," he says shyly and walks closer until he's right behind me, his arms snaking around me and his fingers locking right over my belly. I sigh, all too happy to lean against him and let him hug me tight.

"They're beautiful," I whisper. The air is thick with emotion, all my senses tuned into him when I see another image that hits me like a sudden burst of cold rain. "Are those your parents?"

"Yes," he admits after a moment of hesitation.

For a second, I close my eyes, waiting for the familiar pain to wash over me. The realization of what I've lost, the Band-Aid to be pulled off once again, only this time … it doesn't come. As if I've pulled it off twenty times already, and the glue barely sticks to my skin anymore.

"They'd love to meet you," Henry whispers, and I tilt my head. Unexpectedly, his words don't cause a panic. No, instead, I find my insides filling with warmth, and I experience the sudden urge to meet the people who have raised this perfect person behind me.

"I'd love to meet them," I whisper back, and he freezes for a moment in surprise. "Someday."

"Someday," he repeats and hugs me tighter. "How about a movie?"

"You know what?" I turn my head and glance at him over my shoulder. "A movie sounds perfect."

Henry's arm is warm around my shoulders, and the movie is … okay, I guess. Even Jensen already left the room, too bored with it. We settled on an action-filled, uncomplicated movie, but I stopped paying attention a while ago.

All I can focus on is the way his fingers are tracing slow circles on my hip. Each exhale brushes the top of my head, and I'm hyperaware of the slow, steady rise and fall of his chest, the tow of us breathing in rhythm without even trying.

He's so close. So familiar. And I want him so badly I could scream.

Thank God he apparently shares the same sentiment—he keeps glancing at me, his gaze staying on me longer and longer.

"You know, you're pretty distracting," he finally murmurs against my hair, and I can't help but chuckle.

"More distracting than explosions and semi-good acting?" I ask, turning to look at him with what I hope is a charming smirk and not a *please take me now* expression.

Instead of an answer, thumb and index finger find my chin, and he turns my face, pressing his lips against mine in a soft, searching kiss. He's testing the waters, but I've already cannon-balled in.

I kiss him deeper, turning my body until I'm in his lap. His hands immediately find my ass and give it a tight squeeze that makes me grin into our kiss.

My fingers slide up his chest, chasing the sound he makes—a low growl that vibrates against my palm as he pulls my core flush against him. A sound somewhere between a gasp and a giggle escape my mouth.

"Way more," he whispers and kisses me again, his tongue demanding entrance to my mouth and kissing the sanity right out of me.

I can't help but shiver, burying my hands in his hair as a tiny moan falls from my lips right onto his.

God, I want him. Badly.

"You're so sensitive," he mumbles with a grin, dragging his mouth down my jaw and kisses a path toward my neck.

"You say that like it's a bad thing," I whisper, already breathless.

"It's a *perfect* thing," he objects, sliding his hands under my shirt. "I love how you respond to me. It drives me fucking insane."

I gasp, tilting my head back, giving him more space, and he doesn't waste a second. His lips find that spot right below my ear that makes my whole body twitch, and I moan when his hands slide higher, warm and possessive and like they belong there.

"Jesus, Henry," I whisper, writhing in his lap, rubbing against his hard cock beneath his sweatpants. It makes my brain short-circuit. That delicious pressure. His heat right between my legs.

His breath hitches, and then he's pulling back only enough to watch me—eyes dark, pupils blown wide, his lips deliciously red from our kiss.

"You're driving me crazy, sweetheart," he says, voice low and rough. "You always do."

I can't help it—I smile, a little smug and aching and completely gone for him.

"Then do something about it," I dare him breathily, biting my lip. "Please?"

And he does. Without hesitation, he grabs the hem of my shirt and yanks it up over my head, flinging it somewhere behind us without a second thought. His gaze drops, drinking me in as if I'm the most beautiful fucking thing he's ever seen.

"Sweetheart ..." His voice falters. "You're so ... fuck, I don't have words for you."

"You don't need to have words," I whisper, already reaching for his shirt. "Just touch me."

That's all the permission he needs. He surges forward and kisses me with enough intensity to ruin me, deep and demanding. One hand cups my breast through the thin lace of my bra while the other slips down, popping the button on my jeans open.

I break the kiss only long enough to murmur, "Bedroom?"

But he shakes his head, breathing roughly. "No. Here. Right now."

He pulls my jeans down my hips, and I get up to quickly shimmy and kick them off. My heart thunders, and my skin prickles as his gaze burns into me. He takes my hand, and before I know it, my back is on the couch, and he's climbing between my legs.

The air is electric against my skin, and then his hands are on my thighs, parting them, pulling my thigh over his shoulder and pressing a kiss to my skin then gently sets it down again.

He sinks down, kissing a slow path up to my stomach, and glances up at me as he hooks his fingers in the waistband of my panties.

"You want this?" he asks, voice so quiet it sends shivers down my spine.

"Yes," I press out without any hesitation. "Fuck, yes."

He smiles, mischievous and loving all at once, and pulls them off unceremoniously. He leans in and—holy fucking shit.

The first flick of his tongue makes me moan softly, hips bucking, and he groans against me as if he *lives* for it, like nothing makes him happier than my pussy.

"Just like that, baby." His tongue is slow and steady, circling my clit just right, and every time I gasp or whimper, his grin widens.

"So sweet. You're so fucking responsive. I could do this all night."

His hands are firmly on my thighs, holding me open. He drives me further into madness. Every movement under control. I grab his hair, bury my fingers in it. Hold on tight. All I can feel is him.

His mouth. His hands. His breath on my wet pussy.

Every thought melts away.

"Fuck, Henry. Gonna come!" Moaning, I dig my fingers deeper into his hair. He doubles his efforts, moving faster.

"Do it," he mumbles, slipping a finger inside me. The way he glances at me through my legs should be criminal. "Come for me, sweetheart."

So I do, and when it ripples through me, it's not quiet. It tears through me in waves. I shout his name, loud and messy, but he doesn't stop. He keeps licking me through it, keeps whispering how beautiful I am when I come, how proud he is of me, how much he loves hearing me fall apart this way.

Eventually, I have to push at his shoulder, trembling and breathless. I think I'll explode for real if he keeps it up. He kisses my inner thigh, then my hip, then kisses his way back up my body, eyes shining with pride and mischief.

"You're ridiculous," I pant, grinning like I've lost my mind, which, to be fair, I probably did somewhere around the second flick of his tongue. "Completely unfair. You know that, right?"

Henry stares at me as if I told him the earth is flat, eyebrow lifted curiously. "Unfair?"

"You're out here pulling Olympic-level mouth work while I'm just trying to survive a Tuesday," I say breathlessly, making him laugh.

"You were thriving a second ago."

"Thriving is generous. I was feral. I think I levitated at one point." I bury my hands in his hair and pull him in to kiss him hard. "But don't think I'm not retaliating."

"God, please retaliate."

I tug at the waistband of his sweats. "I'm about to. You can keep talking, or you can help me get these off."

He obliges, lifting his hips as I strip him down and *wow*. I'm still somehow surprised by how *hot* he is, even now. His hands slide to my thighs as I turn us around and settle over him, but I pause, only hovering, teasing.

"You're not going to monologue about how pretty I am like this?" I raise a brow, a smirk tugging on my lips, rolling my hip over his cock. "No emotionally repressed love confessions? No poetic metaphors? Really slacking on the praise today, babe."

His hands tighten on my hips, eyebrows creasing in pleasure.

"You're the most beautiful thing I've ever seen," he presses out, biting the inside of his cheek. "And I'm about two seconds away from begging."

"That's better," I say with a grin, and palm his cock, keeping it steady as I finally, *finally* sink down onto him. As if I haven't been waiting for this all afternoon.

We both groan, and his head falls back against the couch, exposing his neck, and I lean in close, licking a path from his Adam's apple to his ear.

"God, I love this part," I whisper seductively, rolling my hips, only enough to make him twitch inside me. "The part where you lose your mind and forget your own name."

His laugh turns into a moan when I move, my hips slow and steady. It doesn't take me long to find a rhythm that makes him moan incoherently beneath me. And he lets me take my time, hands trailing up my back, eyes locked on mine. Telling me I'm the only thing that exists.

"Fuck, baby … look at you," he breathes, his tongue flicking out to wet his lips. "Riding me so good. I don't even know how I lived without this."

"Probably very boringly. With a tragic lack of orgasms."

"Oh, *definitely*."

I lean in and kiss him, slow and messy. "Then stop talking and let me finish what you started."

He doesn't argue, his grip tightening on my hips, giving me more support as I ride him faster. One of his hands lets go, but only to wander over my front and palm my breast roughly, before tracing a path to my pussy and circling my clit.

And when I come again, I come hard and loud while digging my nails into his shoulders. He follows right after, swearing into my mouth in a messy kiss, hands gripping me tight, as if he never wants to let go.

We collapse in a tangled, sweaty heap on the couch. A car explodes in the movie we completely forgot existed, strangely symbolic for the orgasm I just had.

I rest my head on his chest, catching my breath, legs still shaking, muscles burning after the workout I put them through.

"Okay," I mumble. "I vote next time, we skip the movie and get to the part where you turn me into a sentient puddle right away."

"Agreed," he says, brushing his fingers through my hair. "Although … I did kind of want to see how it ends."

I glance at the screen. "Spoiler alert: Guy punches another guy, fucks the pretty woman, and then something explodes. Boom. End credits."

"You're very wise."

"I contain multitudes. Especially post-orgasm."

"God, I love you," he says and presses his lips against my hair.

And suddenly the world stills. But then, just as suddenly, it explodes into a burst of color, my heart racing in my chest and tears springing into my eyes.

"Really," he confesses, and I glance at him, brain caught in a circuit. "I love how you ramble when you're nervous. How you try to hide it with sarcasm, but your eyes give you away every time."

"So you're saying my eyes are snitches?"

He chuckles. "Total snitches. And right now, they're telling me you feel similarly. But I'd really like to hear you say it."

I laugh, but it's wobbly, turning into a sob. Because the realization settles within me—he means it. He's not only saying it in a post-coital haze. He *means* it. And I know he does, because I saw it coming.

And I feel it back. I've felt it for weeks now, but I didn't want to say it first because … what if he didn't? What if he suddenly realized Marissa and Jay were right? What if I scared him off? What if I scared *me* off?

But here we are. Still tangled up on this stupid couch, bodily and emotionally naked, and it feels right. I belong here, on top of him, in his house, in this exact moment.

"I love you too," I say finally. Quiet. Steady. "Even if you think my eyes are traitors."

Chapter 34

Nic

"You don't look as happy as you should be," Lauren points out.

We're strolling through the streets of Wayward Hollow, soaking in the crisp autumn air after helping Amanda upload some pictures of new furniture to her website. It has rained the past few days, and even now, the sky is hidden behind thick layers of clouds that might be announcing an apocalypse.

Just what I need: some end-of-the-world vibes.

"I don't know," I say with a nervous shrug, my cold fingers playing with the hem of my shirt. "Everything went too good to be true." A deep sigh falls from my lips, and I shake my head.

"Marissa got her comeuppance on stage? Then she and Jay get arrested after it took Erik forever to build a case?" I lift my eyebrow, wondering if she doesn't see it. "It's very teenage rom-com made by Disney in the two-thousands, isn't it?"

"Now that you say it," Lauren agrees, tilting her head as she thinks. "That doesn't have to mean it's too good to be true."

"The 'everybody claps' happy end might be a cliché for a reason. And maybe it's nothing, but a part of me keeps waiting for the other shoe to drop," I explain, stopping by the flower shop to stare at their bouquets. Not that I could ever put up any flowers in my house without the ghostly or living cats pushing the vase off wherever I put it. But hey, I can have a look, right?

They have the most beautiful autumn wreaths in their window, and I can't help but stare at them, mesmerized. That could work. Then again, Chaos can also push frames off the wall—she'd probably get a wreath off its nail too.

"God, this is beautiful. Buy it," Lauren says, like the little devil on my shoulder that she is, but I shake my head.

"They're fresh flowers. It's going to sound irrational as fuck, but they're going to die at some point in the near future, and I can't deal with"—I make a vague motion with my hand—"sadness."

"Chaos never really left, though, did she?" Lauren points out, and I shake my head.

"That's different. Flowers can't exactly haunt me."

"Touché," she says with a giggle, and pulls me away from the window, linking her arm with mine again.

"Why do you think this whole thing isn't over?" Worry seeps through her voice, but I can only shrug.

"I can't pinpoint it. It's a gut feeling. The two of them, they're *lucky*," I try to explain, my voice turning to disgust on the last word. "Really damn lucky. I mean, how else do you think they've made it this far without landing themselves in jail or six feet underground?"

"I don't know. Maybe their gaslighting abilities? And being somewhat attractive?" Lauren says, tapping her lips as she thinks. "Nope. Can't think of any other reason."

"For some reason, the universe has decided that those two would be its favorite people. Especially Marissa." I lay my head back and take a deep breath. "Marissa loses her job? The next, way better opportunity comes along a day later. She has a car accident? It's minor enough for nothing to happen to her. But by chance, it's a rich dude who throws enough money at her to buy a new car, to settle without involving the police or insurance."

"Damn," Lauren curses and I nod.

"It's infuriating."

"But I can't imagine this is something that luck is going to pull her out of," Lauren says, but I shake my head.

"Trust me. Stranger things have happened." A shiver runs down my spine like a bad omen knocking at the door, but I push it aside. "Now, enough about those two. I'm probably overreacting; I need to manifest that this thing is over. No more doubts."

I close my eyes and take a deep breath, trying to shake the negative energy off me. And when I open my eyes again, I'm calmer. I ignore the amused expression on Lauren's face.

"How is your house coming along?" I change topics quickly. "Are you regretting the DIY approach yet?"

"Oh, hell yes! Started to regret it one hour in," Lauren says way too quickly, and I burst into laughter.

"I'm afraid that craftsmanship is not one of my yet-to-be-discovered talents. So far, I've put a chair together backward, my table collapsed the moment I finished putting my food on it, and a bunch of stuff I ordered isn't getting delivered anytime soon," she adds, making a vague gesture with her hand. "Some boat got itself stuck in some kind of canal that apparently is *super* important for furniture delivery. Who knew?"

"Oh, wow, luck is really on your side for this one."

"You have no idea." She exhales a deep sigh. "For now, I have my bed, I have a couch … and a lot of blank walls to stare at."

"My slightly less-blank walls are always there for you, along with my two extremely dumb kittens who adore you."

"Oh, come on. They aren't that dumb," Lauren says with a pout, but I shake my head, biting back a chuckle.

"You know how Pumpkin gets whiny when I'm gone? Yesterday, she turned to the window when I sat on the couch, and I swear to God, after fifteen seconds, she started meowing. I'm telling you, she had a full-on heartbreak." Lauren's lips press together as if she's swallowing an *awww*, her eyes wide as I continue.

"And when I called her name, she turned around, and bam"—I snap my fingers—"everything was okay again. I am 100 percent convinced that in those fifteen seconds, her itty-bitty little brain completely forgot I was there. And then she got sad."

"That just means she loves you!"

"I know she does," I say with a giggle. "And I love those two as well. Ten out of ten. If I had to, I would die for them, but it doesn't change the fact that they both have the IQ of a pebble."

"Hopefully you won't have to die for them anytime soon," Lauren interjects, and I roll my eyes.

"Not planning on it, but thank you, I guess." We never talked about it, but instinctively, our legs bring us to Caleb's café to end our stroll with a nice, warm coffee.

"Who else would I talk to in this town?" She grins, and I nudge her with my elbow.

"What about Caleb?" I lift my eyebrow at her, noting her cheeks turning even darker.

"He's not exactly a talkative guy, in case you haven't noticed." She tries to play it cool, but I've known her long enough to know she's faking it.

"Oh, he is though," I point out, narrowing my eyes at her. "Maybe not quite with words, but I think he's pretty expressive."

"Maybe I haven't really paid attention to that," Lauren says, lying through her teeth as her blush deepens even more.

I giggle and nudge her with my elbow again. "You should go for it, girl."

"One day, maybe." She breathes out a deep sigh. "But today is not that day. I'm living vicariously through you. That's enough for now."

She opens the door to Caleb's café, and I watch her walk in, confused. It would be so much fun. We could have double dates. But I guess if it's not meant to be right now, it's not meant to be.

Taking a deep breath, I follow her, greeting Caleb behind the counter with a happy little wave that he only answers with a grunt, and make my way to our usual table.

Chapter 35

Nic

"Kieran!" I whisper-shout over the other murmuring patrons at Caleb's, waving him over to our table.

His face lights up when he sees us, and he quickly waves at Caleb before making his way over to us.

"He's basically a golden retriever with tattoos, isn't he?" I whisper as I watch him weave through the tables.

"Oh, absolutely," Henry says with a chuckle and takes a sip of his coffee.

"You're so right," Lauren adds, turning around to watch him too. "I can totally imagine him having a fluffy golden tail wagging behind him."

He slides into the booth next to Lauren, and the two immediately fall into a heated discussion about our Friendsgiving dinner. Both have extremely strong opinions about what food we should have.

"No, no, no, I think we should *fry* the turkey," Kieran demands immediately. Lauren rolls her eyes, taking a deep breath before launching into a tirade about why baking it would be better. Her strongest argument is that none of us have ever fried a turkey, and it's much more likely to burn to a crisp than come out edible.

"How was your day?" I ask Henry softly, leaning my head against his shoulder.

He's such a touchy man. The moment I'm close, his arm sneaks around my shoulders or my waist, like he can't help himself. He always pulls me in, and always presses a kiss to the side of my head or my forehead as a part of our greeting ritual now.

And as much as I love holding hands, this? This wins. It's warm, snuggly, and has the tiniest hint of possessiveness, his way of silently telling the world, *She's taken, move along*.

The forehead kisses have quickly become my favorite gesture of his. God, I'm spoiled. Here he is, showing the whole world I'm his, while I don't even have a proper nickname for him yet.

Babe. Honey. Muffin.

They're all just … not hitting right. But I'm determined to find one.

Because the way he calls me sweetheart? It gives me warm fuzzies.

I kind of live for it, and for his possessive streak. Especially now that a few nosy paparazzi pop up in town from time to time, clearly bored and hoping for another scandal.

Too bad for them, the most exciting thing they've caught is me walking Jensen, visiting Henry at work, and the two of us strolling around happier than a Hallmark couple, arm in arm, unbothered and utterly uneventful.

Come to think of it, it's been a few days since the last one showed up. Maybe they finally had enough.

"Oh, you know"—he grins—"the usual. There was a sheep that got stuck in a fence that had some superficial wounds. A horse with a pebble in its hoof, a cat that needed its claws clipped. And a cow about to explode. The usual."

"Hold on, hold on," I say, turning in my seat to glance at him, gently petting his hand as I repeat slowly, "A *cow* about to *explode*? I'm going to need details on that."

"Some cows have digestion issues that lead to a buildup of gas," he explains patiently.

I listen closely. God, I never thought I'd care about cow farts this much, but I'm hanging on to his every word as if there's nothing else I'd rather know.

"And then what? They just *pop* like a balloon?"

"Before that can happen, we put in a small vent to let the air out," he explains, and my face stretches into a grimace, nose scrunching as I try to imagine that. "Back in college, a few guys tried to light the escaping gas on fire, which would work in theory, I guess, but our instructors quickly jumped in."

"That sounds painful," I point out and he nods.

"Not as painful as being so bloated you're about to explode." He smiles and steals the little biscuit from my saucer.

"In the afternoon, a woman came in with the cutest bunnies," he whispers, his eyes drifting to Lauren and Kieran, who are now deep in a debate about the best mashed potato recipe. "All long ears and fluff. One of them was brown, with light sprinkles all over its front. Totally reminded me of cinnamon."

"Aww. Maybe they were brothers in another life," I say dramatically, and he grins.

"Maybe."

My eyes drift toward the front door when the bell chimes, and I freeze for a second, surprised to see Erik walk in wearing his uniform.

"What is he doing here?" I whisper, eyebrows knitting in confusion. Henry follows my gaze, and frowns.

"Huh. I thought he stopped drinking coffee after two."

"Seriously? How do you know that?" I ask, surprised, shaking my head when he only gives me a pointed look, the corners of his mouth twitching. "God, in this town, everyone's up in everyone's business. I love it."

"Hell yes we are." Henry leans closer, whispering in my ear in a low voice, "I know that Mr. Peterson had a New Year's resolution to stop drinking coffee entirely. He lasted about two days." His grin turns evil. "The whole town also knows that our cute, kind flower shop owners are really into BDSM."

My eyes widen. "How in the *hell* do you—?" I can't even finish the sentence, staring at him, mouth agape. *That* kind of gossip also makes the rounds here?

Then again, Lauren and I *did* wonder if the town's dark secret was an underground kink commune.

"That's not important," he says, but I quickly shake my head in disagreement, narrowing my eyes at him.

"If anyone in this town *ever* finds out about *our* sexual preferences …" I hiss and point my index finger at him. "I'm going to feed you to the fishes. I'll tell everyone you demand to be called 'Mommy' or suckle your thumb when you come."

"All right, all right," he laughs, hands raised in surrender. "I'm not telling a soul. Calm down."

"Hey, Nic, do you have a minute?" Erik suddenly appears at our table and I glance up at him, surprised.

"Sure, Erik, what's up? Grab a chair, take a seat." His eyes scan the rest of the table before he shrugs and does exactly that.

"I'm guessing y'all don't have any secrets from each other?"

"Well, actually …" Lauren says and looks at me with a mysterious glint in her eye, and I just know she caught the tail end of our conversation.

So I throw a piece of my napkin at her. "No, we don't," I say louder than she did, turning my focus back to Erik. "Is everything okay?"

"I thought you should know. Someone posted bail for Jay and Marissa," he explains, his fingers drumming against the table.

My blood runs cold. For a moment, I forget how to breathe, and I instantly turn to Lauren, shooting her a glare that says *See? Second shoe dropped.*

"How?" is all I can ask, Henry's arm around me tightening its hold.

"We were going to hold them until tomorrow," Erik explains patiently. "The plan was to transfer them back to LA, where the actual crimes occurred. Since their co-conspirators would be there, and … well, we don't have the resources in Wayward Hollow to handle a case of that scale. But before we could do that, someone paid their bail, and we had to let them go."

"You *had* to let them go?" I ask, arms crossing tightly over my chest, hugging myself. "Erik …"

"I'm sorry." He lifts his hands apologetically. "I promise, Nic, there was nothing I could do. But the court date in Los Angeles is set for next week, and if they don't show, they will have a shitload of problems."

His lips lift in a sad smile.

"I've given them a very strong suggestion to leave town and not come back. But if they do, and they harass you again, please tell me immediately. I'll be all too happy to throw them right back into a cell, and I'm pretty sure half the precinct would cheer."

"So … I see they've been a pleasure in jail," I blatantly fish for information, but he shakes his head.

"Trust me, you don't want to know."

"I really, *really* do," I reply with wide puppy eyes, all but begging to know more. "This is the first time anyone besides me has seen their dark side. Let me have this joy. Hopefully, they embarrassed themselves."

"I still can't tell you how she demanded to have her holding cell decorated, claiming the feng shui was all wrong and that the 'energy in there was tragic,'" Erik says as he gives me a pointed look.

"Honestly, I can kind of respect that," Kieran points out, making the whole table burst into laughter.

"Or how she might have staged a one-woman protest by dramatically lying on the floor until someone brought her herbal tea. She lasted an hour."

I snort. "You're kidding."

"And, of course, I absolutely cannot tell you that she kept quoting legal dramas and saying 'Objection!' every time someone spoke. Including other inmates."

He gets up and glances at us over his shoulder, lifting his hand for a wave. "Totally cannot tell you any of that."

"Oh, yes." I grin, still imagining the whole thing vividly. It's softening the sting that came with knowing she's currently walking free. "Such a shame you couldn't tell me. Thank you, Erik."

"Of course," he says, turning and leaving.

"Shoe dropped," I can't help but point out to Lauren. I knew something would happen, knew the universe would extend another hand and pull her out of a shitshow she created. I just knew it.

Kieran and Henry glance at me, confusion written all over their faces, while I take a deep breath.

"Well … though I can't imagine they did, let's hope they learned their lesson," Lauren says weakly, in an attempt to cheer me up.

"You know, I've always admired your optimism."

God, I hope she's right.

Chapter 36

Henry

"Can we stay in and cuddle?" Nic asks me with wide eyes, her gaze darting between the couch and me. "I don't feel like being in public."

She's been crestfallen ever since Erik gave us the bad news, most of her usual spark has dimmed. As always, she tries to mask it with sarcasm, but I know her better: she's tired. Tired of dealing with her ex, tired of her sister, tired of never being able to check that box and be done with it.

It must be exhausting, never getting the clean break she deserves. Just when she starts to move on, something always pulls her right back into the mess.

"Of course," I assure her quickly, following her to the couch. Jensen, Pumpkin, and Cinnamon are already waiting for us there, glancing up from their naps as we join them.

I'd wanted to take her on another proper date. A quiet, cozy restaurant a few towns over, run by Iona, the sweetest Italian woman you'll ever meet, who also happens to make the best pasta within a five-hour radius. And yes, I absolutely wanted to impress Nic. But the moment Erik opened his mouth back at Caleb's, I knew that today wasn't going to be the day for that.

There is too much going on in that beautiful head of hers, too much anxiety for her to enjoy herself. What she needs right now is love, to cuddle with her cats and, hopefully, me, and some quiet as she processes her emotions.

"Come here," I say, lifting my arm once I'm settled on the couch. Without missing a beat, she grabs her blanket, drapes it over us, and snuggles into my side. The moment I pull her closer, her whole body relaxes against mine and a deep sigh falls from her lips.

"What are you in the mood for?"

"I don't care. You decide." She hands me the remote. "I don't want to use my brain."

She might claim she doesn't care what we watch, but I've learned to read the signs. A little nose wrinkle? Not a fan. Slight eye-widening? That's a maybe. Any kind of seat adjustment? That one's a winner—she's invested.

And after the day she's had, I figure it should be her pick, even if she won't verbalize it. So I scroll through our options, gauging her responses until I land on a cartoon. Sure enough, she snuggles even closer into my side, putting one of her legs over mine.

"This one sounds interesting," I say and press play.

"Really?" she asks, lifting her eyebrow at me, surprised. "I didn't take you for a cartoon guy."

"No, I totally am," I lie through my teeth, tossing the remote aside and pulling her other leg over my lap as well, drawing random patterns on her knees with my thumb.

It doesn't take the animals long to join our cuddle-ball. Jensen lies down over my feet, the not-so-little heating pad that he is, while Cinnamon climbs into Nic's lap and Pumpkin … well, Pumpkin is currently trying to climb the wall, not very successfully.

"God, that cat," Nic mumbles, watching her jump up. "Sometimes I watch her, and I could swear there's not a single thought behind those little eyes."

"Not a thought, but plenty of dumb ideas," I agree with a chuckle and watch as Pumpkin diverts her attention to her reflection in the window, promptly hissing at it.

Suddenly, Jensen bolts upright and takes off, sprinting out of the room while barking loudly.

"What the—?" I start, already on my feet, my heart rate picking up.

Then I hear it. The unmistakable sound of someone fiddling with Nic's front door lock, then a *thud* as that person tries to push or kick the door open.

My eyes snap to hers. She's completely still—wide-eyed and frozen in place, pale as a ghost.

"Are you expecting anyone?" I ask, my voice low, already scanning the room for a weapon.

She shakes her head.

"I have a gun," she whispers, and quickly jumps up, to run over to her cupboard, fumbling with a key hidden under one of the books and unlocking a drawer.

"You're not handling a gun in this state," I hiss when she takes it out with trembling hands, and she hands it to me.

I take it carefully, fingers steady despite the way my pulse is picking up and echoes in my ears. Dad taught me about guns in my teens. *"Just in case,"* he'd said. It hasn't come in handy until today, and holy fuck, am I now glad that he taught me.

I eject the mag, check the chamber, then give the slide a slow rack, to make sure everything is moving how it should.

It's in decent shape. Not new but well-kept. I slide the magazine back in and click the safety on, keeping the barrel pointed low.

"Go upstairs and lock yourself in a room," I whisper as we slowly and quietly make our way to the hallway, peeking around the doorframe to see what's going on. But all we can see are shadows.

"Henry, I'm not leaving you down here alone," she hisses back, furrowing her eyebrows and shaking her head.

I stare at her for a beat. Then nod. Quietly and resignedly. She's stubborn as hell. I'd be lying if I said I didn't find it oddly reassuring now. I take a deep breath and straighten up. Trying to exude self-confidence. I take a step into the hallway. The gun raised, aimed at the front door.

"Stay outside! We're armed!" I call out loudly, forcing myself to take deep breaths and keep my hands steady.

"Fuck you!" I hear a slurred male voice reply and shoot Nic a glance. Two words and we both know exactly who is trying to break in. Who is kicking down her door.

Pumpkin is hiding somewhere in the living room, but Cinnamon is next to Jensen. Her fur puffed up like a feather duster. Her ears flattened and tail twitching with laser focus on the door. Jensen is next to her. He doesn't move. He's coiled tight. A low growl rumbling deep in his chest.

"I'll say it one more time," I shout, rolling my shoulders as I prepare for the inevitable. "I have a gun. Go away now, or I'll shoot!"

But instead of an answer, the door bursts open, nearly tearing off its hinges from the pressure of Jay kicking it in. He looks feral: bloodshot eyes, wild movements, and anger seeping from his every pore. I'm not sure what he's on, but the guy is not sober.

"He kicked down the door, Erik. Please hurry," I hear Nic whisper behind me, and I breathe a quick sigh of relief. My brain had gone straight to defense mode—I hadn't even thought of calling the police.

"Stay right where you are!" I warn Jay, aiming the gun at him, but he shakes his head, taking a step toward us.

"I'm not leaving without what I deserve!"

I'm not even sure what his plan is. He doesn't have a weapon, only lifting his hands as if he's about to challenge me to a boxing fight. I bet this whole thing made a lot more sense in his head.

"Well, you're not taking anything from here," I snap, aiming straight at his groin, hoping that will stop him, but apparently, he's not overly concerned about his reproduction possibilities. What the hell? You'd think a guy would be somewhat protective of his dick.

Jensen is about to snap, growling and baring his teeth at the intruder.

"Don't you fucking tell me what to do!" Jay snarls, stumbling closer. "You fucking hillbilly son of a bitch!"

He grabs a vase blindly, weighing it in his hand to gauge its weapon-potential. Before I can act, he lifts it to throw it at me—and that's when Jensen launches. One loud bark, and then within the blink of an eye, his teeth are buried in Jay's arm.

"What the fuck?" Jay screams, surprised and in pain, staggering backward as Jensen refuses to let go. Did he seriously not see the big, snarling husky right in front of him?

"Get your fucking dog off me!" he shouts, letting the vase fall to the ground, where it shatters into thankfully big pieces and waves his arm, trying to shake Jensen off. But it only makes him bite harder. "This fucking hurts!"

"Why would I call him off?" I reply calmly, ever so slightly lowering the gun, silently relieved that I won't have a human life on my conscience today. And because my aim is really not the best.

"You said they weren't home!" a second voice snaps, and that's when I realize that Marissa is there, too, peeking around the broken doorframe with horror once she spots all the blood.

"Get your dog off me!" Jay whines, a stream of blood running down his arm. "He's going to tear my arm off!" I know this situation is serious and all that, but that almost makes me grin. Does he think dogs tear off limbs like alligators? God, I wish they did.

"Why do you always mess things up?" Marissa continues to curse at him. "Get out of my way, you idiot," Marissa snarls, trying to push past him, and trudges inside as if she owns the place.

I lift the gun again, about to tell her to get the fuck out, when I notice a warm presence next to me.

"Get out," Nic says coldly and steps up next to me, arms crossed in front of her chest. "We're armed. You're trespassing. And I think you underestimate how happy it would make me if Henry shot you."

"You don't mean that," Marissa says, with that same venomous smile she wore on stage at the autumn fair. Yet there's a tinge of desperation in her voice. "You have no idea what you—oh my God!"

Cinnamon—sweet, tiny, usually lazy Cinnamon—has *cannonballed* onto Marissa, claws extended as she digs them into her skin, scratching up her arms and Chanel shirt.

"This is awesome," Nic whispers, and I can only nod. The spectacle could be right out of a cartoon. "This has mad 'mob tries to kill the beast, and the furniture attacks them' vibes," she continues, clearly reading my mind and I chuckle.

"The live-action one though," I point out, making her giggle. I watch Marissa and Jay, ready to step in if they manage to grab one of the animals. But before they can do anything but whine and shout, the flicker of police lights appears in Nic's driveway.

"Oh, thank God," Nic whispers, and I finally lower the weapon completely, putting it on the ground in front of us.

"Henry, call off Jensen!" Erik shouts from his car, clearly fighting off his amusement at the scene.

I whistle sharply, and almost instantly, Jensen releases his grip, trotting over to me with blood on his chin and a proud smile. He's earned a pile of treats. I never trained him to attack, but he knows that whistle means *stop everything*.

Thank God he obeyed.

"Nic, would you mind getting your cat?" Erik asks, the corner of his mouth twitching as he radios for EMTs. Nic steps closer to Marissa, catching a scratch or two herself as she pulls Cinnamon off. As soon as Cinnamon realizes the attack has ended, she wriggles out of Nic's hold and darts into the living room.

"I assume they were trespassing?" Erik asks, and Nic nods immediately. I brush past them to carry Jensen over the spot where the vase broke. I don't want to risk him getting any small shards in his paws.

"Yes."

His eyes flick to the busted lock. "Destruction of property?"

She agrees again.

"Well, then, you're under arrest," he tells Jay, trying and failing to keep the amusement from his voice as he cuffs him. "Again."

"I need a doctor!" Jay exclaims dramatically, trying to wriggle out of Erik's grasp.

"Hell yes he does," Nic mutters beside me. "The *mental* kind."

Marissa is seething, steam practically coming from her ears, and there's a perfect, deep scratch down her face.

"You're under arrest too," Erik says, cuffing her. "Good thing I brought a backup pair. I had a feeling ..."

"You will regret this," she hisses at Nic, who only stares at her blankly, arms crossed in front of her chest.

A new influx of blue lights round the corner to her driveway. This time it's an ambulance, though. Damn, they're quick! Must be a slow evening, apart from pet-prevented break-ins. Erik brings the handcuffed couple over to them, to let them have a look at their injuries, and I see the exhaustion on Nic, weighing her down like a physical weight.

"Hope it leaves a scar on her face," she mumbles, and I put my arm around her shoulders, watching her slowly relax.

"We'll be gone in a bit," Erik assures us and pulls out his notepad. "Can you come in tomorrow to give a report?"

"Do we have to if I've got camera footage?" Nic asks, pointing to a pet cam in the hallway, and Erik quickly scribbles down an email address.

"Please send it here. The more we have, the better, so I recommend you still come in. Let's make this airtight."

"I got it." Nic lets out a deep sigh. "Thank you, Erik. And sorry for the trouble. See you tomorrow."

He catches up with the EMTs, but I decide that this has been enough action for tonight. I walk Nic into the living room, handing her the gun after engaging the safety so she can lock it up again.

Then I return to the hallway, quickly cleaning up the shards of glass, Hoovering the spot for good measure, and inspecting the door. To my surprise, it still closes and even locks properly—apparently Jay knows a thing or two about picking a lock. I'll have to make sure to get a deadbolt installed here.

When I return to the living room, I find Nic buried beneath a mountain of fur. Jensen is curled against her side, Pumpkin is on her chest, and even Cinnamon is perched nearby, a little shaken up. But her eyes are distant, fixated on something beyond the window, or maybe this realm.

"It's over," I whisper and drop to the couch beside her, pulling her into my arms and kissing the top of her head. "I've got you, sweetheart."

"I know," she murmurs through sobs, her tears soaking my shirt. "Thank you."

"Nothing to thank me for," I reply, kissing the top of her head again and holding her tighter. Though this time, it's for my sake. The adrenaline rushes out of me, making my hands tremble and a cold shiver run down my spine.

Fuck. I'd do anything for her.

Jensen jumps off the couch, nudging his nose against Nic's knee and she wipes away her tears before sliding off the couch and to the ground to hug him.

"You're my little hero," she coos exhaustedly, completely unbothered by the traces of blood around his mouth.

"So now even Jensen gets a nickname, and I still don't have one?" I tease her and get on the ground as well. Cinnamon joins us, rubbing her fur against my thigh, and I quickly scoop her up and hug her to my chest, where I she purrs happily.

Even through her tears, Nic shoots me a mischievous look.

"How about Gandalf? After this 'You shall not pass' stunt, that seems fitting. Or how about Rambo?" She tilts her head, probably thinking of even worse nicknames. "James Bond? I could shorten it to 'Jamie.'"

I shake my head, but the giggle that escapes her lips?

It's the sweetest damn sound I've heard all day.

Chapter 37

Nic

"To freedom. Again." Lauren says solemnly and lifts her coffee to the middle of the table.

"To freedom," I chuckle and clink my cup against hers. "Let's hope this time it lasts."

Kieran and Henry lift their mugs to join in. I just got the news that Jay and Marissa were transferred back to the city. Only this time, with no chance of bail and a few extra charges tacked on that will hopefully keep them locked up for a good long while.

Knowing their luck, I was half-expecting them to wriggle their way out of it somehow.

"I can't believe it's over," I whisper after taking a sip of my coffee, snuggling against Henry's side. "I stopped believing Marissa would experience any consequences somewhere between second grade and having to share my birthday cake with her."

"No more sense of impending doom?" Lauren asks, amusement playing at her lips, and I nod slowly.

"I'm still paranoid from time to time, but no, no more impending doom looming over me like a persistent dark cloud." I sigh happily and run my fingers through Jensen's fur. He's resting his head on my knee, whining for a treat, and since he went ahead and turned into a beast to defend my home for me? He's getting all the treats I can sneak to him.

"My parents don't care enough about me to show up at my doorstep, even with Marissa behind bars. And sure, they probably wouldn't have complained if her and Jay's plan had worked out and they'd gotten their hands on some of my money. But it's not as if they ever *needed* it."

I take a deep breath, curling my lips into a smile. God, I can finally breathe again. It's like a couple of gargoyles that had found a home on my shoulders have finally flown away, only leaving behind some cracks in my foundation that will hopefully heal with time.

"So, what's your plan with your newfound freedom?" Kieran asks curiously, throwing his biscuit up in the air and catching it in his mouth.

"I honestly don't know." I sigh, fingers tapping against my warm cup. "Playing with my two and a half cats, wondering if Chaos will lead even more animals to me." I take a sip of my coffee, cursing when it burns my lips. "Hell, maybe I'll pick up reading again. Now that my brain can grasp letters again instead of only pretending it does while I'm actually worrying about those who shall not be named."

Then I turn to Lauren. "How is your new hobby search coming along?"

Jensen is shuffling under the table, making his way over to Kieran, who's all too happy to entertain him. Henry presses his lips against my temple, then gets up to hang out with Caleb.

"Do you think he decorates his café for Christmas?" Lauren asks, eyes darting around the room.

"He didn't for fall," I point out, and she makes an agreeing, humming noise.

"It's a shame. Some winter decorations would be so cute in here. But anyway, hobbies." She grins as she turns her mug in her hands. "Can't say the search is going well. So far, the hobbies I've tried include falling into desperation over IKEA handbooks, cutting off circulation in my fingers while trying to knit, and burning milk in my attempt to make the perfect hot chocolate. Oh, and I tried my hand at tarot, but Amanda seemed like teaching me was about to give her an aneurysm, so I gave that up."

She rolls her eyes, and I can't help but giggle at that visual.

"Reading though … reading works." Her lips tug into a grin. "I might not have the bookshelves yet, but I have three ceiling-high stacks of books in my library and a cozy armchair setup."

"Library?" Kieran's head pops up, and he looks at her, surprised. "Huh. I still have an empty room in my house. That's a great idea. If you figure out how to build those IKEA bookshelves, let me know. Or better yet, once you've got the hang of it, you can build some for me."

She shoots him a glare that says, *over my dead body*. "Only if you film and then publish one video that I get to decide on."

"Welp, good thing there are YouTube tutorials," Kieran presses out with a nervous chuckle before he turns to talk to Jensen Ackles again.

"That's what I thought," she grumbles, before her face suddenly softens. "You look happy, Nic," she says with a smile, and I nod. My eyes find Henry, who is leaning against the counter casually, laughing at something Caleb said, and I bite my lip.

He's so effortlessly handsome. I still can't believe fate, or rather, Chaos, threw him my way. Much less that he wants to stick around after everything that happened over the past few weeks.

"I am," I assure her, my gaze darting back to her, still smiling widely. "I really, *really* am."

"You deserve it," she whispers and reaches over the table to squeeze my hand.

"As do you." I squeeze her hand right back, and the smiles we share with each other convey the same sentiment.

I'm so glad we moved here.

Later that evening, Henry and I are once more cuddled up on the couch, buried under a warm blanket and our animals as we watch a new movie. It's some kind of remake that's not even coming close to the original, but it's entertaining enough.

I have my cheek pressed against his chest, feeling it lift with every breath. His heartbeat thumps under my ear. This is slowly but surely becoming my favorite pastime—being with him, a bad movie running in the background, cuddling my cats.

"You make the best pillow," I tell him lazily, my eyes falling closed, and I hide a yawn in his shirt.

"And you're a great human equivalent to a plush toy," he mumbles, his chest vibrating with a chuckle as his hand starts slowly running up and down my arm.

The sound pulls my lips into a grin. It's low and hearty and about my favorite sound in the world.

Once the movie ends, we stay the way we were, cuddled up and enjoying each other's presence while the flames crackle in the fireplace. Cinnamon is cuddled into my lap and Pumpkin into the crease of my elbow, and Chaos is a warm presence on my shoulder. Jensen has his head on Henry's knee, eyes closed as Henry runs his fingers through the fur on his head. Our little family.

"I have something for you," Henry says suddenly, his voice soft but tinged with something that makes me blink my eyes open and glance up at him.

"It's not even my birthday," I murmur, brow furrowing as I push myself up to meet his gaze.

"I know," he says with a grin, but there's a flicker of nerves behind it that makes me pause.

My head tilts. “Why do you sound as if you’re about to confess you secretly adopted a goat in my name?”

“No goat,” he assures me and leans over the edge of the couch, finding something in his backpack he brought along that holds a change of clothes for tomorrow. I’m still nervous about staying here alone, especially at night.

Even though my door is in relatively good shape, no thanks to Jay, I ordered a new one, and Henry ordered about seven hundred additional locks. Until they arrive, though, he has insisted on staying at my place, and I can’t say I’m opposed to that.

It’s also a little scary, though. Because I might get used to it.

But now he’s not pulling clothes out of his backpack. No, it’s a photo album.

I blink at him, confusion tugging my brows together as I notice his fingers trembling ever so slightly when he hands it to me.

“Thank you,” I say slowly, turning it over in my hands. It comes out more as a question than a thanks.

“I just thought …” he starts, mumbling as he rubs the back of his neck, his gaze darting around the room. He makes a move to pull his arm from around my shoulders, but I shake my head and tighten my grip, keeping him right where he is.

“Okay, what’s going on?” I ask gently. “You’re acting like you handed me a cursed ring, and now I’m going to turn into a frog.”

His laugh is short, but I catch the anxiety still flickering behind his smile. Why is he that nervous?

“So … I know that sometimes you struggle with cutting contact with your parents and, you know, with everything that happened,” he explains softly. I open the first page, and when I see the first picture, a small gasp falls from my lips. Emotions form a knot in my throat.

"And I thought you should have an album with memories and little reminders that you have a new family here who love you and will always be here for you."

"Henry," I say, my voice breaking as I flip through the pages.

There are pictures of Lauren and me, smiling at each other while deep in a conversation at Caleb's. Of me asleep on the couch, with Jensen, Cinnamon, and Pumpkin cuddled against me.

There are images of all of us hanging out at Caleb's and a selfie Henry and I took by the lake. I study a picture he must have snuck during our bonfire—his face prominent in front as he's taking the selfie. The rest of us behind him, completely oblivious, sipping on our beer and enjoying a carefree evening.

"Henry," I whisper again, glancing up at him with glossy eyes. "I don't know what to say."

"Say you love it."

I nod, tears overflowing. "I love it." I turn to him and cradle his face in my palms. "I love you."

"I love you too," he whispers, and I bury one of my hands in his hair, pulling him close for a kiss that I hope conveys the tsunami of emotions threatening to drown me.

What did I do to deserve him?

When he breaks the kiss, there is so much love shining in his eyes, such a radiant happiness on his face, that it's almost making me cry even harder.

I might have thought Chaos was a bad omen, a sign from the universe telling me that everything will only get way worse.

But it turns out, she was the turning point of my life changing for the better. I hear a purr right next to my ear, and I never wished quite as much as I do now that I was able to hug her.

"Thank you, Chaos," I whisper.

Henry glances at me, confusion written all over his face, but I shake my head.

I finally found my place.

And while some wounds will take a very long time to heal, there's no better place for that than Wayward Hollow, right here by Henry's side.

Epilogue

Nic

"Oh my God, it smells like something is burning." Lauren sprints past me to the kitchen right as the doorbell rings, a panicked singsong on her lips. "Don't burn, don't burn, please don't buuuurn!"

"One second!" I shout toward the hallway. Now where is …? Ah. Pumpkin is sprinting toward the couch, and I run after her, quickly scooping her up and making my way to the door while keeping her in a tight hold. "Sorry to make you wait, but this little menace has turned into an escape artist," I say with a grin, greeting Kieran with a hug, Caleb with a happy nod, and finally, my boyfriend with a kiss.

"Is something burning?" Kieran asks immediately, and I shrug, trying to keep Pumpkin from wriggling out of my hold. He's holding a pie dish, and I can't help but try to take a peek at what he brought to our Friendsgiving. I think it's an apple pie. Nice.

"I don't think so, but Lauren just stormed to the kitchen, so …"

"Oh, for fuck's sake," Caleb mutters and immediately brushes past me, folding up his sleeves.

"Chaotic afternoon?" Henry asks with a grin tugging at the corners of his mouth, and I nod, not able to avert my eyes from his lips.

"A tiny little bit," I say with a flirty grin. I kick the door closed behind him and set down Pumpkin before I walk up to him. My hands wander up his arms until I interlace my fingers behind his neck. "But what else is new?" I ask in a whisper, and he amusedly shakes his head.

"True," he mumbles and leans down for a short kiss full of smiles before I let him go again and gently pat his shoulder.

"Go on inside. I'll be right there." But first, I get on my knees to greet my favorite husky. "Are you hungry already, my little hero?" I ask him in a baby voice, catching Henry staring at me from the corner of my eye. "What are you looking at?"

"Just you. On your knees," he shoots me a wink, and my cheeks flush. "It's hot."

"You're very hot from this angle too," I admit, wiggling my eyebrows. "Maybe we should revisit this conversation later."

He leans down, lifting my chin for one devouring kiss before he tears himself away with a sexy smile, winking at me over his shoulder as he continues to the kitchen."Damn. Your owner's going to be the death of me," I whisper to Jensen and lean my forehead against his. He lets out one of his signature awoo-woos.

When I go to the kitchen, with Jensen following close behind, I find Lauren leaning her elbows on the kitchen island, watching Caleb with narrowed eyes and a pout on her face as he has taken over the stove.

"Everything was going fine," she says, annoyance in her voice. "I swear I can cook."

"Sure you can," Caleb says over his shoulder placatingly, and I stop Lauren from reaching for an apple to throw at his head.

"God forbid I want a little crisp aroma to my mashed potatoes," she mumbles under her breath and crosses her arms in front of her chest.

"Mashed potatoes aren't supposed to be crispy," Kieran feels compelled to add, ducking right as she throws a tangerine at him.

"The recipe I'm using is begging to differ. And they're my mashed potatoes. If you're mean to me, I won't share." She narrows her eyes at him, and he lifts his hands in a defensive gesture as he puts the tangerine back where she took it from.

"Of course, I mean, what an interesting concept." Sarcasm is dripping from his voice, and the grin on his face is only a tad too wide to be taken seriously.

Lauren opens her mouth to retort, but I quickly change the topic before this Friendsgiving ends in a fight about mashed potatoes.

"How's the turkey coming along?"

We've never really celebrated Thanksgiving with our families, so this is the first time Lauren and I have set out to make a whole-ass turkey from scratch. Well, minus the raising a turkey, slaughtering it, plucking its feathers, and removing the organs. We spent days obsessing over recipes, watching tutorials on how to properly cook a turkey and what common mistakes to avoid. Hell, I even bought a meat thermometer. I printed out the recipe, stuck it to my fridge with a magnet, and we followed it meticulously, step by step, along with a video tutorial.

"Let me check," Henry says, giving my ass a quick squeeze as he walks past me, much to Lauren's amusement.

"Get a room," she whispers, and I only stick out my tongue at her.

"Honestly? It's looking good," Henry says, after sticking the thermometer into the bird. He's much less squeamish about that than Lauren and I—one of the many perks of dating a vet.

"You sound surprised." I narrow my eyes at him, and he quickly lifts his hands in surrender.

"Just pointing out the obvious, sweetheart."

"Sweetheart!" Lauren exclaims in a whisper and excitedly hits my shoulder with a force that makes me wince. "God, you two are so cute."

"How much longer does it need?" Kieran asks, turning around as he tries to find a timer in the kitchen, but all the times we need to track are in Lauren's phone.

"Turkey needs another ten minutes," she explains and lifts herself off the kitchen counter to peek over Caleb's shoulder.

"What else is on the menu?" Kieran wonders and peeks over Caleb's other shoulder. "Anything we can help with?"

"There are mashed potatoes, mac and cheese, beans, stuffing," Lauren enumerates, while Henry takes his favorite spot behind me, laying his chin on my shoulder and hugging me around the waist from behind.

"And there's pumpkin pie, pecan pie, your apple pie, and some kind of strawberry tiramisu recipe I found online for dessert," Lauren continues, eyes darting around the room.

"TikTok?" Kieran asks, with his eyebrow raised up to his hairline and Lauren nods solemnly.

"TikTok."

"What is that supposed to mean?" Caleb asks over his shoulder, the skepticism in his voice making Henry chuckle.

"That means it's either going to be amazing," Kieran starts.

"Or horrible," Lauren adds with a giggle. "Then again, the ingredients didn't make it sound disgusting, so we'll see. I hope you all brought containers for leftovers."

We shoot the shit for a few more minutes until her timers go off one by one. Then the guys play rock-paper-scissors on who has to get the turkey out of the oven without letting it fall.

Lauren and I shoot each other a knowing glance. It's not as if this thing weighs thirty pounds. Even we managed to lift it without too much difficulty.

"Be careful!" Kieran exclaims when Caleb pulls it out unceremoniously, but he only rolls his eyes as he sets the whole thing down on the kitchen island.

"Do I really look like I would let a turkey fall?"

Kieran's eyes pointedly jump to his broad shoulders, and I catch Lauren staring at Caleb's biceps.

"You've got a point," both of them admit at the same time, and I shake my head at their antics. From the corner of my eye, I see Cinnamon sneaking closer to the kitchen door, eyes on the turkey, so I quickly rush everyone along.

"Come on, everyone. We set our Friendsgiving up in the living room."

Lauren and I might have gone a little ham on the decoration. It looks like an autumn-bomb exploded in my living room. Garlands are hanging everywhere. The table's set with little pumpkin decorations and orange bouquets, leaving just enough space for all the pots and dishes we're bringing to the table in a food parade.

As we sit down, Jensen takes his usual spot by the window while he lets the evening sun shine on his pretty brown fur. Cinnamon is walking under our chairs, rubbing herself against our calves and shins, her miserable-sounding meow an indicator that she's hoping for some scraps.

Meanwhile, Pumpkin is trying to climb up the leg of my pants. I scoop her up, press a kiss to the top of her head, and put her into a box that is high enough that she can't jump or climb out of it.

"You're going to jail, little one," I coo to her as I set her down. "Because otherwise, you're going to find a way to climb up the table to walk over our food. And Lauren and I worked too hard to have your little dirty paws in everything."

"You'd think you don't feed her with how she's acting" Kieran points out with a chuckle when I return, and I roll my eyes.

"God, you should hear her if her food is a minute late. She's such a drama queen."

I sit down next to Henry and Lauren, happy that the cooking portion of the day is finally over and we get to eat now.

"Can we please not do the thing where we go around the table and state what we're thankful for?" Caleb asks gruffly, but Lauren's eyes sparkle as if she hadn't had that idea before.

"No, I think we should totally do that."

"I'll go first," Kieran volunteers, eyes darting around the table solemnly. "This year, I'm thankful for new friendships." Then he glances to his left, where Lauren is seated.

"That's a good one." She nods and taps her chin as she thinks. "I'm also thankful for new friendships, new strength and for this food." She grins and turns toward Henry.

"I'm thankful for old friends"—he looks at Caleb—"new friends"—his eyes dart to Lauren and Kieran—"and the best girlfriend in the world." He lifts my hand and presses a kiss to the back of it, making me blush and giggle nervously.

"I'm thankful for a new chapter, found family, and the best boyfriend I could ask for," I add. I purse my lips for a kiss, which he happily gives me, even if it makes Kieran groan and Lauren whisper, "get a room."

Finally, everyone looks at Caleb, who has his arms crossed in front of his chest, his expression anything but amused.

"You are all ridiculous," he mumbles and shakes his head. "I've got nothing to add to that."

I see Lauren open her mouth, probably to tease him, but I quickly shoot her a glare that makes her remain silent, though not without a pout.

"Fair enough," I say pointedly. She narrows her eyes at me, but all her pouting is forgotten when I say, "Let's eat before it gets cold."

And as we eat a meal that turned out amazingly good, joking around and playfully fighting over the wishbone, a warm fills me from within. The feeling makes the smile on my face stretch wider and brings tears to my eyes.

A feeling of belonging.

A feeling of home. Of family and a future that is so damn bright, I wish I had it in my wildest dreams.

"What's that?" Kieran asks, and everyone at the table suddenly goes silent. Lauren and I shoot each other a glance.

Kieran jumps up, trying to follow the scratching and whines. He comes to a stop right by my window front, his eyes widening.

"Nic, I don't want to alarm you, but there are like three kittens out here. And a puppy."

"Happy Thanksgiving, Chaos," I say with a giggle as Henry jumps up to take a look at them. And as everyone huddles around the adorable little creatures, cooing at them and already coming up with names, I know that this is my place. Here in Wayward Hollow, with friends, animals, and a little ghost cat sneaking around my calves.

Thank you so much for reading A Love Like Pumpkin Spice! I hope you enjoyed your time in Wayward Hollow! If you did, I'd really appreciate you leaving a review or rating on Amazon or Goodreads. It really helps indie authors like me a lot!

If you're hungry for more, sign up to my newsletter on my website for a bonus epilogue from Henry's POV – And there will be even more bonus chapters, and exclusive character art in my Patreon!

Acknowledgements

A Love Like Pumpkin Spice was truly a team effort and wouldn't have been able to release without a lot of people! Meaning a lot of 'Thank Yous' have to go out!

The first and always biggest one goes to my dad, who's letting me do my thing without breaking into 'Child, what are you doing with your life?' monologues… too often. He'll never read my books (Thank God!) but he's by far my biggest cheerleader!

The next one goes to Avery who tolerates my word-vomits and ramblings for a genre she neither reads nor writes in (sorry not sorry).

Eternal gratitude goes out to Austria Bestie for swooping in like a… princess in shining armor to save me typography-wise. My God-child for being the cutest and fluffiest creature on earth. And to Ireland bestie for the emotional support and contagious optimism. To Taylor Swift for being the boss queen she is and showing us that no dream is too big. ♡

A huge thank you goes out to everyone who has helped me make A Love Like Pumpkin Spice the best version it could be: EJL Editing for their great story- and writing feedback, LoveNotes for handling ARC's, @melxartz who did a stunning cover, Kat who hunted errors with her hawk-eyes.

The biggest thank you, however, goes out to you: My readers.

Thank you so much for picking up A Love Like Pumpkin Spice! I hope you had as much fun getting to know Wayward Hollow as I had writing it into existence. Thanks to you I get to write and share my stories with the world and I will forever be grateful for that! ♡

What's next?

Want to spend Christmas in Wayward Hollow?

A Love Like Christmas Time is Lauren's and Caleb's story – get ready for some grumpy-sunshine goodness! More furry friends, more cozy vibes, and a lot of fun ♡

A Love Like Christmas Time on Amazon

Also by Hailey Frost

Curious about my other books?

Reimagined – Read in Kindle Unlimited!
Eight years ago, her best friend became a famous rockstar… by stealing her song! Now they run into each other again, and old wounds re-open…

Dynamic Contrast – Read in Kindle Unlimited!
First he steals her parking spot, then it turns out he hates dogs! Yet she can't resist his charme when she starts working for him…

Counterpoint – Read in Kindle Unlimited!
After a bad break-up Harper decides to move back home, looking forward to the trip… until her brother makes her take along his best friend on her roadtrip. The one who rejected her as teenager…

Breakdown – Read in Kindle Unlimited!
When the world keeps piling on worries, the last thing she needs is her former best friend reappearing in her life… or not?

Siren's Heart – Love at first Sight – Read in Kindle Unlimited!

The last thing Millie expected of the charity football match her pop duo is performing at, is falling in love. And much less at first sight…

Siren's Game – Love in the Spotlight – Read in Kindle Unlimited!

When their friends start dating, Kayla and Asher find themselves in a pickle. Now they need to pretend to be a couple to distract the media. But what happens when their game turns a little too real?

Summer Haze & Tokyo Craze – Read in Kindle Unlimited!

Lily has worked hard to become CEO of the Siren's talent agency. But what if her falling in love with the CEO of her rival company threatens everything?

Bright Smile & London Eye – Read in Kindle Unlimited!

When Lexie's world starts to crumble beneath her feet in a city that doesn't feel like home yet, her friends are there to catch her… and the handsome stranger who she found having a panic attack in front of her bakery.

Winter Glam in Amsterdam – Read in Kindle Unlimited!

Summer has better things to do than join her family for a trip to Amsterdam… but the handsome audiobook narrator with the deepest voice she's ever heard sure seems glad she came along.

Blue Eyes & Paris Vibes – Read in Kindle Unlimited!

Abby never expected to grow to like Paris… or the handsome, yet rude stranger who ran her over at the train station.

Find me here!

Come say 'Hi!' ♡

All my links:

Printed in Dunstable, United Kingdom

67387068R00194